THE
COLOR
OF AIR

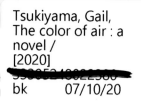
THE

COLOR

OF AIR

A Novel

GAIL TSUKIYAMA

HARPERVIA

An Imprint of HarperCollins*Publishers*

THE COLOR OF AIR. Copyright © 2020 by Gail Tsukiyama. All rights reserved. Printed in the United States of America. No part of this book may be used or reproduced in any manner whatsoever without written permission except in the case of brief quotations embodied in critical articles and reviews. For information, address HarperCollins Publishers, 195 Broadway, New York, NY 10007.

HarperCollins books may be purchased for educational, business, or sales promotional use. For information, please email the Special Markets Department at SPsales@harpercollins.com.

FIRST EDITION

Designed by Terry McGrath

Library of Congress Cataloging-in-Publication Data
Names: Tsukiyama, Gail, author.
Title: The color of air : a novel / Gail Tsukiyama.
Description: First edition. | New York : HarperCollins, [2020] |
Identifiers: LCCN 2019060263 (print) | LCCN 2019060264 (ebook) | ISBN
   9780062976192 (hardcover) | ISBN 9780062976208 (trade paperback) | ISBN
   9780062976215 (ebook)
Subjects: LCSH: Domestic fiction. | GSAFD: Historical fiction.
Classification: LCC PS3570.S84 C65 2020 (print) | LCC PS3570.S84 (ebook)
   | DDC 813/.54—dc23
LC record available at https://lccn.loc.gov/2019060263
LC ebook record available at https://lccn.loc.gov/2019060264

20 21 22 23 24   LSC   10 9 8 7 6 5 4 3 2 1

For all the Hilo Aunties who have graced my life
And in memory of Emily Lee

[T]he very color of the air in the place I was born was different, the smell of the earth was special, redolent with memories of my parents.

—NATSUME SŌSEKI

THE
COLOR
OF AIR

Mauna Loa

November 21, 1935

1

MANGOES

The sky threatened rain as Koji Sanada approached the green bungalow where the pungent scent of rotting mangoes mingled with a hint of smoke, the bitter remnants of the preharvest cane burning that drifted down from the surrounding plantations. He knew it all too well. Sugarcane had been his life since his family first arrived in Hilo, Hawai'i, by way of Osaka, Japan, in 1895, along with all the other immigrant workers who had flocked to jobs on the island's sugar and pineapple plantations. Koji had been ten years old, the older of two children and the only son. He had immediately embraced the wildness of the island as his own, so different from his traditional Japanese upbringing. Along the way, the three years his parents had been contracted to stay before returning to Japan had turned into a lifetime.

Koji walked up the dirt path to the house he knew so well. It was here on the Big Island near the growing community of Hilo that he found a new home at the Puli Plantation, along with years of backbreaking work, toiling under the hot sun, the wind and rain, the tremors and quakes, and it was here on this island of five volcanoes that he'd also found Mariko Abe.

He paused to look around Mariko's yard now and felt a dull ache at having let her down. The garden, always her pride, was wild and overgrown without her. He meant to come pick the mangoes and take them to Nori at the Okawa Fish Market, but once again time had gotten away from him. He continued up the path to see her beloved mango tree, planted by her grandfather but now empty of fruit. It had been wet and muggy all week, and the moist ground was heavily blanketed with leaves and rotted fruit, only the dark seeds of a few fist-size mangoes still recognizable. It always amazed Koji how quickly the earth could reclaim its own.

Close your eyes. He thought he heard Mariko's voice again. *Now, what do you smell?* When they were young, she'd taught him the mangoes were ready to pick when you could smell their fragrant melon pineapple aroma, while they were still firm to the touch. Her tree always yielded the sweetest mangoes in Hilo town. Koji smiled to think Mariko knew mangoes the way he knew sugarcane, and he felt a sudden sharp longing that was just another form of grief. She had died two years ago and it still felt like yesterday.

Another tremor underfoot shook Koji from his thoughts. The island had been restless with waves of slight tremors for the past two months, and he worried that they foreshadowed something bigger and stronger. So far, nothing had come of them, but the island's history said otherwise.

"It's just the island hiccuping," his mother used to say, to coax the fear out of his younger sister. Koji hoped it was nothing more now that Mariko's son Daniel was finally coming home from the mainland after more than ten years of study. The last time Koji had seen him was during his mother's final months. Since her death, time had played tricks on him, moving both too fast and too slow without her. He couldn't help but feel as if part of Mariko was returning to him with her son, reawakening long-buried memories. Koji walked to the woodshed where Mariko kept her gardening tools. He quickly cleaned around the tree before going up to the house, where he was certain to find Nori making sure everything was ready for Daniel's return.

The steps up to the front porch creaked underfoot. Koji was back at the house for the first time in two years, heat and moisture leaving slivers of cracked paint peeling from the trim and railing. Mariko's chair, where she had often sat and sewed, looked weathered and forlorn. Koji slipped off his shoes, pulled open the screen door, and stood at the threshold looking in. The package he came to deliver was in his pocket. He swallowed and felt another tremor. *Go on*, he told himself. He heard movement coming from the kitchen and choked back the familiarity. It wasn't her, he reminded himself; it was Nori. He took a deep breath and stepped into the house.

2

WATCHING OVER HIM

Nori Okawa stood in the kitchen of Daniel's childhood home—the faded, weather-beaten green bungalow that had been left to Mariko by her mother and now belonged to Daniel. The house had been one of Mariko's most cherished possessions, built by her grandfather after he had emigrated from Japan. "It holds our family spirits," she always said, "keeps them alive." And it was within walking distance of downtown and the Okawa Fish Market. Nori's ongoing care of the house was evident in the thriving orchids, in the spotless kitchen, in the clean bedsheets and dusted shelves of his room. For the past few weeks, word had spread through the community about the welcome home party for Daniel at the Okawa Fish Market. Everything was ready for his return.

Nori and the Hilo Aunties had been excited all week. Daniel's letter said he would arrive back in Hilo on the steamer *Lanai* that evening from Oahu. Nori knew how proud Mariko would have been. Her son had left the island at eighteen for a mainland education, and was returning a full-fledged doctor. Daniel was one of the first Japanese in his medical school and the first Hilo boy to become a doctor. The entire community knew how hard he had studied to be accepted into a mainland university.

Along the way, his triumph had also become theirs. There'd been so many obstacles—from cost to the distance—but Daniel did well on his exams, and his high school teachers had written him glowing letters of recommendation. Along with the scholarships he received, it felt destined to be.

Nori smiled. Daniel was returning a big-shot doctor now, who hadn't been seduced away by Chicago and all the big-city temptations. Even when Daniel was a boy, Nori knew he would succeed and make them all proud—he was driven in that way, a good student who cared for every stray dog or hurt animal, even before he realized he wanted to be a doctor. Along with her two boys, Wilson and Mano, who had followed their father into the Okawa family fishing business, she always considered Daniel to be her third son, more so after Mariko had passed away from cancer. She knew it would have to be his own decision, but Nori had selfishly hoped that he would return to Hilo town. So many other young people who left for Oahu, or the mainland, had forgotten their Hilo roots only to return as strangers, or not at all.

Nori felt another tremor just as she leaned over to put the last plate into the icebox. She had filled it with a few dishes Daniel liked—chicken and taro, *lomi-lomi* salmon, and coconut *haupia*, the sweet gelatin he loved as a kid, just in case he was hungry during the night. She didn't dare to make his favorite, Portuguese chicken, which no one in Hilo made as well as his mother. Nori straightened and suddenly felt Mariko's presence right there in the kitchen with her. She was still everywhere—in her stained teacup in the cupboard; in the empty chair against the chipped Formica table; in her faded, flowered apron that still hung inside the pantry door. They had shared so many important moments right there in the small, warm room ever since they were young girls. Nori wiped her hands on a dish towel and once again heard the echo of their voices circle around her.

The kitchen was always the heart of Mariko's house. It was where she had first told Nori she was pregnant with Daniel. She appeared pale and tense that morning, so afraid her husband, Franklin, wouldn't be ready, that he'd be angry with her. But he surprised them all, and was happy when he returned from a job on Maui and found out about the baby. "A boy," he'd said, "I can feel it." At about the same time Nori had discovered that she was pregnant with Mano. "We're having twins," Mariko was the first to say. Nori had never seen her so content, ever hopeful that Franklin would finally settle down.

"I know you can hear me," she said aloud, replacing the dish towel on its hook. "Don't worry, Mari, we're watching over him."

"Who are you talking to?"

Nori's heart jumped; she turned to see her old friend Koji Sanada, muddy shoes in one hand, standing in the doorway. She hadn't heard him come into the house. She smiled now to see him, wearing a T-shirt and baggy work pants. He'd always been like a brother to her. Nori was an only child of pineapple-picking parents who barely noticed her and had eventually drank themselves to death. They'd all grown up together in the tightly knit community, watching the rise of the sugar plantations and the growth of Hilo.

"To myself," she said, and looked away flustered. "What are you doing here and not at the market?"

Nori knew the locals were already gathering there.

"I wanted to leave this here for Daniel," Koji said. He placed a wrapped box on the kitchen table.

Nori smiled. She knew it was most likely another railcar—an addition to Daniel's favorite train set that Koji had started building with him when he was a seven-year-old boy. Every year since, he had added to it.

"He'll be happy to have it waiting for him," she said.

"Is there anything else that needs doing before he arrives?"

Through the years, Hilo town had weathered many ups and downs, and Koji was someone on whom the locals could always depend. Now, just past fifty, he was still in better shape than many men a decade younger, solid and muscular. He'd grown up and worked on a sugar plantation since his father was hired by John Dillingham back in the late 1800s, when many of the big sugarcane plantations were started. "Sweetness runs through my blood," he liked to tell her. Koji knew more about the cane work than most of the *lunas*, the mostly Portuguese foremen who oversaw the workers. He was a legend in the fields, his skill becoming mythical over the years. He was known as the fastest cane cutter on the Big Island, and still held the record of cutting twelve hundred pounds of sugarcane in an hour. After twenty years of cutting cane at the Puli Plantation, and even as age and later injuries slowed him down, the owners had asked him to stay on to run the sugar train.

"Everything's done here," Nori said.

"Mariko would be happy to have him home, yeah?"

"Very happy," she said.

"I'll take the sugar train back up to Puli once the cane is unloaded at the station. Come back down to the market in the truck afterward." Koji ran his hand over his short, graying hair and looked around. He stood a moment lost in memory. "The place looks good."

Since Mariko's death, Koji had stopped coming to the bungalow. Before then, he was there every Sunday helping Mariko to fix one thing or another, spending time with the two of them at harvest end, and later, when Daniel came home at Christmas every year. They were his family, but now he kept to himself. While they had all mourned her death, Koji's loss felt all the louder in his silence.

Nori smiled. "Don't be late, yeah."

"Haven't I always kept the train on schedule?" Koji said.

"Always a first time."

"I'll be there."

Koji lifted his hand in a wave and stepped out the back door. Nori watched as he pulled on his shoes before thumping down the stairs. She waited a few minutes in the quiet kitchen, but Mariko never returned.

3

RISING WINDS

The winds had risen by the time Koji brought the sugar train back to the Puli Plantation. Over the years Puli had become one of the largest sugar plantations south of Hilo, several thousand acres not twenty miles up the mountain from town. From the train barn, he walked past the sugar house and mill, up the road to his small tin-roofed wood cottage that overlooked the cane fields. Only after all his work was completed did Koji really feel the sharp tug of excitement at Daniel's return. He wondered how long it would take for Daniel to slow to the island rhythms again. Daniel would have to readapt to living in a small island town with its sudden midafternoon rainstorms; the muggy heat and fierce winds; the dense, green blankets of foliage; and the hovering, dark volcanoes that loomed over everything. From the moment Koji set foot onto the black lava rocks as a boy, he knew that the island was a living organism and they were simply guests.

The winds grew stronger now, pulling at Koji, ghosts urging him back to the cane. *I still have to change and drive back down to Hilo,* he thought, even as he turned around and began to walk back down toward the fields.

≈

The air stilled for a moment followed by the rustling of cane leaves.

"You're going the wrong way, yeah," Razor Takahashi said, meeting Koji at the edge of the field, a sweat-slick layer of cane dust on Razor's face, a pint-size bottle of whiskey in his hand. The trade winds rose and had the tall cane swaying back and forth like hula dancers. The northern fields were the last of the fields being readied to be burned.

"Just need to walk a bit," Koji said.

"Can't get enough of the cane, eh?" Razor said and laughed.

It was true. Koji often felt a pull toward the cane. It was in his blood, the only life he'd known, and the place where he felt most at home. It was something he knew Razor understood.

Razor took a swig from the bottle. He reached out and offered Koji a drink. "What time is Daniel coming home?"

Koji shook his head and smiled at his old friend. "He's arriving soon. I better go. I'll see you soon, yeah. Save some for me," he added, pointing to the bottle before he walked into the sugarcane field.

When Koji turned back, Razor was already gone from sight.

≈

Razor had been his first real friend at the plantation. Their lives before then had been uprooted when his father lost their small rice farm in Yamaguchi Prefecture in western Japan after a series of bad business deals. "Isn't sugarcane just another type of farming?" his father had reasoned. "A three-year contract offering steady pay and free housing, and we'll return to Japan standing firmly on our feet again." All Koji remembered was how weak his legs felt after sailing across the ocean for more than three weeks aboard the *City of Tokio*, weaker than standing all day bent over in their wet rice paddy field. It was early morning when they'd arrived in Hilo, the town shrouded in mist, reminding him of the Japanese village in a folktale his mother had read to him and his sister. Koji imagined the spirits from those stories had followed them all the way across the ocean. Even the same dark and foreboding mountains stood tall in the distance.

A dockworker unloading the ship followed his gaze. "That's Mauna Loa, yeah, Hawai'i's version of Mount Fuji," he'd said. "There are four more volcanoes that make up the island," he added. "No need to worry, eh. Only three of them are active."

Five volcanoes on one island.

Koji was immediately captivated.

His family's papers were quickly signed and collected at the harbor by Japanese-speaking immigration officers. After, they were herded into a tent for a quick health clearance, poked and prodded by Japanese doctors hired by the plantations before they were packed onto horse-drawn wagons with the other new arrivals, squeezed so tightly together that Koji could hardly move in the breathless heat. From there they were bumped and jostled for two hours through dense forests of ohi'a trees, shrubs, and thick, overgrown foliage, and then up a winding, treacherous mountain road to their new home at Puli Plantation.

By the time they arrived, Koji was hot and sweaty, his body sore and bruised from the rough plywood wagon. His legs no longer felt anything. He sat up when the wagon jerked to a stop at the front gate of the plantation and the driver yelled out in awkward, practiced Japanese, *"Homu, suito homu!"* Home, sweet home! Beyond the gate, not more than half a mile down a dirt road, the driver pointed to three separate wind-weary clapboard buildings that housed the plantation office, the school, and a store. Farther down the road stood a larger building, the sugar mill. And past the mill, as far as the eye could see, were acres and acres of tall, billowing sugarcane.

His family had remained quiet and apprehensive, while Koji could hardly contain his excitement. He wanted to jump down from the wagon and run the rest of the way, but he felt his father's tight grip on his shoulder and knew to stay put. His mother held on to his younger sister in the back of the wagon, her face pale and thin from weeks of seasickness. They were surrounded by the sticky buzzing heat, the low, dark sky threatening rain, and the endless sea of cane. He remembered that his mother had leaned toward his father and whispered in Japanese, "So big and endless, but where is the beating heart?"

They were one of many Japanese families squeezed into the cane grass huts, huddled together at the northern end of Puli Plantation. There was no running water or electricity, and the outhouse was in the yard. His mother and father were put to work cutting cane and clearing away the cane trash, while ten-year-old Koji and his sister went to the one-room plantation school. He was a restless and distracted student until he began working as a "hoe hana," weeding and loosening the endless rows of dirt to plant cane under the hot sun, watching the cane cutters along with Razor and other boys his age whose families had also emigrated from Japan. Through good times and bad they all lived together in a cluster of similar grass houses that comprised the Japanese village. While their tightly knit Japanese enclave continued to grow, and was aptly named Kazoku, or Family Village, Koji noticed that they were also kept separated by acres of cane fields from Chinese and Filipino and Portuguese workers and their villages on the plantation.

≈

Koji kept moving between the rows of waving cane, known to grow as tall as twenty feet high before flowering. Most of the cane workers had already come in from the fields for dinner, walking back to their separate villages scattered around the plantation. Those who still had the energy after a day in the fields might tend to their own small gardens, or go down to the river to bathe, talk stories among their own, and drink moonshine made from ti root. By four the next morning, they would be up and starting the day all over again. Koji had lived the same routine for so many years he could do it in his sleep. Hadn't he survived a lifetime at the Puli Plantation through hard work, keeping to himself, and staying out of trouble? He'd spent his life surviving, and in the end, the lingering guilt still pulled at him, still laid blame. Koji looked out toward the overworked cane fields, knowing the earth needed to be turned over every so often to be renewed. He felt the same. This plantation and these fields had been his life, punctuated by trips down to Hilo town as a boy, and later, to see Mariko and Daniel. After Franklin left, he vowed to take care of them. They were all that ever mattered to him.

The day was turning to dusk—gray and grainy—neither day nor night. What did he see? Koji always felt it was the most revealing moment of each day—the flickering candle just before it fluttered out, leaving everything in darkness. "Last chance daylight," his father used to call it, "just before the spirits come out." He only hoped the spirits would come out to guide him now, just as they always had. Koji walked deeper into the field, the trade winds blowing wildly, the swishing, rustling cane frantic all around him. It didn't take long before he heard their singing again, their ghost voices rising softly at first, and then louder. The songs sung by the Japanese women workers rose upward and were carried above the tall stalks, while the singers themselves remained hidden among the cane. They sang the *holehole bushi* work songs filled with all the small joys and great sorrows they'd suffered, deceived into leaving their homeland for a better life, fueled by empty promises as they stripped the dried cane leaves from the stalks ten hours a day. It was during the days before the fields were burned, and all the clearing was done by hand. It was what Koji loved most—what drew him back to the cane—the beauty and the sadness of those singing voices and the stories they told.

> *Where do I belong? Where is my home?*
> *Is it in America, or should I return to Japan?—*
> *I thought Hawai'i would be my home.*
> *Hawai'i, Hawai'i the place of my dreams—*
> *But what a nightmare—*
> *My tears stain the sugarcane like rain.*

Koji's mother had sung the work songs with the other women, their heartbreaking laments of being far from their homelands and families, tricked into grueling and endless work in the fields by false promises of money and housing as the sun beat down on them, as the wind howled and slapped, as the rain soaked them to the bone, and as steam rose from the muddy ground. The babies strapped to their backs felt like deadweight, a growing burden, another mouth to feed. They were left with thoughts of deepest despair . . . *My baby is better off dead.*

Koji stopped walking, just as he had always paused from his cane cutting to listen to the songs. He closed his eyes and imagined their voices being carried by the wind all the way to Hilo town, their sad and melodious laments soaring through the air before they disappeared over the ocean and back to Japan.

When the singing finally quieted, Koji opened his eyes. He was standing alone in the field. All the secrets he had kept over the years suddenly nagged at him, like the itch of an old wound. The ghost songs were reminders of all the years gone by, his life spent on what he always considered sacred ground. Leaving the formalities of Japan, he had welcomed the untamed island, the long summers of boyhood, the backbreaking work in the cane fields, the plantation life he had never left because it was all he'd known. When Koji turned to walk back to his house, it was Mariko's lone voice that stayed with him.

It's time he knows the truth. You can't protect him forever.

4

THE OKAWA FISH MARKET

Nori hurried back from the green bungalow to the Okawa Fish Market, across the road from Hilo Bay. One of the two-story clapboard buildings on Kamehameha Avenue, it had formerly been the Hilo Town Bar. She passed the older, two-story S. Hata Building, and the S. H. Kress & Company Building, where all the wealthy haole ladies, whose husbands managed the plantations and ran the banks, came down from their big houses up the hill to have lunch and shop for the latest fashions. The buildings gleamed in their Art Deco newness, both products of the sugar wealth in Hilo town during the past forty years that had kept the town growing, and dimmed all the small family-owned businesses of her childhood. Nori swallowed her rising anxiousness and pushed through the crowded streets. She didn't want to be late to Daniel's party.

Since the stock market crash six years ago, there had been other changes. The once-quiet downtown streets were noisy and restless, teeming with agitated Chinese, Japanese, Filipino, and Portuguese men waiting desperately for work on the docks. Nori heard that thousands of Filipino workers had already been sent back to the Philippines by the plantation owners, but it was hard to tell as she slipped by so many sour, unwashed bodies, avoiding eye contact as she picked up her pace and clutched her basket close.

"Lady! Lady," someone called out to her, but she kept moving.

In the past few months there'd been countless drunken fights, a stabbing down on the docks outside of Hoku's Bar, and the window of Ching's Laundry had been smashed by a brick in the middle of the night. Nori remembered a time when it never crossed her mind to lock the market's door after dark. Closed meant *closed*. Now things were different.

Still, as Hilo town continued to grow around her, the one thing that hadn't changed for three generations was the Okawa Fish Market. Every morning, varieties of succulent tuna and snapper, moonfish and swordfish had been caught and brought in, still thrashing, by the Okawa fishermen, first by her father-in-law, and her husband, Samuel, and then, as soon as they graduated from high school, her sons Wilson and Mano. Even now, when Nori stepped into the cool, dark market, the heavy sea salt fish pineapple mildew odor sent her right back to the first day its doors opened twenty-five years ago.

~

Nori had married Samuel Okawa right after they graduated from high school in 1904. They were both seventeen, and she became pregnant with Wilson almost immediately after they moved into his family's house close to the wharf, staying in Samuel's boyhood room. He began working full-time with his father as a fisherman, while she helped his mother at the family fish stand. Nori worried about Samuel going out to sea, taking the boat out in rough waters, confronting unexpected storms or unforeseen injuries. She nourished her courage with old deities and all the fishing lore passed down through generations, but her heart raced with every month's full moon, which carried another meaning: the currents would be rough in the morning. Unrelenting, unpredictable, unforgiving, the sea was governed by Kanaloa, the god of the ocean. Samuel lived by reading the weather signs, watching the currents and the cloud formations, a language Nori learned to decipher during her first year of marriage. It was a skill that was as suffocating and illuminating as it was frightening and life-saving.

Six years later she opened the fish market. Nori had just turned twenty-three in 1910 when she urged her husband's family to expand the simple lean-to that sold the freshest fish in Hilo down by the wharf into a larger market. Samuel and her in-laws resisted. "We're fishermen, why make more trouble, eh?" her husband had argued. Nori simply smiled and remained insistent. She'd given him two sons in the past five years, and was ready for something more than just changing diapers and waiting for her husband to return home each day bringing the rank smells of fish and sweat. No matter how much her husband protested, she knew he would eventually relent. Samuel was a good, hardworking man, whom she'd known and trusted since he was a boy sitting next to her at Queen Lili'uokalani High School, but Nori had all the business acumen in the family. Hadn't she been the one to put away enough money to buy the building and start the market in the first place?

The new Okawa Fish Market opened two months later. Nori, Samuel, and the boys moved into the upstairs apartment, away from her in-laws for the first time. Nori loved Samuel, and marrying him young was a way to escape the memory of her own uncaring parents. But another weight had been lifted when she had a place of her own, away from the watchful eyes of her mother-in-law, a good woman who expected things done her way. "Do like this, yeah," or "No, no, not that way." For the first time in her life, Nori felt like a bird released from its cage. She bought two large iceboxes and used the long, whiskey-stained koa wood bar as a counter where customers could sit and eat. She had shelves built that lined the walls and stocked essential grocery items—canned foods, sacks of rice, beans, sugar, salt, and flour. "Survivor foods," she called them, along with boxes of matches, cigarettes, sweet and salty dried plums, and candies at the front checkout counter, just in case a customer had forgotten to pick up something at Oshima's grocery store, or worse yet, a natural disaster had rumbled through the island, leaving them completely cut off from the rest of the world.

Soon, besides selling the famous Okawa fresh fish, Nori cooked and baked in the small kitchen in back—relatives coming in and out to help—and also sold hot coffee, soda pop, sushi, sweetbread, coconut tarts, red bean buns, and whatever else could be quickly downed while working on a boat or sitting at the counter. She began serving breakfast and lunch when she saw how the locals liked to linger at the market every day, as did a pack of homeless, mostly congenial dogs waiting for daily scraps. Tables and chairs were set up not only in the market, but also out back in the yard for those who wanted to sit and linger longer. All considered the market an extension of their own homes. It was *ohana*, family run and founded by one of their own, and it quickly became the main gathering place in Hilo for island news and gossip.

And business promised to become even brighter in the months ahead. The railway station just down the street was expanding service to sugar mills north of Hilo along the Hamakua coast, which would soon bring in more customers as the sugar and shipping industries continued to grow. Nori was overwhelmed. She'd never expected the market to succeed so quickly, consuming all her time and energy. Every evening she put her boys to bed and headed straight for her own. Before dawn every morning Nori was downstairs at the market mixing, rolling, and baking loaves of sweetbread, breaking eggs, and frying Portuguese sausage and bacon for the dockworkers and hungry fishermen who flocked there for breakfast before they returned home to sleep. While Nori was grateful for the Okawa Fish Market's popularity, she was unprepared for all the work it involved. By her second month in business, she hired her cousin, Jelly, to work the counter full-time, and Jelly's fourteen-year-old son, Nobu, to do the stocking and heavy work, while other relatives took turns watching the boys upstairs as the market continued to grow.

≈

By the time Nori reached the market all the locals had already gathered for Daniel's welcome home party. She sent her sons, Wilson and Mano, down to the docks to wait for Daniel to arrive, while her childhood friend Leia Natua, along with her sister Noelani, Jelly, and Samuel had laid out platters of food on the koa bar. Beer and soda pop were flowing freely. Nori was especially happy to see the jar of mango jam she'd made from Mariko's mangoes on the bar. She and Leia had gone over to the house and picked most of the mangoes in early August, the last of them used in the jam now waiting for Daniel. But the biggest surprise was that the famous Okawa Fish Market bulletin board, which hung across the entire back wall and which was usually covered with ads and announcements, was now also decorated with a banner of big block letters across it that spelled out WELCOME HOME, DANIEL!

The hum of voices grew and laughter filled the air. Nori looked around the room at faces she'd known for most of her life, all the while missing Mariko, the one person who should have been there for her son's homecoming. When the floorboards quivered beneath her feet, Nori imagined it was Mariko trying to return again. She paused, waiting for the tremors to end, but instead of slowing, they grew in intensity. All the voices hushed as a rumbling, quaking movement took possession of the building. In the next moment, the entire building seemed to be rocking, ceiling fans swaying from side to side, cans and bottles toppling from the shelves in small explosions of shattering glass.

"Everyone outside!" Samuel yelled.

Suddenly Nori realized that she hadn't seen Koji in the crowd. He was always the one they turned to in emergencies. In her panic, Nori couldn't think of what to grab, and reached for the jar of mango jam, just as Samuel grabbed her arm and pulled her toward the front door.

5

BEAUTY AND THE BEAST

Koji had just finished changing his clothes when the tremors resumed. He waited for them to pass but they only grew stronger, so he ran to his truck and headed back down the mountain to Hilo town. What he had been dreading had finally arrived. Like all the locals, he understood that living on an island created by volcanoes meant accepting both the beauty and the beast. You couldn't have one without the other. Koji bumped along the unpaved roads, passing fields of sugarcane, descending through huge stands of koa and *hala* trees with their thick, monstrous aerial roots, wondering which of the island's beasts was rearing its ugly head this time. Suddenly his truck swerved as if he had a flat tire. Koji braked and stopped in the middle of a red dirt road, only to realize that it was the ground shifting his truck from side to side. He watched the ohi'a tree branches swaying, leaves falling to the ground in defeat. Koji was helpless to do anything but wait it out. Time slowed. Was it a minute or two or three before the quaking eased and the ground stilled? He waited a moment longer before he started up the truck and kept driving.

Hilo was a good forty miles away from the foothills of Mauna Loa, but they lived under the threat of the volcano while it slept—mostly forgotten—until something deep down ignited and the fire goddess Pele rose and roared to life. It must have been the tenth time Mauna Loa had erupted since Koji first set foot in Hawai'i. Some eruptions were barely a whimper, while others demanded attention. Given the months of tremors preceding it, this looked to be one of the big ones. If Mariko were still alive, he would have gone to the green bungalow first. While her spirit never physically returned to him, he often closed his eyes and felt her there, even heard her voice, but he never saw her. Instead, he headed directly to the fish market. Koji was running on adrenaline. Twenty minutes later, when he reached Kamehameha Avenue and turned the corner toward the market, a crowd had already collected in front. He was relieved to see that the downtown area looked almost undamaged. Koji parked and ran toward the crowd, wondering if Daniel had arrived yet. He stopped when someone yelled, "Mauna Loa! Long Mountain's smoking like a chimney!" Koji watched with the crowd as great plumes of billowing white smoke surged into the sky.

He remembered seven-year-old Daniel once pointing up at a cluster of cumulus clouds with great excitement. "There's Aopua'a," he'd told Koji gleefully, "right there, you see, that's the mama pig with all her piglets huddled around her. Uncle Samuel says it means a quiet day of good fishing with no storms."

But Mauna Loa was not about to remain quiet today. In the next moment, Koji watched the piglets scatter as the bloated white cloud soundlessly spread across the sky. A sudden shifting underfoot shook the ground again, and the nervous onlookers stared at one another and then back up at Mauna Loa. Even the air seemed to pulsate with their helplessness. The great white plumes of smoke turned an ash-filled dusty brown before emerging white again, only to be chased away by a spewing red-hot curtain of lava that blew from the fissures hundreds of feet into the air.

"Pele using her fire to let us know who's boss, yeah!" yelled a local in the crowd.

As soon as Koji saw Nori and the other aunties standing outside amid the crowd, he relaxed.

"You're here, yeah," Nori said, happy to see him.

"Any damage?" he asked.

"Just some broken bottles," she said.

"What's that?" He eyed the jar in her hands.

"Mango jam," Nori said. "The mangoes from Mariko's tree," she added.

Koji felt something inside of him slowly dissipate, something hard in the middle of his chest. He wanted to reach out and hug Nori.

Instead he asked, "Daniel?"

"He hasn't arrived yet."

Another eruption colored the sky. Koji was captivated by the raw power of Mauna Loa. He knew all they could do was worry and wait. It was just the beginning; the real fear was the unstoppable flow of lava, the searing slow-moving rivers of fire that could continue to flow for months in any direction. Just nine years ago, memories of the 1926 eruption, which had buried the village of Ho'opuloa Makai on the other side of the island, still haunted—the lava that crossed roads and fields, setting trees, shrubbery, houses, and anything else in its path on fire with a chorus of popping and sizzling methane bursts, could now be heading toward Hilo.

As if she read his thoughts, Nori asked, "When will the geologists know the direction of the flow?"

"I'm sure they're keeping a close watch, yeah," Koji said. "It won't be long now."

Most of the locals stayed on at the market, waiting for word.

As darkness fell, fountains of lava continued to spew from the fissure. The air grew oppressive with the stink of sulfur, clouds of ash, and the red-hot beast that illuminated the night.

6

HOMECOMING

Daniel Abe stood on deck and watched as Hilo town slowly appeared in the twilight, watery and indistinct. Even from a distance he knew the town by heart, the paved road and railway tracks running the sixty-five miles along the Hamakua coastline for the trains that carried sugar from the plantations, or goods and passengers all the way from Paauilo through Hilo to Glenwood, stopping just eight miles from the Kilauea volcano. On the left he could just make out Reeds Bay, next to Hilo's deepwater port, while to the right lay the crescent-shaped Hilo Bay. And directly across from Hilo Bay, running along Kamehameha Avenue, stood the rows of two-story clapboard buildings that housed the downtown businesses, including the Okawa Fish Market. Beyond downtown the sprawl of houses had inched closer to the foot of the volcanoes Mauna Loa and Mauna Kea.

The steamer engine droned on as the boat bobbed against the waves, dipping to one side and back. A door opened and closed. Most of the passengers had retreated into the main cabin. Daniel was almost home and he finally felt like he could breathe again. He leaned against the railing and watched the gulls circling above, tasting the salt spray on his lips, on his tongue as the warm wind picked up. He'd forgotten how simple, how welcoming it was as the steamer approached Hilo and lifted the weight of Daniel's ten years away.

In grand succession, he had received his medical degree from the University of Chicago's School of Medicine, followed by his residency, and the offer of a position at the University of Chicago's Medical Center. Daniel had proudly accepted, knowing that so few Orientals were ever given the opportunity. He remembered the feeling of triumph, thick and warm, something he had strived for ever since he was young, watching his mother sew for others, scrimping to save, always half hoping deep down that his father would return to them. But he never did.

In Chicago, Daniel was a respected mainland doctor at a prestigious hospital, where many of his colleagues had no idea where Hilo town was. He was ashamed to admit how easy it was to leave his old life behind, embrace the new, and allow himself to believe he was special. When his mother was dying, he'd gone back home, but he hadn't been ready to return to Hilo for good. At the time, he didn't know if he ever would. Eighteen months later, it took one wrong diagnosis and a costly mistake to bring Daniel home again.

His life in Chicago had been fast-paced, filled with raucous city sounds: screeches and shouts, automobile horns and gunning engines, all to be replaced by the comforting echoes of his childhood: the buzzing of mosquitoes; the loud *haw* of the nene geese; the wind whistling through the banyan trees; the lapping of water; and the chirping, rustling, wailing sounds of the rain forest. Only then did he realize how Hawai'i remained an enduring spirit that had seeped into his body and flowed through his veins. "Might not be a fancy big city, yeah, but home comes from within," his mother reminded him when he first left for the mainland. Her absence still stung, but his homecoming had also rekindled thoughts of his childhood, including his father's distant voice that now returned to him like the constant buzz of a mosquito.

"Why is the island so noisy?" Daniel had once asked his father as they walked along the Wailuku River. He was a boy of five and had so many questions.

"The island voices are talking to us," his father had answered.

Daniel studied the pale white zigzag caterpillar scar that ran along his father's left side squirming toward his back, a fall onto jagged lava rocks when he was a bit older than Daniel. He wanted to reach out and touch it, make it disappear. He thought his father suddenly looked sad.

"What are they saying?"

His father shrugged. "Things you wouldn't understand."

Daniel grew hot with impatience. He'd wanted his father to explain it to him. *Tell me.* He could still taste the words on the tip of his tongue, but his father's quiet moment of attention had vanished and he'd turned away.

The following year he was gone. If the island voices were what told his father to leave them, then they were the same voices that had called Daniel back home.

≈

Daniel stood stunned at the railing of the steamer, heart racing as his eyes followed the billowing smoke erupting from Mauna Loa. Moments later, it was followed by the bright blood orange curtain of lava that shot upward toward the darkening sky. Daniel felt the boat rock beneath his feet as a horn blew and passengers filed onto the deck to watch the erupting volcano. This was a homecoming Daniel hadn't expected, though eerily coincidental, since he'd been born in the early hours of another Mauna Loa eruption, in 1907. When he heard the steamer's engine reverse, the rumbling quieted, and he hoped they wouldn't turn around and head back to Oahu. He was so close to home. He thought of Uncle Koji and his Hilo Aunties, realizing that this might be exactly like all the boyhood stories Koji had told him, how the island could rise at any time and remake itself, destroying all that was man-made.

Daniel watched the surge of lava rise and fall, rise and fall, until the molten liquid pooled and flowed down over jagged lava rock like streaming tears, hot and blistering.

It was as beautiful as it was terrifying.

7

Waiting

Koji stood just inside the screen door of the Okawa Fish Market. A good two hours had passed since the first eruption, and everyone remained indoors waiting for news from the geologists at the Volcano Observatory Center. Outside, the air thickened with heat and the noxious smell of rotten eggs. Wilson and Mano hadn't returned yet, leaving Koji to wonder if Daniel's steamer laid waiting just outside the bay, or if it had returned to Oahu. He knew Daniel wouldn't be happy about turning back so close to home. Koji was reminded of a younger Daniel, so smart and curious, asking questions that he wasn't always able to answer.

Over the years, Koji had remained the closest thing Daniel had to a father. As boys, Koji and Franklin Abe were once as close as brothers. Whenever he and Razor could get away from the plantation, they'd spend all their free time down in Hilo with Franklin, who always took the lead with his smooth-talking, easy ways. He was a good-looking hapa: a mix of Japanese, Portuguese, and Filipino on his mother's side, while full-blood Japanese on his father's side. When they were young, he seemed invincible. But when Franklin's mother unexpectedly died, and

his father returned to Japan and remarried, he was seventeen and
chose to stay in Hilo. Frank had always been restless, but it seemed to
intensify from then on, and later it was Koji who remained a constant
presence in Mariko's and Daniel's lives after Franklin had abandoned
them.

≈

Through the screen door of the market, Koji saw a glimmer of light
moving through the hazy darkness, growing sharper as Gus Yamamoto's
boy came into view, flashlight in hand. Gus had a phone at his gas
station down the street, and Koji hoped his son was bringing news the
locals at the market had been waiting for.

He pushed open the screen door and the boy dashed in.

"The geologists at the observatory just called," he announced, his
voice rising with importance. "They say the lava is flowing toward
Mauna Kea volcano and away from Hilo town."

The news was met by rousing cheers from the waiting crowd of locals,
but he didn't see Razor.

Koji looked at the faces of his longtime friends, their anxious air
lightened by the news. They never took the island for granted. They
lived on sacred ground. What Koji loved most about his Hilo family was
their toughness, generations who had withstood so many hardships and
disasters. Even through the difficulties of the Depression, Hilo's local
community had maintained their everyday lives, fishing, hunting, and
bartering to make ends meet. They were survivors.

"We dodged another bullet, yeah," Samuel said, handing him a beer
from behind the koa counter.

Koji nodded. "Lucky this time."

"Now let's hope the boys arrive soon," Nori added.

Koji heard the worry in her words. The room hummed as voices rose
with relief and laughter. Before Koji could respond, he turned toward
the whine of the screen door opening and watched as Daniel stepped
into the market just ahead of Wilson and Mano, the three of them

talking and joking like boys again. Wasn't Koji once that young and full of spirit? Nori and the aunties were the first to pull him into their hugs. Koji stepped back to steady himself when a smiling Daniel turned his way. It was *her* smile, just a glimpse, but enough that he felt the warm rush of the past return to him.

8

In the Quiet

It was late by the time Daniel returned home from the market. He stepped inside the green bungalow for the first time in more than two years, closed the door, and stood a moment in the quiet of the darkened room. In the air warm as breath, the slight scent of his mother's perfume lingered, or so he imagined. Before his mother died, she told him to scatter her ashes in the wind from Pilani Point. "Finally get to see the world, yeah," she'd said. She smiled and Daniel could only nod his head, his throat so dry he could hardly speak. Tonight she was the only one missing at the party, the only one who would forgive all his mistakes. When Daniel switched on the light to see the spare and comfortable living room, a small part of him still hoped his mother would be standing there waiting for him.

All night at the party, laughter and words had flowed with the ease of music. Seeing his Hilo family again, Daniel realized just how much he had missed them. He was happily slapped on the back and pulled into tight hugs by the locals as the room suddenly vibrated with their energy, Mauna Loa momentarily forgotten. Daniel knew every inch of the market, having crawled as a baby across the wood plank floor of the vast room, racing along in diapers with Mano. Born weeks apart, they were as close as twins growing up. Here he was, surrounded by the Hilo aunties and Uncle Koji, so unlike the cold or curious stares directed his way in Chicago, where he hated the whispers, the occasional remarks that followed him as he walked down Michigan Avenue or Rush or Division Streets, "Slanty Eyes," or "Chop Suey Louie," or "Ching Chong Chinaman go home." His blood boiling, gut pulling, he had pushed past the insults and kept going.

No use in causing trouble.

At the university, where he'd been the lone Oriental in his medical school class, the voices were more inquisitive yet just as invasive "Where are you from?" his classmates asked, "China? Japan? Philippines?" They were more interested in *what* he was instead of *who* he was. He'd gone from a town where everyone knew him to a city where no one did.

When he'd finally proved himself and was offered the prized position at the medical center, it wasn't just about getting the job; it was about being recognized for *who* he was.

～

Daniel woke with a start. Confused at first, it took him a moment to remember he was home in Hilo, awakening in his old room, where the relics of his childhood remained. His books and baseball trophies still filled the bookcase above his desk, his well-worn, oil-stained glove and bat lay tucked away in the closet, and his beloved anatomy chart, pin-pricked and faded, detailing every artery and organ of the human body, remained tacked to the back of his bedroom door.

It was still dark outside, his room quiet and stuffy with the window closed against the hovering volcanic fog. Nevertheless, the scent of rotten eggs seeped in through the cracks and crevices. Mauna Loa's eruption last night was just another reminder that the gods would always have the final say. While the Volcano Observatory Center kept a close watch, the locals knew they would simply have to wait for Pele to calm down again.

Daniel's own birth was forever tied to Pele and Mauna Loa. His mother liked to tell the story of how he was born unexpectedly at home on the night of an eruption. Daniel had arrived two weeks early, while his father was away working at a construction job on Maui, leaving his twenty-year-old wife alone as his son began to push into the world. If Mauna Loa hadn't erupted, Uncle Koji wouldn't have come down to check on his mother, finding her in labor. "Mauna Loa erupted in happiness and not in anger the night you were born," she always said. "Means Pele will always watch over you."

Is Pele watching now? Daniel wondered. *And if she is, is Mauna Loa erupting in happiness or in anger at my return?*

≈

Sleep was fruitless. Daniel heard a rooster crow, a dog barking in the distance. He turned on the light to see that the clock read just past 4:00 a.m. It was midmorning in Chicago, and if he were still there he'd most likely be at the hospital looking at charts, starting his morning rounds. It would be a typical day, just like that early morning the four-year-old was brought in to the hospital with a slight fever and loss of appetite. She'd been lethargic and vomiting, her parents said, all flu-like symptoms. Daniel checked all her vitals, gave her a small dose of aspirin, told the parents to keep her hydrated, and sent her home. The little girl returned two days later, unconscious after suffering a seizure. Daniel's thoughts turned over and over in his memory. What had he missed on her first visit? Had he been too complacent, too quick to dismiss her symptoms as the flu when he should have been more thorough? He'd been tired, working an extra shift in the emergency room with patients still waiting. Not long after the little girl returned she'd gone into cardiac arrest and stopped breathing. By the time they resuscitated and stabilized her, she had suffered permanent brain damage. What Daniel assumed was a case of the flu had triggered something else, an abnormality sparked by his giving her aspirin. "You couldn't have known," his colleagues reassured, unable to look him in the eyes. It could have been any one of them, and the relief that it wasn't could be seen in their fleeting gaze. There wasn't much he could do except to make the child as comfortable as possible. Daniel had seen fatalities before—death was a part of his profession—but he couldn't help but feel his mistake had damaged the little girl's life in a way crueler than death.

Daniel quit his coveted position at the hospital, refusing to be branded the Oriental doctor who had made the tragic mistake. All that he'd worked so hard for was suddenly gone.

He had nowhere to go but home.

~

Daniel got up and rummaged through the hall closet until he found the box he was looking for and carried it to the kitchen. He looked out the window; the stark gray light of dawn had begun to filter its way through the soupy fog and ash that hung in the air. He flicked on the light, made a pot of coffee, and set to work. The box held his entire train collection, divided into smaller oblong boxes. One by one he opened them, the power box, the metal tracks and train station, the Lionel railcar numbers 1 through 13, given to him by Uncle Koji over the years. He added the latest addition, the new railcar Koji had left for him. Daniel remembered all the hours of happiness the train set had given him. He blessedly felt like that boy again snapping the metal tracks together on the kitchen table and lining up each railcar behind his favorite number 5 engine. He connected the wires to the power box, plugged it in, and pressed the switch.

Nothing happened.

He reconnected the wires and made sure the screws were tight. "Please," Daniel said aloud, stirring the quiet. "Please."

Suddenly nothing felt more important to Daniel than the train moving forward. He pressed the switch again. The power box buzzed. The light flickered and then remained green as the train began its wobbly start, click-clacking around the table once before picking up speed.

GHOST VOICES

MARIKO, 1914

I light the kerosene lantern and set it on the table. The kitchen is suddenly aglow again after we were left in darkness. Outside, the storm rages on with the wind punching and moaning, striking down everything in its way. I only hope the house is strong enough to withstand it. I should feel better with the lamplight, but the shadows grow and seem to be lurking as the wind and thundering rain become deafening. It started out as a typical rainstorm, but it grew in strength as the evening wore on. Earlier in the day, Nori and Samuel asked if I wanted to stay with them. "No need, yeah, it's just a rainstorm," I said. "Daniel and I will be fine." Now it's too late, the storm has grown into a typhoon, and it's too dangerous for us to leave the house. I look up to see Daniel standing in the doorway, watching me.

I open my arms to him. "It's going to be okay," I say. "It's just a storm, it blows in and out like breath, yeah, and then it's gone."

He nods and comes to me for a hug. He's tall for seven years old.

There's a sudden loud crash in the yard and I hurry to the window. It could be Daniel's bicycle, or a chair left out, or a fallen tree limb. I hope and pray it isn't the mango tree and already grieve at the thought. I can taste the succulent fruit on the tip of my tongue. I can't see anything outside in the dark and driving rain.

Something suddenly hits the window hard and I jump back awkwardly, as if I've been pushed. And just as quickly, Daniel is there, arms around my waist. "It's just the wind," I say, thankful the window hasn't broken.

The wind howls painfully and the rain falls in torrents, as if all the gods are crying at once. Beyond Hilo town I imagine the roar of the ocean waves pounding furiously into Hilo Bay, flooding the roadway and railroad tracks, stealing tethered boats from the wharf, and thrusting them out to sea. As with so many other storms, we'll wake up to a mess—severed branches like torn limbs, roof shingles, siding, and unrecognizable ocean debris littering the flooded streets and shops and leaving muddy pools everywhere. In the end, I know it doesn't matter as long as no one is hurt.

I take the lamp and sit down on the sofa with Daniel. He snuggles up to me and I try to read to him, but the storm wins again by drowning out my voice. I stroke Daniel's hair, rub his back, and feel him finally relaxing in my lap when we're startled by something just beyond the noise of the storm, a thud, thud, thud that makes Daniel quickly sit up and listen. It takes another moment before we both realize that someone is pounding on the front door.

"There's someone—"

"Don't open it, don't open it," Daniel says, a small plea. He pulls at my arm, frightened all over again.

I think of the knife that was in the drawer of my bedside table, the one Franklin left for our protection now gone. "It's all right," I say, pulling Daniel closer. Even if it isn't, even if I'm frightened too, even if my first thoughts are: Where is Franklin? Where has he been the past year? Where is he when we need him the most?

I open the door slowly, but it's snatched from my hand by the wind and slams against the wall as if the storm itself has entered the house. The wind and rain whip into the living room. Then, as if carried in by both, Koji rushes through the doorway and shoves the door closed behind him. I can't believe he's standing there looking like a crazy man, drenched and muddy in an old raincoat and hat.

I've never been so happy to see anyone in my life. And there's something more that has dashed in with the storm: it's the first time since Franklin has left that I've felt a stirring in me beyond anything more than just gratitude. I shake the thought away.

"Uncle Koji!" Daniel shouts, and runs to him.

"Careful, careful," Koji says, "You'll get wet and muddy, yeah."

"How did you get here?" I ask.

He takes off his boots and raincoat and drops them by the door, but not before he pulls a brown box out of his coat pocket.

"I have my ways," he says. "Wanted to make sure the house was still standing. Big storm, yeah?" He looks down at Daniel. "I know you're taking good care of your mom, but sometimes it's good to have two men watching over things."

Daniel nods. He relaxes into Koji's hug.

I can't help but smile. "Let me get you a towel," I say. "Don't want you getting sick on our account." From the moment Koji steps into the house, it's as if all of our fears have left.

I return to see him handing the box to Daniel.

"What is it?" Daniel asks.

"You won't know until you open it, eh."

Daniel looks at me and I nod. Rain continues to thunder down, but my little boy no longer seems to notice. He opens the box to find a metal railroad engine that looks just like the ones that rattle through the Hilo train station, the ones he's loved since he was a toddler.

He holds it up for me to see. "It's an engine," he says. Marveling, he inspects its intricacies, the shiny black paint, the smokestack, the electric lamp, and the red cowcatcher on the front.

"Not just any train," Koji says. *"It's a Lionel number five steam engine. There are thirteen in the set, and I thought you might like to start collecting. We'll get you some track, yeah. One day you'll have them all."*

"What do you say?" I remind my son, raising my voice above the noise of the storm. I look up and catch Koji's eyes before glancing shyly away.

"Thank you," Daniel says. Across his face blooms a big smile that I haven't seen since his father left.

As Koji explains to Daniel how the engine runs I can feel the darkness lift, while outside, the storm continues to howl and rage.

CARRYING ON

November 23–25, 1935

9

SANCTUARY

The trade winds had stopped for two days after the eruption, leaving a hazy gray curtain of volcanic fog hanging across Hilo. The air stewed with heat, and everything simmered in shadows. Nori kept the market open, knowing many of the regulars would still be scurrying through the veiled daylight, bandanas tied over their mouths and noses like bandits as they made their way to the market for companionship and the latest news.

Over the years the market had provided a place not only for Nori's Saturday afternoon game of hearts with the Hilo Aunties, but also for the old-timers to play cards and dominoes every day in the yard out back, reminiscing about the biggest fish they had ever caught, or the prettiest girl they'd ever courted, until it was time for them to head back home. Nori always made sure to have a fresh pot of coffee, guava juice, and bowls of rice crackers available for them. She'd lost track of how many times their wives had thanked her for giving them a place to congregate, keeping them out of the house. Nori knew it was just as much for her own sake. Since Samuel had retired from fishing after a back injury a couple of years ago, he spent a considerable amount of time out in the yard with the old-timers and out of her way. She had seen Samuel more in the past two years than in all the years they'd been married.

Now that Samuel was retired, she still worried about Wilson and Mano going out to sea every morning. Nori held back her fears and concerns when both of her sons followed their father into the family business. It only proved that the Okawa blood was stronger than hers. Even the eruption hadn't stopped them.

"With all the rumbling from Loa, the fish will be scared right into our nets, yeah," Mano said, making light of her fears.

But Nori was always waiting, waiting for when the ocean would rise or the island would rumble with fire and split open, taking everyone she loved from her.

≈

By the third morning of the eruption Nori was relieved to see the sky had cleared. Overnight, the winds had blown the volcanic fog west, toward the other side of the island. As soon as the lunch rush was over, Nori left Jelly to watch the market and hurried to visit her old friend Leia, and her mother, Mama Natua.

Outside, the sun was warm and the smell of smoke and sulfur lingered. The streets were crowded again, groups of men smoking and playing cards on the sidewalk, hoping to get work down on the docks if they waited long enough. Nori hurried through the crowds and walked up Ponahawai Street toward the Natua house. She usually visited eighty-three-year-old Mama once a week, bringing her the salty dried plums she liked to suck on, but missed seeing her last week because of the eruption.

Today nothing could keep her away.

When Nori was young, she liked to pretend Mama was her real mother. Her feelings hadn't changed over the years; Mama would always be special to her, loving and no-nonsense, the woman who had taught her what family meant. From the time Nori was six years old, slight and dark-eyed, a mix of Japanese and Portuguese, Nori knew by the tone of her father's or mother's voice if a fight was coming, the sharp sting of ti root alcohol souring the air, followed by that rising pitch that made her stop whatever she was doing and listen, waiting for the waves to come crashing to shore. "Not picking one more damn pineapple," her mother started, followed by glass shattering on the floor or against a wall. As their voices grew louder, Nori would quickly climb out her bedroom window, or slip out the back door and hurry along the road to Mama Natua's house, the small cluttered bungalow with a screened-in front porch to keep the mosquitoes away. Nori had spent much of her childhood in and out of the Natua house, playing with Leia and her younger sister, Noelani, and staying overnight when her drunk and volatile parents had a particularly bad fight and the hitting began.

Nori slowed down when she saw the sagging roof of her paint-stripped, childhood house, black wattle and barbwire weeds swallowing it up whole. Her muscles tensed and her stomach churned like that young girl again in no hurry to get home, black and blue blotches peppering her arms and legs like dark clouds. Her mother liked to pinch and push, slap and shove, while her father sat, too drunk to stand. Going home every day meant becoming invisible to them and staying out of the way, and it meant not being able to see Mariko until the next morning at school. Mariko had been her best friend, the keeper of all her secrets from elementary school until her death, while Mama had been her home. Nori caught her breath and shook away the sad memories. Her parents were dead now, the road to the Natua house the last thread tied to her childhood, and with it, Mama Natua, whose mind and body were fading.

〜

Nori found Leia in the kitchen, a half-strung lei hanging from her arm. Tall and amicable, Leia had a quiet strength most missed but Nori held dear. Hadn't she been the older sister who always protected her? She was a younger version of Mama, a nurturer, and had inherited her lei stringing skills. Mama Natua was once celebrated as the best lei maker in Hilo town, creating beautiful garlands from the island's natural bounty, and was well known for weaving traditional open-ended ti leaf leis coveted by hula dancers from all the islands. The locals always joked that "Mama Natua could make a beautiful lei made out of tin cans!" Nori loved watching Mama Natua's hands in constant motion, while the Natua porch and kitchen always resembled the outdoors—baskets of flowers, ti leaves, fern fronds, seashells, even seeds piled high on the table—the air thick with sea salt, or smelling sweetly of everything from pine to pikake when Nori walked in, her bare feet sliding across traces of sand on the wood floor. It was no different now.

"How is she doing?" Nori asked.

"She has no idea Mauna Loa has erupted," Leia answered.

"Better that way, yeah."

Leia nodded, and peeked into the basket Nori carried to see a banana bread and ono butter mochi. "Thank you for this," she said, and led Nori into Mama's dark, warm bedroom, which smelled stale and medicinal. "Lately, she doesn't like the room too bright," Leia whispered.

Nori nodded. When her eyes adjusted to the dimness, she saw white-haired Mama sitting in an old armchair.

Over the years, Mama had stubbornly refused to see a dentist or a medical doctor. She didn't trust modern medicine. She believed that all the medicine she needed came from the plants that grew all around her. Nori hoped she might consider letting Daniel examine her since she'd known him since birth.

Once majestic, Mama was now a shrunken and wrinkled version of herself sitting in the chair. Her hands still moved in front of her as if she were stringing together the leis that had been worn by everyone from well-known hula dancers to the movie star Shirley Temple to Queen Lili'uokalani. It was believed that pure Hawaiian blood flowed through Mama's veins too, even if it had been thinned by generations of outside marriages. She'd always been their closest connection to the old Hawaiian ways.

Mama Natua looked up. "You come home, Noelani?"

"Mama, it's not Noelani. It's Nori. You remember Nori," Leia said.

Mama Natua looked from her daughter to Nori. "You change your hair, yeah?"

Nori instinctively touched the back of her hair, peppered with gray. "No, it's the same, Mama."

"Where your bangs?"

Nori smiled. "Mama, I haven't had bangs since I was seven years old."

Mama Natua watched her suspiciously. "I don't know you," she said, turning away.

"Of course you do, Mama," Leia said. "It's your favorite, Nori. Little Nori from up the street. You've known her all of her life."

A look of bewilderment washed over Mama Natua's face.

"Look what I brought you," Nori said, hoping to bring her back. She took out the bag of salty dry plums. "I know it's your favorite." She opened the bag and put one in the palm of her hand.

"Nori such a smart girl, yeah," Mama said, slipping the dry plum between her lips and sucking noisily on it. "Sometimes she looked so sad. Broke my heart."

Nori looked at Leia.

"Good days and bad," Leia said softly. "She comes and goes."

"You know my younger daughter, Noelani? She's away in Honolulu for secretarial school. First one in the family to leave the island, yeah," the old woman said, as she sucked on the dry plum and smiled.

"Mama, that was a long time ago," Leia explained. "Noelani's home now and working at the Kailua Plantation. She'll be by later to see you."

"Why you cut your hair? Makes you look old," Mama Natua said.

"Mama," Leia pleaded.

"I won't cut it so short next time," Nori said, appeasing.

It didn't matter what Mama said now, Nori thought. *I am getting older.* She would be forty-nine in a few months. Would she one day forget everyone and everything, her mind a blank canvas? Nori shook the thought away. Instead, she smiled, pulled a chair over, and sat down next to the woman who had saved her childhood. She glanced at a photo of Mama and Uncle Nestor by her bedside, taken just after they married, both so young and beautiful. Nori reached for Mama Natua's hand, her fingers tracing the deep grooves along Mama's open palm before she placed another dried plum in it.

Mama stared at her for a moment. "I know you," she said, her eyes brightening.

10

FIRE AND ICE

Daniel stayed mostly indoors during the first two days of the eruption, getting reacquainted with his surroundings while the volcanic fog blanketed him in a sleepy haze that slowed time. As soon as the air cleared, Daniel was outside walking along the outskirts of downtown, quiet streets lined with small, single-story clapboard houses with rusted corrugated roofs and sun-bleached walls, both foreign and familiar at the same time.

He used to walk home this way every day from school, but now everything appeared much smaller than he remembered. His old high school and the baseball field looked faded and run-down, and the bleachers where he sat with Maile, his high school girlfriend, sagged in the distance. All those weekends spent with her at the beach or Wailuku River, along with Wilson, Mano, and other high school friends, smoking and drinking whatever could be pilfered from their parents without getting caught. Daniel tried not to think of Maile when he was in Chicago, but here, she was everywhere. She'd been the only girl for him back then. The last he'd heard from her was a card she'd sent after his mother passed away. She was living in Honolulu

and engaged to be married. All at once, his mother was gone and so
was Maile. He had no right to hope for anything from her, but he'd
still felt grief-stricken.

Daniel picked up his pace. After so many years living in Chicago,
his body still hummed with the traffic and noise bouncing off the tall
buildings. A part of him had been apprehensive about returning to
Hilo, anxious that he wouldn't be able to adjust to the unhurried island
quiet, only to arrive in the midst of a different kind of turmoil and
chaos with Mauna Loa's eruption. He was quickly reminded that the
island was just as volatile and unpredictable as anything a big city
could offer.

What Daniel didn't miss about Chicago was the cold. He still felt
the icy wind against his cheeks, chapped raw and red, his fingers so
cold he could barely get his key in the door. He had shivered through
so many frigid winters dreaming of warm Hilo mornings that smelled
sweetly of papaya and guava, pikake and ginger flowers. It was what
he longed for most when he walked along the shore of Lake Michigan
bundled up like an Eskimo during the long, dark winters that felt like a
scentless, icy purgatory. His first winter there, he couldn't imagine how
people lived in such cold.

Instead, Daniel had returned to a gray veiled sky of smoke and ash
and the scent of sulfur that was finally being carried away by the warm
trade winds. Still, he felt calmer to be home, away from Chicago and
the turbulence of the hospital, the knot in his stomach loosening. Daniel
walked toward downtown, along ghostly streets that were once lined
with new markets and small restaurants opened by the influx of workers
coming for the plantation work.

Before leaving for his first year of college, he had walked down these
very same streets, smelling the sweet aromas of baking bread topped
with butter and sugar from the Villanueva Bakery and the rich, fragrant
scent of *pan de coco* that wafted from the doorway of De La Rosa
Cakes, making his mouth water. Back then, everyone from the plantation owners and workers to the missionary families and the locals
shopped at the bakeries. The crowded streets came alive at night with

a colorful mix of languages, foreign foods, and the rhythmic, pulsing music of Filipino bands playing in the growing number of clubs and bars that had opened. Now, six years after the stock market crashed, there were only the empty, run-down storefronts with their faded signs written in two languages, one English, the second either Japanese or Portuguese or Tagalog.

Daniel turned down the street toward Kalakaua Park, directly across from the Federal Building, still the biggest and sturdiest structure in Hilo, and the first built using reinforced concrete, back in 1917. It had been inspired by all the sugar and cattle wealth, a stately Renaissance Revival design that still appeared out of place. Auntie Nori always thought it was showy, just like the haoles who built it.

"What would you prefer?" Uncle Samuel had asked. "Two grass huts?"

Auntie Nori stopped for a moment. "One would do," she answered.

Daniel smiled at the memory.

The Hilo Spring Festival at Kalakaua Park was one of Daniel's favorite events as a boy, the annual celebration that brought out not only the Hilo community and bigwigs, but also the plantation and dockworkers. Along with Wilson and Mano, he couldn't wait for the festival every April, excited by all the food and games and the shave ice stand manned by Uncle Samuel. For days beforehand, the aunties prepared their best dishes: the Natuas' *kalua* pork, Auntie Nori's butterfish *lau lau,* his mother's Portuguese chicken, long tables laden with food the locals brought to share. Everyone ate until their stomachs bulged, and then they ate more. It was the one day of the year that brought everyone together, the park bursting with music and *hau'oli.*

Daniel crossed the street to Kalakaua Park and stopped short as a flock of birds burst from the banyan tree and into the sky. Ominous shadows lay under the large, beloved tree, its thick, gnarled roots fanning out like a road map. He looked again to see that sleeping bodies were nestled between the roots. Some men had blankets, while others lay curled up into themselves. He had just turned to leave when a large, thick-bodied, mud-colored dog came out of nowhere and charged at him, barking and growling with such menace, Daniel paused, heart racing, looking for anything to protect himself with. He grabbed a branch on the ground and stepped back, ready to swing, when, all of a sudden, the dog yelped in pain as a rope around his neck choked him roughly back with the force of his own momentum. Daniel quickly stole away from the salivating, panting dog and the sleeping men, who scarcely stirred.

In Chicago, Daniel had seen hordes of weary people living on the streets with nowhere to sleep and little to eat, but still, he was startled. He was reminded of what Uncle Koji had told him the night of his homecoming party when he asked how the plantations were doing in these hard times.

"Puli and the other cane plantations have been lucky, yeah. No matter how bad it gets, everyone still wants sugar in their coffee. Not the same for our *hala kahiki* brothers. Most of the pineapple plantations have had to shut down."

"On all the islands?"

Koji sipped his beer and nodded. "Hard times, eh," he continued. "We were lucky, yeah, the sugar plantations didn't fire us. Cut our salaries and stopped hiring from overseas. But the cane workers, mostly still got their jobs. Never mind the Depression, the mainland's still addicted to sugar."

Until now, Daniel hadn't seen how the Depression had hurt Hilo in the same ways. He glanced back at the crowded park, so far away from the jubilant festivals of his childhood. Daniel shook his head; it was obvious things had changed even on the Big Island. He turned down the street and walked toward Hilo Bay.

If he hurried, he might catch Uncle Koji at the train station.

11

THE SUGAR TRAIN

Koji guided the sugar train down the mountain, wiping sweat and coal dust from his face with his bandana. It was stifling in the cramped engine car, even after Pedro, his fireman, stopped shoveling coal into the fire. He began coughing again, and looked up at Mauna Loa, still shrouded in a massive gray plume of steam and gas and ash that rose into the sky and drifted toward Kona. Yesterday's sun had been muted, the sky darkened by fog and a dusting of volcanic ash that cast everything into shadows, the dull, gray air hard to breathe. Today Koji was relieved that the trade winds had returned as the train traveled toward Hilo and the station. As long as the lava flowed away from the sugar plantations and Hilo, the sugar train continued its twice-daily runs, despite all-powerful and unforgiving Pele.

The Hawaii Consolidated Railway ran three different train lines through Hilo, the main thread connecting all the mill towns from Mahukima to Kohala to Niulii. One line transported passengers from along the Hamakua coast. Another carried freight and goods to the warehouse down by Hilo Bay. The third line ran the narrow-gauge sugar trains. From March through November the sugar trains worked nonstop, either transporting sugar from the northern Hamakua coast mills to the port, or, like Koji's train, traveling up and down the mountain carrying sacks of refined sugar from the Puli Plantation mill down to Waiakea, the deepwater port at Hilo Bay to be stored at the wharf warehouse, or loaded directly onto an awaiting steamship heading to the mainland. Every time Koji climbed up to the engine car, he was reminded of when he and Razor were teenagers at the end of the harvest season, catching rides up and down to Hilo on the sugar train. He'd learned everything he could from the engineer, Salvador, never dreaming that so many years later he would be the one running the train. When the train left Puli and rounded the cane fields, Koji thought he glimpsed Razor, only to look again and see it wasn't him.

Koji leaned out the engine window as the train slowed on its approach toward Hilo's clapboard train station, with its simple ticket office and waiting room with wooden benches. He pulled the slippery cord to sound the whistle. Steam hissed as a plume reached toward the sky. He saw Daniel standing on the platform in the same spot where he'd waited for Koji when he was a boy. As the train rolled to a stop, Koji leaned farther out the window and raised his hand.

Just like old times.

≈

Daniel had just turned six, too young to understand what had happened when his father abandoned them. By the time Daniel was eleven or twelve, he was often waiting at the train station for Koji, wanting to know everything he could about Franklin. They sat on the old wooden bench just across from the tracks and talked, while Koji waited for his crew to unload the sacks of sugar from the railway cars and cart them across the road to the harbor.

Then one afternoon when Daniel was thirteen, he finally said, "Tell me how I'm like my father."

Koji looked at him and gathered his thoughts. He paused to light a cigarette. "On the outside, you look a lot like him. Tall and skinny, dark eyes and a thick head of hair, movie-star island-boy good looks," he said. He inhaled and exhaled smoke. "You're athletic like him; you got his speed and agility. His stubbornness, too. The rest, everything on the inside, comes from your mother. Lucky for you, yeah," he added.

"Why did he leave us?" Daniel had asked bluntly. "Was it because of me?"

Koji's eyes widened with surprise. He sucked on his cigarette, taking his time to answer, smoke rings rising into the air and disappearing. "Oily hands," he finally said. "Shame your father could never hold on to anything. His leaving had nothing to do with you. He let the only two good things in his life slip through his fingers, you and your mother. Some men just like that." He dropped the cigarette and snuffed it out angrily with the toe of his boot. "He looked for ways to lose things. Lucky for me, yeah, I get to see you grow up and make your mother proud."

Koji shook his head at the memory. How could he have given Daniel such a rational explanation for something so irrational? At the time, Koji had confided in Razor that he wanted to tell Daniel that his father was a bigger son of a bitch than any of them realized. He wanted to fuel the boy's anger, but Razor helped him to understand that he couldn't do it. Neither of them would feel any better, and it only would have made Mariko's life more difficult. Days, weeks, months turned into a year, and Koji saw Franklin's absence in the deepening lines on Mariko's face, and how the light in her eyes had dimmed, breaking his heart too.

~

In the station, Koji sounded the train whistle again: a short, short, long wail filled the air, the same greeting he used when Daniel was young. Moments later, he jumped down from the car in his T-shirt and baggy pants.

"Look who's here," he said, and wrapped his arms around Daniel in a big hug.

Daniel smiled. "Good to see you, Uncle Koji," he said. "I wanted to thank you again for the new model railcar. Looks just like your engine."

"I thought it might remind you of us hardworking folks."

"It's the best one yet," Daniel said.

Koji shook his head. "You say that every time."

"It's the truth, they're all the best," Daniel said. "I've missed getting to sit down with you and catch up."

"Our schedules keep changing daily since the eruption," he said. "Never know where I am lately." Koji scowled. He hated not keeping the train on schedule.

"So much has changed since I've been gone," Daniel said. "I was at Kalakaua Park . . . saw the men sleeping there."

"Shame, yeah," Koji said. "But the sugar business keeps going, eh." He gave a guilty shrug and changed the subject. "But I want to hear more about you. How you doing? You know your mother would be so happy to have you home. She'd be so proud, yeah. A doctor."

Daniel shifted from one foot to the other, his smile momentarily disappearing. He pulled out a handkerchief to wipe his face before meeting Koji's gaze again. "I've been thinking," he said. "Maybe I made the wrong decision."

"Coming home?" Koji asked. It was the first thing that came to mind. He always wondered if Daniel would ever come back after Mariko was gone. There was always the big city in him, and no one was more surprised than Koji when Daniel's letter arrived saying he was on his way home.

Daniel shook his head. "Medicine."

Koji looked at him stunned, not knowing what to say. Wasn't becoming a doctor what Daniel had wanted ever since he was young? Doctoring was in his blood. He labored through all the letters and applications involved in getting into a good mainland university, helped by scholarships. Mariko was ecstatic when he was accepted into medical school after all his hard work, even though she worried about the cost. Her seamstress work barely covered her living expenses, but Daniel had applied for grants and worked part-time, and Koji had insisted on helping with the rest. "An investment, yeah," he told her. "I may need a good doctor one day." Mariko encouraged Daniel every step of the way. His success had always been hers. "Imagine, yeah, a Hilo boy returns a doctor," she liked to say. "I know Pele's watching over him." Daniel was the first local boy he knew with a medical degree from the mainland.

"Did something happen?" Koji asked. He saw a fleck of anguish in Daniel's eyes and then it was gone.

Daniel shook his head. "It's . . ." he began, but then said, "It's just that I've been holed up in the house for the past few days. Too much time to think," he added.

"Never a good thing, yeah," Koji teased.

Daniel managed a smile.

Koji sensed his uneasiness but didn't push. Something had to bring Daniel home from that big, fancy hospital in Chicago. Koji watched Daniel but he quickly looked away, just as he always did when he was a boy and wasn't ready to talk. Instead, Koji smiled and stepped forward to hug him again, strong and firm.

Koji would never let Daniel slip through his fingers again.

12

THE GREEN BUNGALOW

The morning after Nori visited Mama Natua, she walked down Kame-hameha, past the wharf and up the road toward the green bungalow to see Daniel. She carried a palm leaf basket filled with freshly baked coconut tarts. She hadn't seen him since his welcome home party. With the eruption causing so much commotion, she hadn't even been able to check to see if he'd settled in comfortably. Now that the air had cleared, her impromptu visit also included a special favor to ask of him.

The sky darkened and the air smelled of rain by the time Nori arrived at the bungalow. She knocked on the front door, a part of her still hoping to see a young, teenage Mariko behind the screen when it opened. "About time, yeah," she always said, even when Nori was early. They'd hurried to her bedroom to do homework or gossip about boys and school. School had always been Nori's solace. She loved the peaceful sounds of the class-room, the click, click, click of the chalk on the blackboard, the turning of pages, the wind rattling the windows, and the rustling palm trees outside. She loved math, the solid numbers that made complete sense to her when everything else didn't. Adding, subtracting, multiplying, and dividing seemed like simple rules for life. The classroom walls were painted a soothing pale green, with a clock over the door and speckled gray tiles on the floor.

Nori sat one desk away from Mariko. Between them sat Samuel Okawa, who always smelled salty like the sea, and often fell asleep in class sitting up, his eyes closed, his sudden snore waking him as the class erupted in laughter. When it happened, Nori watched Samuel's cheeks flush with embarrassment and felt bad for him. She wasn't the only one who kept secrets. She learned he'd been going out every night on his father's fishing boat, working in the darkness before dawn while everyone else slept, hours and hours before school started. Only Mariko knew her deepest secret that she loved school and being as far away as she could from home and her drinking, fighting, furious parents, and how she often wished they were dead.

≈

Nori knocked again. A few moments passed before she heard quick footsteps and the door swung open.

"Auntie Nori," Daniel said, his voice full of surprise, "good morning. It's good to see you. Everything okay?"

She nodded. "Everything's fine, yeah. I just wanted to see how you were doing. Haven't had a chance to talk since you returned," she said, and smiled.

"Come in."

Daniel led her toward the kitchen.

As they walked through the living room, Nori realized that Daniel had rearranged some of the furniture, a table moved to a corner, a chair across the room. She had no business being upset by it, but it was a sharp reminder that it wasn't Mariko's house anymore. Thankfully, the kitchen was still hers, except for the train set that covered the Formica table. *Where does he eat?* Nori thought.

"Sorry for the clutter," he said, following her gaze. "I was trying out the new railcar Uncle Koji gave me."

His face was that of a young Daniel again, shy and flushed with embarrassment, so different from her boys who had lumbered into and out of rooms, leaving a mess in their wake without so much as a thought.

Nori smiled. "Nonsense. A house should be lived in, yeah? It's been quiet in here for much too long."

"Thank you for taking such good care of the house . . . of everything," he said, and his voice caught.

And there was Mariko in the room with them again.

Nori placed the basket on the counter while he poured her a cup of coffee. "I was happy to come around and check on things, yeah. Made me feel like I was still visiting your mother," she said.

Daniel smiled. "Shall we sit in the living room?" he asked.

"Can we stay in here?" Nori always wanted to stay where she felt Mariko's presence strongest.

Daniel nodded. "Of course," he said.

He placed the plate of coconut tarts in the middle of the Formica table, surrounded by his train set, then pulled out two chairs from the table for them to sit.

"How are you?" she asked. "I'm sorry we haven't had the chance to really talk. Since the eruption and all . . ."

"I'm fine," he said, then added, "It's good to be home."

"Your mom would be so proud, yeah."

Daniel looked away from her and simply nodded.

Nori saw a nerve twitch under his left eye, a storm lingering just underneath.

"There wasn't a single day your mother wasn't proud of you, and rightly so, yeah. We're all proud of you—not every day a local boy returns a doctor. Big deal, eh." Nori finished what she started to say. She hoped he would tell her if something was bothering him. "Everything all right?" she asked.

"Just trying to figure out what to do next," he finally said.

She watched him for a moment. "You were always the most complicated of the three boys."

"Is that bad?" Daniel asked.

Nori smiled, thinking of Wilson and Mano. "Bad, no. You have always had bigger dreams than my boys. Nothing wrong with that, eh. They're happy chasing fish. All I'm saying is that you've already accomplished so much. You're just back, yeah, there's no need to hurry," she said, and then added, "Your mother would want you to be happy. That's all she ever wanted. Everything else will fall into place."

They were silent a moment. "Thank you for checking up on me," he said.

"Don't thank me yet. I need to ask you a favor."

"Anything," Daniel said.

"Could you visit Mama Natua and give her a quick checkup?"

"Is there something wrong with Mama?"

Where should Nori begin? *Everything is wrong*, she thought. She absently stroked the small scar on the back of her right hand. Everyone in Hilo town knew and loved Mama, only now, Mama no longer knew them. Mama didn't know *her* anymore.

Nori sipped her coffee to clear her throat and said, "She has forgotten so much in the past few years, everything and everyone, yeah. I just want to make sure there's nothing else wrong with her."

"Doesn't she have her own doctor?"

Nori shook her head. "Mama doesn't trust the new ways, always relied on plants and herbs. She's never seen a doctor, doesn't believe in them."

Daniel leaned forward. "Then what makes you think she'll let me give her a checkup?"

"You're not a doctor to her, you're Mariko's boy."

Daniel laughed. "How could I forget? One big, happy family."

"Hilo needs a good family doctor, yeah," Nori added. "We need someone we can trust who understands the community, especially the older folks, not just all these haole doctors who practice medicine here for the warm weather and beaches."

Daniel laughed. "Coming from Chicago, there's nothing wrong with the sun and beaches."

She saw a flicker of mischief return to his eyes. Daniel looked like Franklin, but his smile brought back his mother.

"You joke, but most young folks don't return once they leave."

Daniel's smiled turned serious. He ran his fingers through his hair. "Easy to get lost along the way," he finally said.

"But you found your way home, yeah."

He hesitated. "Yes."

It was all Nori needed to hear. "You'll check on Mama then?"

"Yes, of course," he said. "I'd love to see Mama Natua again." He reached over the train tracks for a coconut tart.

"Thank you."

"What else can you tell me about Mama's health?" Daniel asked, biting into the tart.

Nori sat back and began to tell him everything he needed to know.

13

THE HOUSE CALL

Four days after the eruption, Daniel reached for the screen door and stepped into the Natua porch for the first time in more than a dozen years. The sweet scent of flowers and damp earth hung heavy in the air, bringing back a rush of childhood memories. He was happy to see that nothing had changed. The long wooden tabletop where Mama and Auntie Leia sat stringing their leis was laden with orchids, pikake, kukui nuts, shells, and ti leaves. He walked into the warm cluttered house and followed the voices to the kitchen, where Auntie Leia and Auntie Nori were there waiting for him.

When Daniel was shown into Mama Natua's room, he put down his brown leather medical bag, a gift from his mother when he graduated from medical school, and walked across the room to push the curtains apart, sunlight spilling into the dark and cramped space.

"She likes it dark," Auntie Leia said.

"I'll need the light," he said, keeping his voice low and professional.

Mama squinted at him, sizing him up from her armchair as he pulled a chair over and sat down in front of her. "Who are you?" she asked.

"He's Mariko's boy," Nori said. "Daniel's a doctor now," she added.

Mama stared a moment longer. "You always liked to run around, didn't you?" she said. "Even as a boy, yeah."

Daniel looked up at Auntie Leia. When Auntie Nori asked him to give Mama a checkup, she warned him that Mama could be difficult.

"She's confused, must think you're someone else," Auntie Leia said. "She's been a handful all morning, yeah. Threw a tantrum, didn't want to eat her sweetbread and mashed papaya." Leia shook her head.

Daniel smiled at Mama and asked both of his aunties to wait in the living room while he examined her. During his geriatrics rotation, he saw patients with senility at differing stages. He knew that the less distraction there was, the calmer the patient remained.

"You call if she acts up, yeah," Auntie Leia said as they walked out of the room.

Mama's gaze followed them.

"Mama, it's nice to see you again," Daniel said, pulling back her attention.

He looked her straight in the eyes, keeping her focus on him. When he held out his hand to her, Mama suddenly leaned forward in her armchair and looked closely at Daniel. She reached out to him and he took her hand in both of his, his fingers entwining her wrist, his thumb finding a strong pulse.

"Always a charmer, yeah," she said, pulling away. "Why did you come back that morning by the beach if you were going to leave again anyway?" she asked.

"Mama, look at me. I'm Daniel Abe, Mariko's son." He tried to sort out what Mama was saying. "Mama, do you remember my mother, Mariko? We used to come and visit you when I was a boy. She always brought you the sticky rice wrapped in banana leaves that you liked."

Mama looked at him, her eyes searching his. "Why did you leave your family? I told Koji it wasn't right. You should have gone home, eh," she said, becoming more agitated.

"Who should have gone home?" Daniel asked. But even as the words left his lips, the pieces came together and the realization hit him straight in the gut. She was talking about his father.

"Always such a good-looking boy," Mama Natua mumbled. "Too busy chasing trouble to know how lucky you were, yeah."

Daniel sat listening. He couldn't be certain if Mama was talking about an incident that had really occurred, or if it was a confused memory from the past. Uncle Koji would have told him if his father had returned. Daniel wanted to probe further, but he needed Mama to calm down and focus so he could examine her as thoroughly as possible.

Her gaze drifted away from him.

Daniel had to pull her back. "Mama, do you remember when Wilson, Mano, and I were boys and down at the beach near Reeds Bay? It was early in the morning, just after the New Year, and you were collecting shells for your leis." He looked directly into her eyes, reaching down into his bag and retrieving his stethoscope. "You knew right away we were up to no good," he continued. "Wilson had gotten hold of a string of firecrackers and we had this grand plan of setting them off and scaring up some sand crabs." He slowly placed the chest piece against the neckline of her muumuu, lowering it slowly as he talked, having captured her attention. "When you saw what we were up to, you came running down the beach and put an end to our pranks."

Mama Natua flashed him a smile.

"Can you take a big breath for me? Breathe in and out?" he asked.

Surprisingly, she did as he asked without putting up a fight.

"You were up to no good, yeah," Mama Natua repeated.

"We were," he said, and laughed. He took out a tongue depressor. "Can you open wide for me?"

She did, her breath warm and sour.

"You made Wilson give you our entire string of firecrackers. I thought he was going to actually cry that day," Daniel said. "Do you remember what you gave him in return?"

Mama remained quiet.

Daniel watched her trying to remember. For the first time in months, he felt like a doctor again, a part of him fearful he'd lost his touch. His careful fingers felt the lymph nodes to each side of her neck, pressed along her side and down her spine, her face open and accepting as a child. He looked at her eyes, into each of her ears, quick and careful and efficient. Then he bent down and rummaged through an inside pocket of his bag, looking for something.

"Shells, yeah!" Mama Natua yelled out, a child's excitement in her voice.

"Yes," Daniel said. "You gave him the shells you had collected." He smiled. "And I kept this one." He held up a seashell in his hand, no larger than a pikake bud, coral-colored with rows of soft whorls, collected that day on the beach. It had caught his eye and he picked it out of the pail that day and had held on to it ever since.

Mama reached for it, her eyes lighting up with delight. "You're not Franklin," she said, her eyes focused on him.

"No, I'm not Franklin. I'm Daniel," he said. It was the first time in years he'd said his father's name aloud.

Mama smiled. "You were always a good boy," she said.

~

Mama still needed blood tests and a more thorough exam that Daniel would have to arrange through Hilo Hospital. While Mama clearly suffered from senility, her vitals appeared stable for someone who had never seen a doctor in her eighty-three years. Daniel busily answered Auntie Leia's and Auntie Nori's questions about Mama's health, keeping any questions about his father to himself for a little longer. After so many years, Daniel was surprised how just hearing the name Franklin still affected him, and how quickly his father became flesh and blood again.

As he walked home, Daniel's thoughts were filled with questions. He cut through an old neighborhood, streets lined with small, rickety houses crowded with roaming chickens, stray dogs; a goat eating from a neighbor's toppled garbage. A bare-assed little boy clutching a coconut ran toward a house. If Mama had really seen his father and Uncle Koji together after he'd left them, when did he return? And why hadn't his mother or Uncle Koji ever said anything? As he combed the past for answers, what became abundantly clear was how easily his mother and the entire community had erased all memories of his father from their lives. His mother had stopped speaking of him, while all the tangible objects that belonged to him had slowly disappeared from the bungalow. She'd kept in a box for him a few family photos, a tarnished money clip, and an old slingshot his father had made out of manzanita, but there was little else.

Just before he turned down the paved street that led back to the bungalow, Daniel remembered his father's hunting knife. His mother had kept it in the drawer of her bedside table. She once told him his father had killed a wild turkey in the upcountry with the knife when he was a teenager.

"It's to keep us safe when Daddy's away, yeah," his mother had said. She let him hold it. "Careful, now," she added. It was heavy and sharp and cool in his hand.

His father had left the knife with them for their protection.

Daniel remembered sneaking into her room a few times to play with it, pretending he was the one chasing down a wild turkey in the upcountry. After cutting his finger, he stopped. Over the years, he'd forgotten all about it.

As soon as Daniel arrived home, hot and anxious, he went directly to his mother's bedroom and pulled open the drawer of her bedside table, only to find it empty. Clouds had captured the sun, and a gray light suddenly washed over the room like sadness. Had he dreamed it all? Daniel sat down on his mother's bed, looked around her spare room, and wondered what other secrets she had kept from him.

14

THE HOUSE ON THE HILL

It was late afternoon by the time Koji walked up the dirt road to his cottage from the train barn. At the top of the hill, he paused to wipe the sweat from his neck with a bandana and looked up at the darkening sky, looming gray and heavy. He turned when he heard footsteps to see Razor walking up the hill toward him.

Koji smiled to see his old friend, the slight limp he inherited after breaking his leg as a boy more pronounced. Never fused back together right, Razor explained, though it had never slowed him down and was usually noticeable only when he was tired.

"I was hoping to see you," Koji said.

"Here I am, yeah." Razor stopped and looked toward Koji's house. "Remember when we were teenagers cutting cane," he said, "just dreaming, yeah, to be living in this house on the top of the hill?"

Koji smiled. "Who would have thought, eh?"

"You deserve it," Razor added. "No one could cut cane like you."

"All I did was swing a knife."

Razor shook his head. "Took skill, skill I never had, eh." He paused for a moment before adding, "Another harvest almost over."

Koji smiled. "Not a minute too soon, yeah."

"Still got Pele to deal with, eh."

They both looked toward the mountain. Mauna Loa was still erupt-ing, with no signs of stopping. Puli Plantation was on the southern side of the volcano, too far away from the eruption to feel any real effects, though Koji detected hints of sulfur in the air.

"Not the first time Pele showed her might," Koji said.

Razor nodded, then smiled. "We were just boys the first time, yeah. Remember? The ground kept shaking so they let us out of school. Thanked Pele all that afternoon, yeah."

Koji laughed at the memory. They had tried to catch a ride up closer to the eruption, but no one would take them. Instead, they spent the afternoon playing baseball against the Sakata boys until it was dark. By the next morning, Pele had quieted and they reluctantly returned to school.

"This time's different," Razor said, "feel it in my bones. Pele's not going away so easily. You wait and see, yeah."

Koji didn't disagree. Life on the island could change in a heartbeat. "I've been thinking about staying with Nori and Samuel down in Hilo for a few days after the harvest, spend some time with Daniel."

His plan was to finish up the harvest in the next couple of weeks, do the last of the sugar train runs, and head down to Hilo to stay with Nori and Samuel during the lull. She'd asked him to stay with them several times after Mariko's death, but he couldn't bring himself to remain down in Hilo without her. Now, after two years, he needed a change of scenery. He also wanted to get to the bottom of what was bothering Daniel.

"Sounds good, yeah," Razor said, as if he knew what Koji was thinking. "It's about time, eh."

Koji nodded. "Come in for a while?"

"Nah," Razor said, "just wanted to say hello. Gotta get back."

"See you soon, then," he said.

Razor smiled. "I'll be around."

Koji watched his friend make his way back down the road and to-ward the cane fields before he headed back to his cottage.

≈

Koji turned off the radio and finished cleaning up the kitchen. He looked around the small room, worn and scrubbed, an old table and two mismatched chairs taking up most of the floor space. On the counter were a coffeepot and a single mug. What Koji never told Razor was just how happy he was to have a place of his own after a lifetime of living with others. A few years after his family arrived from Japan, the plantation had prospered and the simple cane grass huts of their Kazoku Village were replaced by clapboard, tin-roofed houses, which Koji's family shared with another family, eleven in all, living in the hot, cramped four rooms until his sister married and moved to the other side of the island, and his mother passed away. By then, his father had been dead for a lifetime, and Koji had been cutting cane for almost twenty years.

≈

Koji had been just shy of his sixteenth birthday when he was given his first cane knife, a blunt-tipped machete that belonged to his father. It was three days after his father had accidentally cut the palm of his left hand, leaving the wound to fester and stink, until it was too late and had to be amputated, his heavily bandaged stump propped up on a pillow like an offering. As Koji stood in the hospital's long, open ward, crowded with two rows of beds, his thoughts couldn't stop circling around his father's missing hand, how it must be as dark as a bruise with shriveled, claw-like fingers. Where was it? Had it been thrown back into the cane field waiting to be hauled away with the cane trash?

"Pay attention out there," his father snapped, startling Koji. "It only takes a moment for your life to change."

Koji began cutting cane that June. After years of watching others cut and stack the cane, he was one of them. He listened to the workers curse the mostly Portuguese lunas who lorded over them on their big horses, unable to pause and stand and take a breath without the luna's whips raining down upon their backs. It didn't matter that they were immigrants too; they were haoles and would automatically be given the higher-paid, better jobs on the plantation. Koji held the heavy knife in his hand and looked out at the tall, billowing cane, the red earth the color of his father's dried blood. The first morning he worked beside two older Filipino men, Efren and Francisco, both good men who knew his father. Less than half an hour later, Koji was sweating and felt the solid weight of the long cane knife straining the muscles of his arm. He gripped the knife tighter and swung it over and over again.

Every *whack* of the machete was a challenge.

Every *whack* of the machete taunted him.

He couldn't disappoint his father.

"Slow down, eh, or you'll faint from the heat before you finish a row," Efren warned him.

Koji was already suffocating. Dressed in gloves and several layers of clothing to protect against the sharp cane leaves, they all wore straw hats against the sun, and bandanas tied over their mouths to keep out the dust. Koji soon sweated through both shirts and the jacket that clung heavily to his back like wet rags. By the end of the day, Koji could barely lift his left arm, and the palm of his hand burned and bled watery pus from his broken blisters. Only then did he realize how much his parents had endured every day since they arrived at Puli, especially his mother, who returned home from the fields filthy and exhausted every afternoon, stripped off her layers of clothing, and began to cook dinner for them. After dinner, she washed clothes, or sewed, or tended their garden before finally finding a moment to rest, while his father went down to the river to drink with the other Japanese men. In the early hours of the morning it began all over again.

Day after day, Koji gripped his father's machete in his callus-hardened palm. It didn't take long for him to find his rhythm among the older men. It soon became evident he was born for cane cutting, a strong, broad-shouldered boy with an easy swing that came naturally to him. Within months, Koji was noticed by the luna as a talented cutter, stacking hundreds of pounds of cane each day. Not long after, his water breaks grew longer while other lunas paused to nod his way. At the end of his first year, Koji stood hot and uncomfortable in the wood-paneled foyer of the plantation manager's big house, clutching an envelope containing his first cash bonus for cutting the most cane by the end of the harvest.

Sixteen years ago, when Koji retired from cutting cane and began running the sugar train, he was given the sugar train cottage to live in. The house on the hill, Razor had always called it. One of the few things Koji had taken from the old house was his mother's small Buddhist shrine, which now sat on his kitchen shelf above the coffeepot. Koji lit a thin stick of incense, watching the dark curl of smoke rise into the air, bringing with it the welcoming scent of agarwood and sandalwood, a reminder of his childhood in Japan, and growing up on the plantation. His mother used to light a stick of incense every morning, praying for the health of her family. The small bundle of incense she bought weekly at the plantation store had been her one extravagance. Once a year, when they were still young, she took Koji and his sister down to Hilo town, where they visited a Buddhist temple and lit incense in memory of their ancestors. "Never forget," his mother said, bowing low, "we are here because of them." Even as a boy, Koji remembered thinking, *No, I'm here because of you and Father.*

His mother had stopped lighting incense after his father's death. Her shrine sat empty and scentless in the corner of their bedroom for years. Koji wondered if his father had been embraced by their ancestors after he died, or did they feel cheated, too, just like his mother did? His father's death came quietly one morning, two years after he'd lost his hand. When they returned home one afternoon from working in the fields, his mother thought his father was napping, only to discover his body stiff and lifeless. It was the first and only time he heard his mother scream, high-pitched and feral. All that had mattered to Koji back then was earning a man's wage to help take care of his family. He wanted to make his father proud, but day after day, the more cane Koji cut, the farther his father drifted, cold and distant, sitting outside their cottage every morning as he watched them leave him behind.

In her grief and shame, his mother hid his father's suicide, and told everyone at Kazoku Village that he had died of a heart attack in his sleep. Koji knew his father's death had been fueled by his own demons, along with a fistful of sleeping pills he'd gathered over the year, but he told no one, not even Razor. Afterward, his mother never honored his father's memory at the temple, and never forgave him for leaving her alone among the endless fields of sugarcane, so far from Japan and her ancestors.

≈

The spirits of his parents never visited him, unlike Mariko and others, whom Koji hoped were his aumakua, spirit guardians, who came to him in times of need. He was reminded of his own weaknesses and past actions every time the spirits were with him, and though he knew it was important to move forward, the notion paralyzed him. Koji shook the thought away, struck a match, and reached up to light the thin stick of incense. He'd never been religious but found himself lighting a stick each evening since Mariko's death. At first it was to honor her, but as time went by, Koji realized it was for his own selfish reasons.

He stepped back and watched as the dark smoke spiraled up, then closed his eyes and breathed in the sweet fragrance that filled the small house, letting the scent surround him. And for a short time, he felt Mariko there in the room with him, a warm reminder that he wasn't alone.

Island Voices

Razor, 1901

My real name is Yoshio, which means righteousness, but I've been called Razor for as long as I can remember. I've always been fascinated by my father's straight-edge razor scraping his cheek every morning, so they gave me the nickname. My father gave me that razor when I was thirteen and I carry it with me always. Three years have passed and I'm still working as a hoe hana, but what I want more than anything, yeah, is to be cutting cane like Koji. I can already feel the weight of the cane knife in my hand as I swing it against the tall stalks with a hard, solid thwack of the blade, watching them fall over like toy soldiers. Now that this year's harvest is over, I hope to be finally cutting cane next season. I can feel it.

Meanwhile, for a few sweet weeks in December, hoes and knives are forgotten and we sneak down to Hilo whenever we can to meet Franklin. Franklin Abe is a friend of my cousin who's a year older and lives down in Hilo. The three of us have become fast friends and Koji and I can't get down to town fast enough, yeah. We help Salvador, the engineer of the sugar train, and the workers load the burlap bags of sugar onto the train, so we can hitch a ride from the mill down to Hilo wharf. We also pay Salvador with loose cigarettes pinched from other workers or a bottle of soda pop or coconuts Franklin has climbed the trees to cut down. We take turns shoveling coal into the furnace and hang out of the open windows, wind whipping our faces. Below, the big ocean spreads out gray and choppy as the sky clouds over and a warm rain soothes our hot skin. Moments later the sun pushes through the dark clouds again, forming a sun shower, leaving us sticky with sweat and laughter.

"Stay out of trouble," Salvador tells us once we jump off at the Hilo train station. We're already halfway down the platform when he yells, "And get back here on time, or you'll be walking back up the mountain. You hear?!"

Outside the station, we meet Franklin and walk to Hilo bay or a beach close by. Koji and I act like we do this every day, like we're town boys, not cane boys. Along the way, Franklin pulls out the slingshot he made from a branch of red manzanita. He's a natural with it, yeah, shattering bottles and clipping mangoes, and even hitting lychees off of trees from twenty feet away. There's not much Frank can't do, and the girls like that, his tall, skinny body, his cocky grin, his pretty-boy good looks so different from us. Koji's strong and quiet. Me, I'm short and persistent. What I don't have in height, I have in stubbornness. Like a dog clutching a bone, Koji teases, never going to give it up. But we can't hide the dirt under our nails, while Franklin has an excitement that draws attention to him.

It's no different today when we meet the three girls down at Onekahakaha Beach for the first time. It's a windy day, the palms swaying, whitecaps on the ocean looking like a thousand white birds on the surface of the water. Koji and I watch the girls walk across the beach toward town, laughing and talking, fishing poles and buckets in hand. Other than Koji's sister, we don't know many girls.

"Three for three," Franklin says, as he tucks his slingshot into his back pocket. "I'll be right back."

We have no idea what he means and just stand there as if we've suddenly lost our tongues. We shyly watch Franklin walk over to the girls, full of bravado and confidence as he talks and laughs with them. Frank can talk himself into, or out of, anything, something Koji and I can't help but admire.

When we return to the plantation later that afternoon, Koji can't stop talking about each of the girls—Nori, the protective one; Leia, the tall, quiet one; and

Mariko, the one with the beautiful smile and a small dark mole near her left jawline. *It's like a period at the end of a sentence,* Koji says. He has stopped right there. My best friend is already so mesmerized he can't see straight, yeah, and I don't have the heart to tell him that while he was standing there watching Mariko's every move, her gaze never left Franklin.

The Past,
the Present

November 25–26, 1935

15

ISLAND BOYS

The little girl lay on the hospital bed and opened her eyes, staring at Daniel accusingly. She never said a word as her body began to shake in violent spasms. He tried to get the attention of the other doctors in the room, but they continued to ignore him, even when he began screaming that the girl had gone into cardiac arrest, only to realize that it was his heart pounding erratically followed by a painful explosion in his chest.

Daniel sat up from bed, sweating, clutching his chest. Switching on the light, he glanced at the clock to see that he was late. He'd fallen back to sleep and into the unsettling dream. He pushed aside his sheet and scrambled out of bed. Wilson and Mano were waiting for him at the wharf. If he hurried, he could still make it down to the dock before the *Okawa & Sons* fishing boat left its berth at 3:00 a.m.

Daniel was winded by the time he arrived at the dock, the troubling dream far away, just as Wilson started the boat's engine and it roared to life. The stink of gasoline along with the briny ocean brought back his last trip out on the Okawa fishing boat with Wilson and Mano more than fifteen years earlier. That morning, however, they had endured rough waters for just over half an hour when Daniel began to feel sea-sick, his stomach roiling and his breakfast rising as he rushed to vomit over the side of the boat and into the choppy sea.

"Best kind of fish bait, *braddah*," Wilson had said, slipping into pidgin, and laughed, almost choking on the sandwich he was eating.

Little bothered good-natured Wilson. He could eat anytime, anywhere, and was at his best on the boat bringing in the fish. Growing up, Daniel watched Wilson and Mano's relationship alternate between adoration and animosity. Wilson, two years older, was big and strong and boisterous, whereas Mano was more introspective and easily irritated by his brother's antics, while thankfully, Daniel created balance by being the one they both listened to.

They were all too different for comparison.

≈

"Look who got out of bed!" Wilson said, waving Daniel to come aboard in the dimness of the early morning.

Once on board, he steadied himself against the boat's rocking motion as Mano threw him the rope tethering the boat to the dock and jumped down after him.

"Let's go, yeah!" Mano yelled.

Moments later they pulled away from the dock, leaving Hilo behind. A cool wind blew. Daniel breathed in and out and watched the dark outlines of a sleeping Hilo town grow farther away. Hovering over the island, Mauna Loa's massive shadow rose toward the moonlight, still smoking, a billowing cloud of steam and gas reaching upward in its dark and dangerous beauty. In the growing distance, Daniel understood what lured the brothers out to sea every morning. He felt completely liberated sailing out into the vast and unpredictable ocean, leaving the rest of the world behind. And for the moment all his anxieties, his mistake and guilt concerning the little girl, the questions of his father's return, even the eruption felt insignificant in comparison.

Daniel was half listening to Mano talking when he caught her name and quickly turned around.

"I said Maile's back from Honolulu," Mano repeated.

Just hearing her name made the past rise with the boat on a sudden wave. He planted his feet to keep his balance. *Maile* rang through his mind, only to still on his tongue.

"She's back in Hilo?" Daniel asked.

"Just the other night," he answered. "Kailani said she came by the house yesterday afternoon."

"You didn't see her?"

Mano shook his head.

Mano's wife, Kailani, and Maile had been best friends through high school. He and Maile had gone steady through their junior and senior years, and everyone assumed they would marry right after graduating, as so many other local kids did. Instead, Daniel left for school in Chicago. They tried to stay together through his first year away, but when Daniel returned the following summer it became awkward between them. He was enamored of his new life in a big city and they no longer seemed to fit. Before he returned to Chicago, they had agreed to take a break. At the time his sadness was quieted by his ambition. "You have to choose what you keep and what you let go of in life," his mother said, remaining neutral, though he knew she already thought of Maile as a daughter. "Just be certain, yeah, I don't want you to regret it later on."

Part of him always had.

"Did Kailani say how she's doing?" Daniel asked. He saw her again, thin and dark-eyed, with the prettiest smile he'd ever seen.

Wilson had cut the engine, and the sudden quiet was soothing. The boat swayed from side to side as Mano gathered the nets on deck.

"Maile's good," he said. "She came back with a teaching certificate. Always smart, yeah. She's staying with her cousin for now."

Daniel hesitated. "Didn't she get married?"

Over the years, Daniel just wanted the best for Maile. He'd made his choice, as his mother said. Still, it bothered him to know that she'd married someone else. He was always busy in Chicago and had a few convenient relationships, but none that came close to serious. Now the thought of seeing Maile again brought a warm flush of happiness.

Mano shrugged. "Last I heard, she broke it off," he said. "You'll have to ask Kailani for the details. She's been asking why you haven't come by yet."

"Tell her I'll be over soon," he said, and smiled.

Daniel helped Mano hook the nets up to the wench and power block before they waved for Wilson to lower them into the water. All the while he tried to remain steady at the news.

Maile wasn't married.

≈

By the time the sun rose, Daniel helped the brothers pull in the nets, heavy with a load of flailing tuna, the rough rope burning against his palms. It felt good exerting a different set of muscles after so many years away. Daniel needed this. Everything seemed alive with movement, the deck bobbing from side to side, the rise and the fall, the creaks and groans of the boat. They stood watching the fish thrash around down in the hold, gasping for water, the silvery glint of skin and scales reflecting off the sunlight before Wilson threw another bucket of salt water over them and closed the hatch.

"Good catch, *braddahs*," he said, grinning at them.

"You're buying breakfast," Mano quipped.

They headed back, and as Hilo appeared in the hazy morning light, the rising smoke from Mauna Loa was now in full view.

"Think it's ever going to stop?" Mano asked.

"Pele can't stay mad forever," Wilson said.

"Yeah, she can," Mano said. "Pele's not like one of your girlfriends you can sweet-talk out of being mad at you."

Daniel smiled, watching the two brothers banter back and forth when he heard a surge of water followed by a sudden violent blow to the port side of the boat that pitched him and Mano across the deck.

They both slid and hit hard against the starboard side, hanging on as the *Okawa & Sons* tilted halfway onto its side and a rush of seawater drenched the deck. Wilson clung to the railing on the upended port side, dangling from the rail as Mano grabbed onto a rope and pulled himself up, throwing his weight toward his brother to help right the boat again. Daniel tried in vain to get up, but the slippery, lurching deck kept him holding on tight. He heard Wilson yelling just as the boat righted, slamming back down onto the water and rocking from side to side until it finally settled enough for Daniel to pull himself up.

"What the hell was that?" Wilson asked as the boat rocked from side to side and he found his footing again. "Look, there!" he then said, pointing toward the water.

They all hung over the side of the boat to see a *kohola*, a young humpback whale, swimming away from them. The whale must have lost his way and ventured farther into the bay than usual, clipping the boat as he turned and swam back out to sea.

Daniel rubbed his shoulder and made sure Wilson and Mano were both all right. They talked happily as they secured the deck. Their bumps and bruises were nothing compared to seeing a kohola up close. Growing up, Uncle Samuel had told them the whales were also known as aumakua, a family guardian of great respect. It was a story they would be telling until they were old men.

"Wait till we tell Dad," Mano said.

"He's not going to believe the boat was kissed by a kohola, yeah," Wilson added.

They were boys again, standing together and laughing with disbelief at the once-in-a-lifetime event. Daniel let out a relieved breath. He could hardly believe he was a world away from Chicago and could leave the anguish behind. He and his brothers had been touched by a humpback whale, and Maile had returned. Daniel looked up. In the distance Pele continued to erupt, watching, reminding him that despite being kissed by a kohola, the fire goddess was still in charge.

16

HIDE-AND-SEEK

Maile had been back in Hilo for two days, awakening each morning to the dry, metallic taste of panic on her tongue. She was safely home, yet couldn't stop worrying that her ex-fiancé might have followed her back from Honolulu. She sat at the kitchen table in her cousin's house drinking coffee, a sliver of sunlight sliding through the barely parted curtains and caressing her wrist. She wanted to get up and make herself something to eat, but just the thought seemed to steal away all her energy. There was no way he could know, Maile reasoned. She was being foolish. She hadn't told anyone she was returning to Hilo.

Still, she couldn't shake the fear.

Maile was ashamed at how naive she'd been. As soon as she received her teaching certificate she was determined to leave Honolulu. Regardless of the eruption and the cancellations of steamers sailing to Hilo, she still found a way home. Her boat had docked on the Kona side. From there, she'd caught a ride to Kohala and boarded a train to Hilo. She arrived back in town at dusk, in the grayish light of despair, when most of the shops were closed and the locals would be at home with their families. She had sneaked back like a thief, trying to reach the safe area without being seen, just like when she played hide-and-seek as a child.

Maile had dated a few young men in Honolulu, but only one had been serious after Daniel, serious enough to marry. He was a good-looking haole—smart and worldly—having traveled throughout the mainland, he'd told her. He was a businessman, a dealmaker who took her out to expensive restaurants and popular clubs she never dreamed of entering. Until they were engaged, he'd been loving and attentive. Afterward, as the weeks rushed into months, his smile turned into a scowl. When his deals began to fall through, he blamed her. The first time he slapped her, Maile smiled at the stinging surprise of it, telling herself it must have been an accident, he didn't mean it. Thinking back, she'd heard the same excuses from the lips of several of her high school girlfriends about their boyfriends. He made her quit studying for her teaching certificate, saying he would take care of her, right before he began following her everywhere just to make sure she was going directly to the store, or to church, or to a girlfriend's house down the block.

"You better not lie to me," he warned.

By the time he'd split her lip with a closed fist and threatened to kill her, Maile knew she had to get away. She waited for her chance and quickly disappeared one morning when he left for a business meeting. She found a job waitressing on the other side of the island, rented the back room in a house owned by a Chinese widow, and vowed to return and finish studying the last five months for her teaching certificate before leaving, hoping upon hope she wasn't worth looking for.

On weekends, Maile found the courage to get out and walk a few blocks, always looking out for him, always fearful that he would find her. The big world that she had once dreamed of seeing became smaller and smaller as she took to spending most of her time in Chinatown, hiding in the older areas of Honolulu with small, run-down buildings and family-owned stores that sold shave ice and reminded her of Hilo, places he would never think to step foot in.

Since her return home, Maile had only visited Kailani. When she heard from her friend that Daniel was also back from Chicago, her heart sped and she felt a dull ache in her stomach as Kailani kept saying, "It's fate, yeah," that they'd returned within days of each other. She couldn't imagine what Daniel would see in her now; he had studied on the mainland and was a doctor, while she'd barely gotten her teaching certificate. Maile watched her friend rattle on happily and couldn't bring herself to tell Kailani she no longer believed in fate or magic or fairy tales.

≈

Maile leaned against the front door. She took a settling breath before she inched it open. Ever cautious, she looked left and then right down the empty road before she stepped out of her cousin's house into the stale afternoon heat. Early in their relationship, she'd been caught by him with her guard down back in Honolulu, and could barely open her tender and bruised eye that throbbed for a week. She had to learn, he'd said. She wasn't going anywhere without asking him first. Why had she stayed after that? She'd been such a fool.

Maile walked toward downtown and the Okawa Fish Market. Pele had quieted for the moment and the sky had cleared. As the streets grew more crowded, Maile began to sweat. The fear and anxiousness made her nauseous. She stopped near a building and turned back to look once, twice, and couldn't shake the feeling that he was there, following her. She swallowed her anxiety and willed herself not to turn around again before she rounded the corner. One step, two steps, she whispered to herself, refusing to let him win. She was determined to leave his ghost behind. All she had to do was think of Daniel and Uncle Koji to remember there was a world of good men she didn't have to be afraid of.

Maile felt calmer as soon as she glimpsed Hilo Bay in the distance, knowing the Okawa Fish Market was just steps ahead. She wondered if the Hilo Aunties were still meeting to play Hearts every Saturday afternoon, and if the old-timers still gathered in the backyard. Maile had missed the market's camaraderie, and she was anxious to check the bulletin board to see if anyone was looking to hire a teacher or a tutor.

She quickly rounded the corner without looking back.

17

THE BULLETIN BOARD

At the end of the day, Nori stood at the cash register, adding up the market's receipts. She was delighted at how smoothly Mama's exam had gone yesterday morning. Even more relieved when Daniel told them Mama was doing reasonably well physically. "A strong pulse," he'd said, "a fighter's heartbeat."

It wasn't anything she didn't already know. Mama was always a fighter.

Then, this afternoon, Nori was taken completely by surprise to see Maile walk in, cautious at first as she peered through the screen door, only to smile wide when she saw Nori. Nori moved quickly around the counter to give the young woman a big hug. "You're here!" she said, stepping back to take a good look at her. She was thinner and tired, or was it sadness Nori saw, a thin line between the two?

"I returned late yesterday," Maile told her.

"Are you staying awhile?" Nori dared to ask. Maile paused and then nodded. She was home. Everything else would follow in time. It was almost too good to be true to have both Daniel and Maile return to Hilo within days of each other.

Nori knew Mariko would have been ecstatic to have both her fledg-
lings back home.

Nori looked up when the screen door whined open, and Kang, a young
Chinese dockworker dressed in a faded shirt, dungarees, and a soiled
bandana wrapped around his neck, hurried into the market, nodded at
her, and walked straight back toward the bulletin board. At least twice
a week he came in, quickly pinned up a few flyers on the board, and was
back out the door again without saying a word or spending a cent, the
slap, slap of his sandals echoing behind him. He was just one of many
union supporters who came in to pin up announcements for the growing number of labor meetings.

Jelly was fed up. "Enough," she said, banging another can on a shelf
she was restocking. "Ban them from coming in if they're not going to
buy anything!"

"It's why we put up the bulletin board, remember? More trouble
than it's worth trying to keep them out, yeah," Nori reminded her again.
"Even Pele hasn't stopped them from organizing."

"Wouldn't hurt to buy a piece of licorice now and then, eh," Jelly
mumbled.

From the front window Nori watched Kang amble down the street
handing out flyers before she walked back to the bulletin board to see
when the next meeting of the dockworkers would be. On a light blue
sheet of paper, black, block lettering announced that another meeting
was being held at the longshoremen's union headquarters down by the
wharf.

COME ALL BROTHERS!
STAND UP AGAINST
LOW WAGES AND POOR WORKING CONDITIONS!
DECEMBER 1, 1935—7:00 P.M. MEETING.
UNION HALL

Nori sighed. If only talking could solve all the problems that were increasingly ending in violence. Like the persistent lava flow, the continuing labor issues were heating up again amid the never-ending Depression. Even though the Immigration Act of 1924 had prevented any more workers coming from Asia to Hawai'i, those who had already worked on plantations continued to rise against the long working hours and low pay. She shivered, recalling past worker strikes that had led to numerous deaths on Oahu and Kaua'i. It felt like a festering boil that would need to be lanced soon. But at what cost? More lives lost? She lost count of how many times she'd warned Razor to be careful when he first became involved.

Nori reached up and pulled down several old flyers from the bulletin board. Every week it grew heavier with announcements. But as fast as the old flyers were taken down from the board, another round was back up.

No one really knew where the bulletin board came from. One morning in 1911, a year after Nori opened the Okawa Fish Market, Jelly and her son Nobu carried it up from the basement. Before she knew it, Nori was helping them tack it up. It spread completely across the back wall.

"Must have belonged to the bar, yeah, though it doesn't look like it was ever used," Nori said, stepping back to see if they'd hung it straight. There wasn't a pinprick on it. "Maybe it'll bring more folks in and out if they can leave messages on it."

"Let me start," Jelly said.

Nori watched her write something on a piece of paper and pin it in the middle of board, the lone slip strangely enticing on the big, empty board. It read, "Leave your message here. If you're reading this, others will too."

Within three months, the Okawa Fish Market became the community's center of communication. The locals checked the board religiously, knowing they could find whatever they needed on it. They'd tacked up everything from newspaper clippings to job openings to items for sale: snippets of white paper offering hope. Entire lives came to cover the board announcing births, marriages, and deaths. By the end of each month, it was blanketed with layers of flittering paper in all sizes and shapes. Nori and Jelly tried to take down all the outdated slips, only to have it cluttered again in days. She had no idea that the bulletin board would become the main conduit among all the locals in the community.

The only thing Nori asked Jelly never to remove from the board was the brittle, yellowed-edged newspaper photo of her, Mariko, Leia, and Noelani, the Hilo Aunties playing Hearts, taken more than twenty years ago. It remained in the lower left-hand corner, the anchor that always held her steady, her eyes immediately drawn to the photo pinned there by Mariko so many years before. Nori's fingers again whispered across their young faces, frozen in laughter. It felt just like yesterday.

≈

The Hilo Aunties had played their first game of Hearts in October 1910—six months after the Okawa Fish Market opened. Nori was just twenty-three and shadow rains lingered that wet Saturday afternoon when she invited Mariko and Leia to come to the market after the lunch rush. Nori missed spending time with her two closest friends. Mariko brought along three-year-old Daniel to play with Mano. Leia was the oldest of them at twenty-five, and she brought along her vivacious and pretty sixteen-year-old sister Noelani, born unexpectedly to their middle-aged parents. Nori served plates of sliced pineapple and sweet mango from Mariko's tree, took out a new deck of playing cards, and announced that they would be playing Hearts.

"What's Hearts?" Noelani had asked.

"A card game, you'll love it," Nori teased. "It's full of scheming at every turn."

Nori had learned the game from some local fishermen, and liked to watch them play because it involved thought and cunning and losing "tricks" so that the player with the lowest score was the winner.

"The opposite of life," she told her friends. She dealt the cards until the deck was evenly divided among them. But when Nori began to explain how the game was played, she realized it was more complicated than she thought.

It took several Saturday afternoons before they all understood how to play Hearts without pausing midway for instructions or to replay a hand. The first time they played a game straight through, Nori rewarded all of them with a cherry cola. With the fish market's success, Jelly sold fish and worked the lunch counter on Saturdays. Still, it wasn't long before her other customers simply came in, took what they needed, and left the money in the King Edward cigar box Nori left on the counter rather than interrupt their card game. As time went by, the children who came in to buy candy began calling them the Hilo Aunties as they lingered and decided whether to buy black licorice whips, or chewing gum, or salty dried plums, and dropped their pennies and nickels into the cigar box.

The name stuck.

The Hilo Registry had taken the photo on the second anniversary of the Hilo Aunties playing hearts together. "Shooting the Moon" the photo was titled, the big thrill of the game capturing all thirteen Hearts and the Queen of Spades in one hand, sending all the game-losing points to the other players. The four Hilo Aunties had been seated at their table staring seriously down at their cards, a differing degree of intensity fixed on each of their faces. But as soon as the photo was taken they had all relaxed into laughter and Noelani had tossed her cards across the table. Nori remembered hearing a second click and seeing the flash of the camera, which was the photo used in the paper.

≈

The following week Nori was sitting in Mariko's kitchen, giddy over seeing themselves when the photo appeared in the paper. "Slow day for news if we're the pin-up girls!" Mariko had said. Daniel and Mano were playing outside. Franklin away again working at another construction job, on Oahu.

A year later, he was gone for good.

Nori glanced over at Mariko's empty chair, her absence still a dull ache. She never thought Mariko would be the first Hilo Auntie to leave the table.

GHOST VOICES

MARIKO, 1913

It's March and it has rained nonstop for the past four days. I haven't heard from Franklin in more than three months. I can't stop pacing from my bedroom down the hallway through the living room to the kitchen and back. Over and over. I'm afraid if I stop moving I won't ever start again, collapsing right here on the floor. I no longer have the energy to be frantic. Now there's only fear and anger coursing through my body and still, still, the sharp longing for him that only fuels my rage. Koji comes by every week to see if we need anything. I know he'd come every day if I asked him to, but the last thing we all need is more confusion. How can two men who grew up together be so different?

I glance down at Franklin's kitchen chair. I can almost see him sitting there, yeah, smoking a cigarette with his morning coffee, trying to pull me onto his lap. My anger suddenly rises like a quick flame and I pick up his ashtray, open the back door, and throw it as far as I can, its landing blunted by the rain and mud. The thick air smells of dying flowers, of misery. Before now, the longest period of time I hadn't heard from him was just short of a week. He later told me there had been an accident on the construction job and he'd been laid up. "Believe me, sweetheart, I had no way to get word to you." I believed him then because it was the first time, and Daniel was still a toddler and he had kissed me, sucking gently on my bottom lip. I begged him then to stay in Hilo. There was talk of a new federal building being built and they would need construction workers. Meanwhile he could work odd jobs or for the plantations. "Doing what?" he'd said, his anger rising. "I'm no knife swinger!"

There were extended absences for a time or two afterward, but never more than a week, yeah, and he always sent money every month to supplement what I would make from my sewing and mending. This time I haven't received anything from him since he was home at Christmas. Franklin left again just after the New Year and I've been alone with Daniel ever since.

By February, I sent a telegram to the construction firm he worked for on Oahu and they were decent enough to have replied. "Frank Abe never returned to work after Christmas." How could he have just disappeared into thin air? I can't help but wonder how many of these inquiries they receive, frantic wives chasing after lost husbands. When did I become one of them? Nori, Leia, and Mama Natua bring food, which appears in the icebox as if it was always there. I feel nothing on most days, dead to the world around me. Except for Daniel.

$$\approx$$

Nights are the most difficult, when the shadows emerge to play tricks on me. Some nights my despair feels like a deadweight pulling me downward, drowning me. I know I'm luckier than most, I have a house. Daniel is asleep in the other room. He's a smart boy of six who has stopped asking about his father after seeing how pale I've become, how I've stopped eating or sleeping much, walking around the house like I'm in a trance.

"Are you sick, Mama?" he asks.

He reaches out and places his open palm against my forehead, mimicking me, and I shake my head and begin to cry. I can't say why I know this time is different, but this time I can feel it in my body, a small, hard seed in the middle of my chest.

This time he isn't coming back.

Another month goes by. I no longer think of where Franklin is or why he has left us. I can't think of a future without him, so I return to the past—one early morning just after we marry and he takes me to see Waianuenue Falls along the Wailuku River. As we walk along the path, thick and dense with foliage, the cool air smells of tinny, damp earth, moisture dripping from the banyan trees, the sound of rushing water falling in the distance. We are enveloped by a twilight composed of giant ferns, blooming wild ginger, and flourishing monstera plants that cocoon us in their own private world. He holds my hand and leads me forward, clearing the way for me to follow. I grip his hand as the damp air rushes at us and the thunder and crash of falling water grows louder. When we finally step out from under the shadows and into the open clearing, the shock of light stuns me.

"Look!" Franklin yells above the roar.

I shade my eyes to see the eighty-foot surge of foaming water crashing down into a dark, blue-green pool. Franklin wraps his arms around me and kisses me as a rainbow arches over the waterfall. Then he steps back and I instantly miss the warmth of his body.

"All for you!" he says with a wave of his hand, making me believe at that moment he's the magician who has conjured all of it up just for me.

〜

By early April, Daniel and I are walking to the Okawa Fish Market for our Saturday afternoon game of Hearts. "Daddy had to go away," I finally tell Daniel.

Nori. Hilo Aunties. Hearts. It's the chant I've carried in my head all through the morning, grounding me. I know Daniel's excited to see Mano and Wilson, which will soften the news and distract him with play.

"For work?" he asks, looking up at me.

I nod. If I don't say the words out loud, is it still a lie?

"When is he coming home?"

"I don't know," I answer, which isn't a lie. "Until he does, we'll be okay, yeah? We have Uncle Koji, the aunties, Wilson, and Mano."

It takes Daniel a moment to understand what I'm saying. I can see it in the way his gaze drifts away from mine in thought. He doesn't answer right away as he normally would, and I don't press. When we turn onto Kamehameha Avenue and start toward the fish market, Daniel reaches over and takes hold of my hand.

You Can't Hide

November 27—December 4, 1935

18

A New Direction

From the train station, Koji walked to the Okawa Fish Market, eager to catch Nori. The day had grown increasingly hot and humid, sweat prickling down the back of his neck as he picked up his pace, hoping she might know what was bothering Daniel. Koji hated to see him troubled. He heard a faraway rumbling and stopped, glancing up toward Mauna Loa. The volcano continued to erupt, smoking and spewing day and night; his only relief was in knowing that it didn't pose any danger to Hilo town.

The streets down by the docks were teeming with longshoremen. Koji edged his way around the groups of men lingering on the streets, stifling and foul-smelling, a chorus of Portuguese, Chinese, Tagalog, and Japanese languages all melded into one indistinguishable song. Even in hard times, everywhere he looked, notices were tacked up calling for workers' meetings and rallies that were open to everyone. Everything felt louder and more insistent down at the docks, while meetings at the plantations were still held in tight secrecy, separated by ethnic groups, just as the owners planned. Even before his family arrived at Puli, workers were kept in their isolated villages on the plantation to keep them from unifying, pitting brother against brother if one faction should strike.

In 1924, Filipino workers striking for better conditions on the island of Kaua'i had turned violent, leaving sixteen strikers and four policemen dead. Months later, the strikers were easily defeated by the wealthy mainland owners. Owners with the fancy names of Alexander and Baldwin, Castle and Cooke, and Theo H. Davies ruled with money and power. Koji learned the striking workers in Kaua'i had been arrested, or fired; their families evicted from the plantation in the middle of the night. Since the Depression, the union had kept a low profile. Now, the increasing union gatherings and the murmurs of strikes were signs of the ongoing battle—but lately, down on the docks it seemed like a raw nerve had been touched, and change felt imminent whether the owners wanted it or not. Hadn't Razor told him this would happen all those years ago?

Razor was twenty when he began attending union meetings, just after his beloved dog, Laki, was found dead, and he was inconsolable. With no proof it was one of the plantation's lunas who had killed his dog, Razor turned his anger toward organizing. He dragged Koji along in those early days, the meetings held in musty, abandoned cabins and dank basements that stank of rot and urine and mildew. Only a handful of Japanese workers showed up back then, nervous and unable to sit still, antsy and cautious, one ear always listening for sounds of the plantation police arriving to break up more than just their meetings. It wasn't long after they'd begun to meet that Mariko had married Franklin, leaving Koji desolate. Through the years he'd always been careful to keep his feelings to himself, and if Franklin knew anything, he kept uncharacteristically silent. Koji stopped going to the meetings and threw all his energy into cutting cane, grateful it left him too tired to think of anything else. The following year, when Koji finally paused to take a breath, he'd become the fastest cane cutter on the island, while Razor had begun recruiting for the unions in the shadows. The more involved Razor became with organizing and recruiting, the farther apart they grew.

Koji was relieved to step into the fish market and out of the muggy heat, away from the crowded press of workers and the memories. He hoped for rain to bring relief. The high-ceilinged market was cool and filled with the hum of voices and laughter coming from the tables in the yard out back. Jelly was at the counter helping customers just as Samuel walked in from the yard and waved for him to join them. Instead, Koji pointed toward the kitchen, looking for Nori. Samuel nodded.

Koji watched Nori from the doorway. She pulled a tray of sweetbread from the oven and poured a glass of guava juice, leaning against the counter and drinking. The air was warm and fragrant compared to the days of unpleasantness outside. As long as he had known Nori, she had taken care of everyone in the community. He'd always admired her strength, especially since her childhood was filled with neglect and loneliness. And though she'd never stepped foot off the island, she had more ambition than all three of the Okawa men put together. Koji rarely saw Nori standing still for very long. She was usually wearing one of Samuel's old shirts and a pair of shorts, but she didn't need fancy clothes to be a nice-looking woman.

When he cleared his throat, Nori turned to him.

"Sneaking up on me again, yeah."

"I let you know I was here," he said, and smiled. He suppressed a cough, not wanting Nori to lecture him to take better care of himself.

She shook her head and poured him a glass of guava juice.

"Waiting for the train to be unloaded?"

Koji nodded and drank down half the glass of juice in one swallow.

"Saw Mama Natua the other day. Daniel gave her a quick checkup. Calm as can be with him," Nori said, transferring the sweetbread onto a cutting board.

"How is Mama?"

Koji felt bad not seeing Mama more often. She was the one who watched out for Nori when she was young, and later kept a close eye on Franklin, one of the few people who hadn't been taken in by Franklin's charm. Still, it was too late; Mariko had already fallen under his spell.

Nori shrugged. "According to Daniel, she's doing fine physically, but she's sinking deeper into her own world most of the time now."

"Mama has everyone's love and support," he said.

"I know," she said in a quiet voice.

Mama's loss of memory was upsetting to everyone in the community, but none more than Nori, who was devastated when Mama began to forget things. Just two years back, Koji found Mama standing on the train platform early one morning barefoot and in her nightgown. "Some folks coming to visit," she told him, only she couldn't remember who the visitors were. Koji stood with her as they waited for one train, and then another, to rumble by before he walked Mama slowly back home with the promise he'd bring her visitors up to the house as soon as they arrived. Leia had been frantically running around the neighborhood looking for her, and was just returning home when they turned the corner. Mama had wandered away while Leia was out back feeding the chickens. Since then, she seemed to be drifting faster and farther away.

Nori cleared her throat. "Good of Daniel to stop by and examine her. There's a first for everything," she said, slicing a loaf of sweetbread into thick pieces.

"Have you had a chance to sit down and talk to him?" Koji asked.

Nori paused before answering. "I saw him a few days ago and asked him to check on Mama. Not long, yeah. Other morning he went fishing with the boys, saw a kohola up close. I think it was special for him. For all of them."

"A kohola, eh. Good for them. Daniel seem all right to you otherwise?" he asked. "Sounded kind of lost when I saw him at the station last week."

Nori stopped slicing the bread and looked up. "There's something, yeah," she said matter-of-factly. "But he seemed happy with the boys and with Mama. Maybe he just needs a little time to settle in," she said. "Mauna Loa has disrupted everyone, yeah, can't imagine how he must feel returning to all of this."

Koji smiled. "You make a good argument there," he said.

"Tell that to Samuel," Nori quipped. She poured more guava juice into his empty glass. "Speak of returning, Maile's back."

Koji sat a moment with the news, a surge of happiness spreading through his chest. "When?"

"A few days—" But before Nori could finish her sentence, a barrage of excited voices rushed in from the market. "What now?" Nori said, putting down the knife.

Koji followed her out of the kitchen to find the Yamamoto boy standing amid Samuel and a group of the locals who had gathered by the koa bar.

"There's news?" Nori asked, raising her voice above the clamor of the crowd.

The crowd quieted and the long-limbed boy looked over at them.

"The Volcano Observatory Center just called down. There's been another eruption. East of the current lava flow, yeah," he said eagerly. "The new flow's moving north toward Saddle Road right above Hilo. They say it's ponding between an old flow and the cinder cone Pu'uhuluhulu." The boy paused to take a breath. "They say if it begins to flow again, it'll be heading directly toward town."

There was a rumbling from the crowd, wanting to know more. The boy repeated himself. Koji felt Nori's eyes on him, but neither of them said a word.

19

One Step Forward

The new eruption above Saddle Road changed everything. Pele now hovered directly over Hilo, biding her time, waiting. Word had spread quickly through the community about a town meeting the next morning. By the time Daniel arrived, the fish market was already overflowing with worried locals, Mrs. Laney, his old high school history teacher, dockworkers, well-dressed haoles he'd never seen before, all pushing into the crowded space. Uncle Samuel's radio was perched on the counter, broadcasting Civil Defense announcements. Voices buzzed through the room. The screen door whined open and clapped shut. Daniel looked around the packed room, searching for Maile among the crowd. Ever since Mano told him she was back, Daniel looked for her everywhere he went, but she remained elusive. He glanced over at the screen door each time it opened only to be disappointed until Uncle Koji walked in.

He watched how Koji's presence settled the room. His mother must have felt the same way when she was with him. It wasn't until he was ten or eleven that he really understood what Koji and his mother meant to each other. It was the way their looks lingered a moment longer across the room, communicating secrets. By then his father had been gone for almost half of his life. His uncle moved among the crowd and stopped to talk to some of the locals. Through the years, Koji had always been the one there to protect them, comforting them with his steadiness. Daniel smiled, hoping to catch his uncle after the meeting to ask him about Mama Natua seeing him with his father.

Daniel sat next to Wilson and Mano as Uncle Samuel stood near the back bulletin board along with a tall, pale geologist from the Volcano Observatory Center, who talked about the latest eruption and the eventual lava flow toward Hilo if it didn't stop. The crowd sat silent and collectively seemed to deflate, slumping in their chairs. Once again, all they could do was wait. Even Auntie Nori seemed out of sorts, keeping quiet and busy by refilling snacks, a serious, thoughtful look on her face as her hands worked quickly from experience.

A low rumbling of voices murmured through the room.

"It's up to Pele like always, yeah," someone spoke up.

Uncle Koji added, "It's not the first time, eh, won't be the last."

"Don't forget, yeah, Hilo has always stood up to whatever came our way," Uncle Samuel encouraged.

One old-timer reminded everyone of the eruption in 1881. "No stopping the lava, yeah. Came oozing down the mountain, splitting into two forks as it flowed into town, snaking through the streets until it stopped dead at Komohana Street, at the intersection of Mohouli and Popolo Streets, as if there were a stop sign. Lucky for us, eh, it ended just a little over a mile from Hilo Bay."

The locals laughed and relaxed. Daniel heard the quick hum of agreement. Just like always, the Hilo community had roused themselves out of their gloom. Whatever was going to happen, they'd find a way through it. They had always put their faith in the natural world, along with the deities who ruled each part of it. It was something he'd missed being in the clinical world of medicine, where life and death revolved around hard, cold facts. Daniel turned when he heard the screen door whine open again, only this time he wasn't disappointed. Maile stole in quickly, her fingers edging the door quietly closed behind her.

Maile stayed near the front door ready for a quick escape, while Daniel turned and struggled to get a good look at her through the crowd. In high school, she had been thinner and taller than most of the other girls, her waist-long dark hair hanging down and hiding her pretty face as she hovered over a math problem or a book. She was always studious and attentive in school, watching and learning while the other girls were lost in their own noise. It was her quiet intelligence that Daniel found most attractive. Maile was invisible to everyone but him. It wasn't until their junior year in high school that she'd blossomed over the summer, emerging from her cocoon and returning to school as if she were some-one new and mysterious who had just arrived on the island. Suddenly Maile was attracting the attention of all the boys. But it was too late; Daniel was already years ahead of them.

≈

The crowd lingered when the meeting was over. By the time Daniel moved through the throng to where Maile was standing, she was gone. He was just as quickly out of the market, the screen door slapping shut behind him. Daniel finally caught up to her a few blocks away. Heart beating, he watched Maile from a short distance as she stood in front of Oshima's grocery store, looking down at the wooden crates of starfruit and papayas on display. It was hard to believe that ten years had passed and here they were, still unmarried, while most of their classmates married right out of high school and now had a passel of kids. Maile appeared thinner, her dark hair now shoulder-length, her cheekbones more prominent. Even if Daniel couldn't see her eyes, there was something sad and forlorn about the way she stood there all alone. And yet, nothing had changed; just the sight of her took his breath away.

Daniel walked slowly toward her and spoke her name softly, "Maile," as if they'd been standing next to each other and he wanted to show her something.

Maile looked up, startled to see him. "Daniel?" she said, glancing nervously around. Her first moments of uncertainty gradually turned to warmth and recognition as they spoke of the eruption, and she smiled as they reminisced about their high school days together.

"You didn't stay in Chicago?" she asked.

Daniel expected the question, shuffled through the answers he could give her, and chose what was close to the truth. "Something unexpected happened to bring me back home. How about you?"

Maile squinted against the sunlight. "Me too," she said.

They walked from Oshima's down to the wharf, the years between them disappearing, the salt-fish air blowing away all the sulfur scents as he pointed out the *Okawa & Sons* fishing boat berthed along the dock, and the new shave ice stall. They caught up with easy conversation that floated comfortably to the surface. Daniel had spent the past ten years moving at a frantic pace, always trying to be the best until he wasn't. With Maile, he felt calm for the first time in a long while—she shared his history and his community. She knew his strengths and his weaknesses. With Maile he had nothing to prove.

After they parted, Daniel walked back to the green bungalow, replaying their moments together. Maile was both the girl he once knew and the woman he knew nothing about. The girl had been shy but always at ease, while this Maile was hesitant, overly cautious. It was just one more mystery he had to untangle.

≈

Daniel woke the next morning filled with energy, a buzz racing through his veins at the thought of seeing Maile again. He left the house early, not willing to wait and worry about when the lava would begin to flow toward Hilo. Instead he kept busy by borrowing Uncle Samuel's truck and driving to Hilo Hospital to arrange for Mama Natua to take some tests. He hadn't been back to the hospital since his mother returned home for the last time. Daniel turned down the paved road that led to the gray, three-story concrete building, now L-shaped with the addition of a new children's wing two years ago. Auntie Nori said it had been funded by a rich sugar plantation owner whose son had been treated at the hospital for dengue fever. Daniel knew it was the closest most locals would come to know the wealth garnered by the sugar plantations, but it was good to see that some of the owners were giving back to the community.

As soon as Daniel entered the busy hospital, the life he had left behind rose before him. The hospital was tiny compared to the large, frenzied, nonstop world of Chicago Medical Center. Still, the similarities were there—the sharp, insistent smell of alcohol and antiseptic, the anxious voices of people pushing for information, the crowded waiting room filled with the worried and the restless. The coughing, sneezing, moaning sounds of the sick brought Daniel right back to those long, sleepless hours of his internship and the hectic years of his residency. Several fans spun the warm air above the reception area as he waited to speak to the nurse behind the desk. Daniel began to sweat, dizzy from the heat and the noise, along with the shameful reminder that it was the first morning in months that the little girl hadn't haunted his thoughts from the moment he woke. Before Daniel left Chicago, he wanted to visit the little girl, but instead stood outside her hospital room door and couldn't bring himself to enter when he heard murmuring voices, someone singing a nursery rhyme in which he recognized the melody but couldn't make out the words. What kind of doctor was he, unable to face up to his own mistake? He closed his eyes and swallowed the sourness rising up to his throat. He didn't want his mistake to become a rash that would never go away, so it became just one more reason to leave rather than cause any more problems for the hospital.

"You okay?" the nurse seated behind the front desk asked.

Daniel opened his eyes again, saw her questioning gaze as he stepped forward, then saw past her to the glint of the shiny chair in the hallway behind her.

~

By the time Daniel left Hilo Hospital, he'd been able to accomplish much more than he had hoped for. His first moments there were focused on trying to catch his anxious breaths and breathe normally so he wouldn't faint. But as soon as he saw the wheelchair in the hallway, he began to focus again, knowing it was exactly what Mama needed. He'd been able to bypass the bureaucracy, not only by telling the administrator he was a mainland-trained local boy who was returning to open his own practice—a lie that came to him too quickly to be completely false; but also because the wheelchair was for his patient, Mama Natua, who was beloved by the community.

Daniel lifted the wheelchair into the bed of the truck, tying it securely to each side, happy that he'd been able to get the chair so quickly. It was the first of many steps in helping Mama regain some mobility, allowing her to get out of her dark room and to sit in the kitchen or the porch or outside in the warm sunlight. And with the ongoing eruption always threatening, it would be essential to her evacuation. Daniel drove slowly over the rutted roads as the wheelchair bounced and rattled all the way back to the Natua house.

Auntie Leia was surprised to find him tapping on the screen door. "Can't remember the last time someone knocked," she said. "Neighbor kids usually walk right in, thinking they're at home, yeah. The day Nori wandered in, I gained a second sister," Leia rattled on.

Daniel smiled. Nori's temperament had always been much closer to Leia's. He guessed having a much younger sister as lively and impulsive as Auntie Noelani could be trying. Noelani had run off to Honolulu and eloped at seventeen, only to return divorced by twenty, and was currently a widow after the death of her third husband. Auntie Leia had been the quiet and steady Hilo Auntie, the one who saw the most and said the least. She always seemed happiest stringing leis with her mother, though he wondered now if she ever wanted more when she was young. Daniel heard that the Natua lei business had grown twofold in the past years, Leia's business skills and intricate stringing praised with the same respect and admiration that was given to Mama.

"Mama always liked a full house," he said.

"Come in, come in." Auntie Leia pushed open the screen door. "Mama just finished her breakfast."

"How is she?" Daniel asked.

"Easy this morning, yeah," Leia said. "She'll be happy to see you."

"One more thing: there's a wheelchair for you and Mama in the back of the truck. It'll help you to get her around easier," he said excitedly. "Out of her room to the porch, even outside. We'll have a ramp built for her. Hopefully she'll pay more attention to her surroundings."

Leia, barefoot and dressed in a flowing muumuu just like Mama wore, followed him to the truck. He untied the ropes and pulled the wheelchair down from the truckbed and onto the dirt with a heavy thud.

"Look at that, eh!" Auntie Leia said with delight. She touched the leather seat. "I've never seen one close up. How did you get it?"

"When the administrator at Hilo Hospital heard I was Mama Natua's doctor, they couldn't turn me down," Daniel said. "She's much loved. Everyone wishes her the best."

Auntie Leia looked at him for a long moment, her eyes tearing. "Thank you," she said, her hand touching the armrest, the leather back.

"Mama still needs to take some blood tests—only way to tell if she has any other existing problems. As my one and only patient, Mama gets my undivided attention," he added with a smile.

Leia looked at him, her smile turning serious. "Will Mama get better?" she asked, her anxiety suddenly seeping out, lingering in the air.

Daniel learned early on that the most difficult part of being a doctor was telling the hard truths.

He shook his head. "There may be moments when Mama will be more lucid, when she'll connect with people and everything around her," Daniel said. "But it'll be temporary, it won't last. There's no cure for senility. I'm sorry."

Auntie Leia nodded. "Hard not knowing, yeah. At least now we know to hope for those moments." She gripped the handle of the wheelchair. "Don't know what we'd do if you didn't come home."

Daniel felt a rush of blood warm his cheeks. "We'll make her as comfortable as possible. I'll give you some exercises that will also help," he said. "Mama may surprise us."

"I hope, yeah."

Without another word, Auntie Leia reached out and pulled Daniel into a quick hug before stepping back, embarrassed. He never remembered her ever being someone who hugged. But in that moment her usually stoic gaze was soft and shy, and he glimpsed how she might have been as a young girl, tall and sweet and awkward.

20

Awakening

Mama Natua felt the warmth of the sun filter through the buckling screen that wrapped around the front porch, like a hand caressing her cheek, hovering over her breast. She must have dozed off. For a moment she thought that her husband, Nestor, was alive again and standing next to her. She looked up. "Where have you been?" she asked. It was her no-nonsense, scolding voice. He always knew her real warmth and loving lay just beneath. When there was no answer, Mama caught herself. He'd been gone for so many years. He had fallen one day and was dead the next.

She was taking a long time to fall.

≈

Mama sat in the chair with wheels that the young man had brought. There was something familiar about him. Her hands had grasped the arms of the chair in confusion when it began to move. She heard her daughter laugh with delight. It wasn't until the young man pushed her out to the porch that Mama's stiff limbs relaxed. It felt as if she were a child again, being carried outside for the first time. The warm air embraced her and a light suddenly flickered on in her head. She wanted to cry when she sensed the slow shift of clarity returning. Her memories were usually scrambled. She saw faces and places that didn't follow in any one sequence and would just as quickly slip away from her, like trying to hold on to water. But Mama *knew* this place. She knew the sweet, earthy smells, she knew the buzzing and scratching sounds, she knew the creaks and cracks of the old floorboards of the porch, even the rich soil that lay underneath them.

Mama looked up when she heard voices from the kitchen, suddenly remembering again that the young man was Mariko's boy. She wanted to tell her daughter and Mariko's boy how happy she was to be back sitting out on the porch again, but by the time the words formed in her mouth they had already disappeared back into the house.

He was asking her daughter so many questions.

"How is she sleeping? Has she gained her appetite back? How are her bowel movements?"

"Off and on all day. Better. Could be better."

Who was this child they were talking about?

≈

Mama stopped listening to them. The porch was always where her heart beat strongest. She closed her eyes for a moment and breathed in deeply, taking in the scents of damp earth and sea salt mixed with sweet pikake and orchids that brought back memories Mama couldn't forget no matter how hard she tried, sticking to her skin like the white sap from a plumeria tree. Mama had strung her leis at the table almost every day for sixty-five years, the last forty with Leia by her side, keeping an eye on the neighborhood as she worked. Nothing got by her. Didn't she know the Kalani daughter was pregnant even before she came to her begging for help? Didn't she stop those Pakai brothers from tormenting that scabby, homeless dog, only to raise him herself to a ripe old age? And didn't she recognize that little Nori up the road needed a home too? She tended to those who hurt, yeah, and had dried enough tears to fill a pond.

The only one she couldn't save in time was her own sweet Leia. All those years ago, there'd been a hurt so bad it stole her voice and she wouldn't tell Mama. Neither Nori nor Mariko would talk. *Tell me. Tell me,* she willed her daughter, but Leia wouldn't or couldn't and never did. Still, Mama knew she'd found happiness now, more talented at stringing leis than she ever was. The mistake that most folks made was assuming that she didn't see anything sitting at home stringing up her leis. But it wasn't so; she saw all the wounded birds. She felt their hurt. She knew they had to fight harder to be happy. They were the ones who always held a special place in her heart.

≈

Mama opened her eyes when she heard a scratching sound. Her gaze followed the path of a green and yellow gecko that had paused and clung to the screen in front of her. She reached out, only to have it scurry away.

The warm wind picked up. Mama heard the hibiscus flowers sweeping against the side of the house and the rustling branches of the monkey pod tree in the front yard. Like an old friend. She breathed another mouthful of air, catching a faintly familiar scent in the wind, just like those preserved black-colored, thousand-year-old eggs the Chinese grocer used to try and sell her. "I'm no fool, yeah," she mumbled aloud. "Buried in clay and ash for a time don't make an egg a thousand years old, yeah, even if it looks and smells like it."

Wasn't the egg, though. Mama tried to remember what the scent was. A thread pulled at her. She suddenly felt that sly, crafty animal creeping back in and trying to snatch away her thoughts again. She could feel it hovering, but this time Mama fought back, tasting her old stubbornness, that quick rush of anger.

"Go away!" she hissed. Mama's hand slapped down hard on the armrest of the chair. "Go away!"

And suddenly the cunning animal slowly crept back at her threats. Mama smiled and sat back in her chair, breathing in and out, only to finally remember what the particular scent in the air was.

Pele had returned.

21

Puli Plantation

The sugar train released a plume of steam, chugging and wheezing up the mountain toward Puli Plantation. Pedro watched the firebox and tossed a shovelful of coal into the fire to keep the pressure balanced as they headed up the mountain. Koji turned back to glimpse the last bit of ocean through the trees before the train slowed down and curved around the bend on its way to the summit. He'd seen the sight a thousand times and never tired of it.

As they approached the plantation, Koji felt the heat through his gloves as he gripped the iron lever and applied the brakes to slow the train for the last few miles. Hot and sweaty, Koji hung out the open window for some fresh air as the train entered Puli, the last stretch of tracks circling around the cane fields that led back to the train barn. The sky gave off a hazy gray light, the air smoky and warm. Koji coughed, spitting up phlegm. The remnants of the morning's cane burning of a nearby field remained in the dark cloud of smoke still lingering overhead. Mauna Loa's eruption did little to disrupt Puli from completing its year-end harvest and getting the sugar on ships to the mainland.

During the past ten years Koji had cut cane, he'd stood hypnotized in those very same fields watching the cane burning during harvest as the heat pressed up against him. Billows of black smoke rose into the sky as flames raced through the fields. The controlled fire spread quickly, consuming the hidden pests and the leafy tops of the sugarcane, returning the ash to the soil as nutrients. The crackle of the leaves and straw rose in a choking cloud—gloomy and serious and stifling. After, the fire was quickly contained and the fields watered down with hoses before the cane was cut. All that was left were the thin stems, their tough outer layer shielding the raw cane underneath. The scorched stalks leaned over like drunken men, felled by the fire that cleared away the cane trash and by the gravity of their own weight.

On those windless mornings during the burning, a blanket of pewter haze hovered in the darkened sky. Koji tied his bandana tightly over his nose and mouth as he moved between the blackened rows to cut the charred cane. His eyes stung and watered, his throat raw and sore from the lingering smoke, thick and acrid, that filled his lungs. When he was finished for the day, his clothes were filthy and any fraction of exposed skin was as dark as coal. Koji felt like he was emerging from another world—one as harsh and as suffocating as any volcano eruption, only all of it had been man-made.

Koji applied the brakes again, slowing the train as it passed the newly burned field, an uneasy feeling rising in him again. Ever since the eruption and Daniel's return, a growing restlessness nagged at him like a dull ache. Koji looked across the blackened cane field and saw himself in its desolation. He'd become acutely aware that he had little to show for a lifetime at Puli. He'd spent the past forty years on the plantation having taken the easy way out, working for lunas who admired his discipline and cutting skills and had even struck up casual friendships with him, while others only saw his worth in the amount of cane he could cut. Deep down he had always prided himself at being the best, which may have been his greatest weakness. The bosses who lived in their big houses on the other side of the plantation had persuaded him to stay by giving him what he wanted, to be left alone and allowed the freedom to come and go. For that he stayed out of trouble and cut all the cane they wanted. Mariko and Daniel had always been his real prize, even if they never really belonged to him. The preferential treatment he'd been given had caused problems with some of the other workers at first. One late afternoon when Koji was returning from the fields, he was stopped by two brothers from his own Kazuko village.

"Who you to get special treatment?" the older of the two asked.

The younger brother jumped in. "I see you buddying up to those bastards. You spy for the boss man, yeah?"

Koji shook his head. He didn't want trouble, but he wasn't about to run away from it either. "I'm just minding my own business, eh. You both should too," he added.

Things escalated quickly from there. Koji couldn't remember which brother threw the first punch, but the fist slammed into the side of his jaw. After that, he made quick work of the older brother when the younger one rammed him from the side, both falling and wrestling in the dirt.

It was Razor who came running, breaking them apart and also getting hit in the melee.

"Dammit! Stop!" Razor yelled. "When you assholes can cut cane as fast as Koji then you can complain, yeah. Not before!"

Even after the bruises faded, things were never the same with the brothers, but Koji ignored them and was always grateful Razor stood by him. In turn, he had let Razor down time and again, missing so many labor meetings, but still his best friend had always returned and understood. Koji looked out toward the fields that hadn't been burned yet, realizing he hadn't seen Razor in more than a week.

As it shivered to a stop, Koji eased the sugar train back into the barn. He parted ways with Pedro and walked back up the dirt road to his cottage, only to pause midway and look down at the wide sweep of fields. They spread out before him like a quilt Mariko might have sewn, squares of flat, burned fields, next to those of growing cane that wouldn't be harvested until next season. The owners kept the cane fields on different yearly rotations to ensure an annual harvest and income. They controlled the plantings, just like they controlled the workers, including him. Koji had conveniently surrendered to a life that Razor worked endlessly to try to change. The years had turned Koji into someone he no longer knew. It hadn't started out that way; cutting cane had been his pride and provided for his family. Now he was only one of a handful remaining from the early years still working on the plantation.

Koji stood and looked across the cane fields, but there was still no sign of Razor.

ISLAND VOICES

RAZOR, 1904

It's the harvest, yeah, and I'm finally cutting cane. Got a new dog too. Wandered onto our back porch and refused to leave, so he's the newest member of Kazoku Village and already family. He's a big, gray shepherd mix, a hapa dog I'm calling Laki, which means Lucky, because he's one lucky dog to have found me, yeah. Every day when I drudge back to the village after work, he's there waiting, nipping at the rope that keeps him from running after me and into the fields every morning.

We've been squatting in the fields cutting all afternoon when I suddenly stop and look up at the sound of laughter, not the happy kind, but a low, guttural, in-the-throat kind of laughter, raw and cold and callous. Been here long enough to know it can't be good, yeah. When Koji sees me he stops, too. We're both sweating in the heat and dust as we stand and pull down the bandanas tied over our noses and mouths and listen. If we're caught by a luna for standing up too long instead of cutting, we'll feel the stinging slap of his whip across our shoulders and backs that can leave oozing, angry red welts for weeks.

Still, we stand.

The laughter is coming from the clearing where the wagons are being loaded with cut cane. A group of Chinese men are gathered there, taunting some

Filipino "Sakada" workers carrying heavy loads of cane stalks across their shoulders. Don't know how the Sakadas take it. If it were me, yeah, I would have shut them up a long time ago. But Koji gives me the eye, reminding me to be careful. He has been cutting cane for almost three years and he tells me to stay alert, to watch everything and remain quiet and cautious while working, tells me who I can trust and who I can't.

"Nothing is as simple as it looks, eh," Koji reminds me. "Trouble can follow you like a shadow, so you need to watch your back, yeah, keep one step ahead."

Koji has the ability to ignore it all, while I see the lies and injustices add up. In the fields every day, I hear the Sakada workers whispering their grievances. "They came to our homeland with lies and promises of work and a better life. No schooling, no matter, they say, put your X right there. Is this a better life? Once we arrived from the Philippines, they gave us da dirtiest, most backbreaking work—burning, clearing, and loading da cane onto railcars, ten hours a day, six days a week. Lucky if we receive ninety cents a day!" I look up to see a luna a row away from us. "No talking in the fields!" he yells, snapping his whip. They want us to lick their boots just like the way they have to bow down to the managers and the managers to the owner. I know what the plantation owners are doing. The bastards. They deliberately keep us separated when we're off the fields so we can't form any alliances. If the Japanese workers strike, the owners pay more to the Chinese and Filipino workers to take their place. I don't like how they pit us against each other. I don't like it at all.

Still, I listen to Koji and we usually steer clear of the fights between the different groups of workers, or with some of the lunas who wield their power with brutal beatings to quash our wills, keep us under their thumbs. They're cruel to be cruel, I say; the smells of fear and blood are what they jack off to.

We steer clear for as long as we can until we can't anymore.

Koji moves first toward the wagons to see what's going on. He already has a reputation for being the fastest cane cutter at Puli, who works hard and stays out of trouble. It's only when we reach the clearing that I see what he must have sensed right away. An older Filipino man, carrying a carefully balanced load of cane on his shoulders, is pushed from behind and knocked down by one of the Chinese men. He falls hard, dropping the cane and hitting the dirt face-first. The ugly laughter rises. By the time the man looks up, I see it's Koji's friend Efren and his face is covered in dirt and the blood that bleeds from his nose.

Koji moves to help him up as the crowd quickly parts and a luna on his big, black horse suddenly hovers over Efren, the lash of his whip slapping across his shoulders and knocking him back to the ground.

Koji hesitates for just a split second before moving toward them.

"You fool!" the luna shouts, raising his whip again. "Get your ass off the ground and pick up that cane!"

It happens so quickly I can hardly believe it, yeah. Koji reaches up, grabs the luna by his belt, and pulls him off of his horse, his big body landing with a hard thud onto the dirt. And just as quickly as the dust danced, the luna is on his feet, hand on the pistol strapped to his hip. But when he sees that it's Koji, his eyes narrow in indecision—reign in his anger—step back, or deal with the bosses. He doesn't look like the forgiving type, but at that moment we both know Koji is one of the untouchables. The bosses want him to stay healthy and strong for all the cane he cuts. He's one of the few they've ordered not to be beaten.

Instead, the luna turns away from Koji to pick up his hat and shifts his anger to the gathered crowd.

"Dammit! Get back to work!" he hisses. "Now!"

The crowd scatters. Efren scurries to his feet and gathers up the cane, while the luna picks up his whip and climbs back up onto his big, black horse, his brimmed hat covering his eyes, so that all I can see is his large nose and bearded chin as we all hurry back to work.

≈

"You the king here," I say, walking back into the field.

Koji doesn't say anything. He grips his machete and looks down the long row of cane ahead of him. I wonder what he thinks about his newfound power. If it were mine, I would have killed that luna, stealing my father's razor from my boot, swinging the blade open and singing it across his throat in one smooth swoop, yeah. But that's me, that's Franklin, not Koji. Never Koji. Instead, he takes a deep breath and I see him reaching deep down inside of himself to call up his monster, eh, that strength that makes him such a fast cane cutter that even the lunas and plantation police won't touch him. Then before I can say another word he begins cutting with such speed I can't keep up.

Every whack of the machete releases his anger.

Every whack of the machete makes him stronger.

I pick up the pace and try to follow.

We have to stay one step ahead.

LOST AND FOUND

DECEMBER 6–8, 1935

22

ASHES

Daniel carefully snapped apart and boxed the metal railroad tracks before slipping each railcar back into its original packaging, all the while thinking of Maile. It had been more than a week since he'd seen her after the meeting at the fish market. Since then, it was as if she'd disappeared back into hiding. He had a mind to stop by her cousin's place just to make sure she was all right, maybe see if she'd have a meal with him. Daniel shook his head; he was acting like they were in high school again.

With his railcars and track packed and back in the hall closet, the kitchen table looked stripped. Daniel had been home for two weeks and knew it was time to clean up his toys, as his mother used to tell him, though his railroad set had been a welcome sight every morning when he walked into the kitchen. His first week back, he watched the railcars click-clack around the table as he stood at the counter eating his breakfast, comforted by them like being in a room with old friends.

Daniel sat down at the table with a cup of coffee and glimpsed his father's glass ashtray sitting on the counter. Earlier, while he was rummaging through the pantry, he was surprised to find it tucked behind jars of dried mango and shaved coconut flakes. His mother had always put the ashtray on the kitchen table when his father came home from a construction job, the thin gray film of ash on the bottom washed clean. It had disappeared for the first time not long after his father had left for Oahu, never to return. Daniel reached for it now, fingering its chipped edge as he set it on the table again. His memories of his father were scant. He was six when he left, too young to realize that those early years were all he'd ever have of the father who bought him gumballs and licorice, and took him to Wailuku River to swim every time he came home from a job.

What did Daniel remember about his father? He seemed well liked by everyone in Hilo town. When they walked down the street, they were always stopped by someone who knew him. He was *Frank, Frankie, Franklin*, all three rolled into one. He was always generous, as if he didn't have a care in the world. He left all the worrying to his mother. When his father first arrived home after finishing a job on another island, he was always happy, buying his mother flowers and taking them out to eat at the Lahaina Diner, only to become anxious and antsy after a few weeks. Even as a small boy, Daniel could feel the air thick with tension, his father roaming around the house like a trapped animal, drinking cups of coffee as he filled the ashtray with his cigarette butts.

There was the one rare afternoon his father stayed home to watch him while his mother went shopping; it was the first time Daniel had been alone with him. His father had hurt his back in a fall on a job and it was the longest period of time he'd ever stayed home with them. "Daddy can't carry you," his mother told him, "so you hold his hand if you go out, yeah." Daniel was no older than three or four and had wanted to run after her as he watched her leave.

They'd sat on the couch, and his father read him a book about a rabbit and a snake who become friends when they have to escape a forest fire together. Afterward his father stood and stretched his back, grimacing with pain, and then said, "Let's play a game."

Daniel watched his father pick up a pad of paper and a pencil from the table, leaning closer to him. He smelled like cigarettes and something sweet and flowery he used to comb his hair with. "This is a guessing game called What Is It? Where Is It?" he'd said. "I'm going to draw something, yeah, and I want you to tell me what it is and where it is. Do you understand?"

Daniel nodded. He'd never heard of the game before. His father began to draw a circle with spears around it. "The sun!" Daniel yelled out, louder than he expected to.

"That's right," his father said. "Where is it?"

Daniel pointed up to the ceiling but he meant the sky. "Outside," he added.

His father smiled, and he felt a warm happiness spread through his body as he anticipated the next drawing. A flower, a tree, a cup, a train, all guessed correctly.

His father paused and lit a cigarette before smiling down at him. "You're a smart boy. You did good, son," he said.

Daniel thought about that afternoon now, remembering it as the first time his father had ever called him "son." He didn't realize how good it made him feel, only to never hear him say it again. It was such a small legacy to leave behind.

≈

Daniel held the ashtray in the palm of his hand. One morning, months after his father had disappeared, he was outside playing in the yard and had found the ashtray half buried in the mud. His mother's face turned pale when she saw him washing it off in a bucket of water. "Give it to me," she'd said, her voice sounding strange, cold and flat. Her eyes were dark and annoyed as she snatched it quickly out of his hands. Daniel wanted to say he was sorry because he'd made her mad though he wasn't quite sure why. Later, when he went inside all the anger was gone and his mother was back to herself. Daniel never saw the ashtray again until this morning. He finished his coffee and stood to put it back where he found it, buried deep in the pantry where she wanted it.

Ever since Mama Natua had mistaken him for his father, Franklin Abe had crept back and lay heavily in his thoughts. The ashtray was just another reminder. It felt as if his father kept returning, only to disappear all over again. Daniel tried to remember when he finally realized his father hadn't left for work, he had left them.

≈

Outside, the sky was clear, the warm wind finally carrying the sweet scents of the pikake and naupaka blossoms he missed. Daniel looked around the yard to see so many tasks ahead of him. The house could use a fresh coat of paint. The garden needed cleaning up, and his mother's beloved mango tree was so much taller than he remembered. He was back now and finally understood what the mango tree had meant to her: it was the living embodiment of their family's time on the island—the past, the present, and the future. It would remain long after they were gone, a reminder of the resilience of life. It was his turn to make sure it continued to thrive. Daniel walked down the dirt path to the main road. It wasn't until he turned the corner that he knew where he was headed.

23

THE SURPRISE

When Maile heard footsteps at the front door, she stopped mopping the kitchen floor and quietly waited. All afternoon she remained in the thick heat of the small house while her cousin was at work. When the knock came she flinched, a sourness roiling in her stomach. She held on to the mop tightly. *All I have to do is stay quiet*, she thought. *Just stay quiet and wait until whoever it is goes away.* Maile stepped slowly toward the front door, taking deep breaths in and out to swallow her panic. She was scaring herself. It could simply be a neighbor, or a salesman, or a Bible-toting missionary recruiter. *He* couldn't know where her cousin lived. She had only mentioned her cousin to him once or twice, in passing. All he knew was that both her parents were dead. Maile's thoughts stumbled over each other. She leaned the mop against the wall and picked up a screwdriver her cousin had left on the coffee table. It was impossible to keep living her life like this, held hostage and afraid. Blood pumping, she used her bandana to wipe the sweat from her face. Her shirt clung sticky against her back by the time she reached for the door and pulled it open, only to find Daniel standing there.

≈

Two days later, Maile was early and already waiting for Daniel on the wood platform at the train station. He wanted to take her on a train ride, he'd said, standing outside her cousin's front door the other afternoon. He had asked her to meet him at the station, looking like the boy from high school, laughter and kindness in his voice. He made her feel like that young girl again. It was the first morning she hadn't thought about anything else, hadn't felt the knot of anxiety in her stomach getting up to face another day. Maile was halfway down the road before realizing she hadn't looked for *him* when she stepped out of the house that morning. And now her fear rose again, having let down her guard. She wouldn't look back, she wouldn't. Even if it was for just this one morning, Maile tamped down her anxiety. She walked straight to the train station without turning, breathless with hope, breathless with anticipation.

≈

The small station shook like a quake had hit when the first local passenger train arrived. The day was airless and already warm, but Maile's heart jumped at the shrill sound of the whistle. The wooden planks reverberated under her feet as the large train rumbled and slowed toward the station. Clouds of steam swarmed around her as the train ground to a stop, wheezing one last time, full of sighs and ticks. The light circled her and changed just as suddenly, tinged with expectation. The quick commotion of doors cracking open was followed by dockworkers, women in bright-colored, loose cotton muumuus, and uniformed schoolkids coming to Hilo from towns along the Hamakua coast, stepping down from the cars and hurrying off to their destinations.

The Hawaii Consolidated Railroad had opened up the small world of Hilo, connecting them to other parts of the island. News of the lava pooling above Hilo hadn't changed any of their daily routines yet, and she watched, amazed at their resiliency and ashamed of her own weakness. Voices echoed from all directions as the scurried movements of the day beginning reminded her of being back in Oahu, sparking a moment of renewed fear.

Maile inhaled and exhaled and pushed it out again.

She waited until the very last passenger disembarked from the train and it stood completely empty. Only then did she sit down and wait for Daniel, the world around her having gone quiet again.

Daniel arrived not long after. Maile looked across the tracks to the platform on the other side and saw him emerge from the small station, looking for her. It took another moment for Maile to believe that all of this was really happening. Just a few weeks before, she'd been walking along the streets of Honolulu's Chinatown, stopping among the sad stalls of pungent salted fish and vegetables wilting in the afternoon heat, never imagining she'd be here now. Maile looked across the tracks and watched Daniel, wearing a white shirt and dark pants, always so handsome, still recognizing his quick, lanky movements, his shorter haircut, and his caring, inquisitive eyes that suddenly looked across the tracks and caught hers. She couldn't help but wonder again why he would still be interested in her. Daniel smiled, then waved to her.

"You're on the wrong side!" he yelled over.

Maile smiled and waved back to him. She hadn't thought about which direction they were heading. She hadn't thought about coming or going; she simply knew it was with someone she wasn't afraid of, someone she knew for years and could depend on. Maile's tongue swept over her lips and she tasted the sweetness of that feeling again.

24

THE SCENIC EXPRESS

≈

**THE HAWAII CONSOLIDATED RAILROAD
ANNOUNCES THE SCENIC EXPRESS.
EXPERIENCE HAWAII LIKE YOU'VE NEVER SEEN IT BEFORE.
RIDE AND DINE IN THE COMFORT OF OUR LUXURY TRAIN CARS.
ENJOY THE SPECTACULAR VIEWS ALONG THE HAMAKUA COAST.
—TICKETS AVAILABLE AT THE HILO RAILWAY STATION—**

≈

Daniel had first seen the ad for the Scenic Express tacked on the Okawa Fish Market's bulletin board the night he returned. He'd thought nothing of it until he saw Maile again. In Chicago, he'd spent most of his days and nights at the hospital, leaving little time to spend his salary. During his residency, he sent money home whenever he could, but his mother was already gone by the time he began working full-time at the

University of Chicago's Medical Center. Even in these lean times, he reasoned he had worked hard for this small extravagance, and there was no one he would rather share it with than Maile.

"Our train should be arriving soon," Daniel said as they waited on the platform.

Other passengers had begun to gather. Daniel recognized the manager from S. H. Kress & Company and his wife, a doctor he'd spoken with at the hospital, and other well-to-do haoles who lived in their big houses up in the hills east of downtown. He glanced down the platform and was surprised to see a missionary minister who'd come by the fish market trying to recruit locals. Daniel wondered how he could afford such a luxury on a minister's salary. The murmur of excited voices and laughter surrounded them, the sweet-scented aftershaves and perfumes of the men and women finely dressed in suits and expensive dresses. He watched Maile watching them before looking down uncomfortably at her faded cotton dress and scuffed shoes. Had he made a mistake?

"Where are we going?" Maile asked, her voice rising just barely above the commotion.

"It's a surprise." Then he smiled reassuringly. "Trust me."

He saw her flinch at his words.

It was only after the gleaming black-and-burgundy train pulled smoothly into the station that he saw her slight apprehension turn to surprise. They were suddenly standing next to the luxurious Scenic Express, the letters spelled out in bold, gold letters on the side of each car. It offered a special sightseeing excursion in beautifully renovated railcars, part of Hawaii Consolidated Railways' remedy to help cut the costs of building the railroad along the Hamakua coast to service the sugar mills north of Hilo. Daniel couldn't imagine the amount of work involved in building a railroad along the rugged coast, rearranging nature to suit their needs. They had blasted through mountains to create tunnels, and built trestles to support the railcars rising hundreds of feet over valleys and rivers.

"I read about the Scenic Express in an Oahu newspaper," Maile said with awe.

They counted six cars. Each large window had thick, velvet burgundy drapes tied to each side. It was beautiful and extravagant. She glanced at Daniel, her face flushed. She looked at the train and remained quiet. A burst of steam was released as the train shuttered and settled.

"Is everything all right?" he asked.

Daniel watched her, suddenly nervous as they stood on the crowded platform among the other excited passengers. He should have waited, done something simple and quiet. Instead he had to show off. Maile shifted from side to side, her brow knitted as if she were worrying over a math problem. Was this all too much for her? He only wanted to take her away from Hilo and the eruption for a little while. He grew warm at the thought that she might refuse to board the train with him as she eyed the fancy railcars and the well-dressed passengers.

"We don't have to—" he began.

"No," she said. "I mean yes, everything's fine, thank you."

Daniel breathed a sigh of relief when she turned to him and smiled, her cloud of hesitation cleared away.

≈

The Scenic Express didn't disappoint. Instead of the hard, wooden benches and sticky gray floors of the passenger trains, the car was wallpapered in a burgundy and gold-leaf crown pattern, sharing matching burgundy lampshades on the overhead lamps and soft, plush gold carpeting underfoot. To each side of the center aisle were white-tableclothed tables set with china, silverware, and wineglasses, each table smartly positioned for gazing out of the large picture windows. They were shown to table twelve, toward the back of the car, as other passengers filled the tables around them.

It was a luxury that couldn't be further from Daniel's sugar train experiences with Uncle Koji, sweating in the engine car, breathing in soot and coal dust, and yelling to be heard above the grinding, chugging train. "Too pretty, eh, for a real train," Uncle Koji would say. Daniel felt a tinge of guilt at the lavishness and cost. He cringed to think of Auntie Nori's retort, "Why pay, yeah, when nature is out there for free?"

But as the scenic train slowly pulled out of the station, all his reservations disappeared. They sat at their white-clothed table and spoke easily, though Maile still hadn't said anything about her fiancé. Daniel knew enough to wait. There was something fragile about her that he didn't want to spook. When the train picked up speed, leaving the outskirts of Hilo and snaking down the Hamakua coast, they gazed out at the wondrous views, bordered by the ocean on one side and the lush, massive mountains on the other. After living in crowded cities surrounded by traffic and tall buildings, they were both seeing the island anew again, pure and wild and untouched. It was hard to believe that just on the other side of the mountain, the burning lava endlessly flowed.

When they entered the first tunnel, the lamps in the train flickered on before the darkness surrounded them. Daniel thought he saw Maile tremble. He heard a collective intake of breath from the other passengers in the car as they were suddenly rumbling through the cool, black night. He looked at Maile's reflection in the dark window, girlish in the dim light, and he could hardly believe they were there, moving straight through the interior of a massive mountain together. Daniel looked down at the silver knife rattling against Maile's water glass. When he reached over to quiet it, his fingers brushed against hers and stayed. Moments later, the sunlight stunned as the train barreled out of the other side of the tunnel and the whistle blew through a cloud of rising steam.

≈

After they emerged from the darkness of the first tunnel, Maile relaxed and seemed her old self again. Not long after, a waiter came with the first course of their lunch, beef consommé.

"What did I do to deserve this?" Maile asked, looking down at her soup in wonder.

Daniel smiled. "It's just a train ride."

Maile shook her head. "The local train is a train ride. This is something else," she said, a smile in her voice. "I can't imagine what Uncle Koji would think."

Daniel laughed, having thought the exact same thing. "He'd hate it. He wouldn't think this was a train at all, more like someone's fancy dining room. He'd also think I was trying to impress you."

"Are you?"

"Maybe a little," he confessed, and smiled. "Let's eat the soup before it gets cold."

Daniel watched Maile sip the broth, then look up at him and nod. He tasted it next, warm and salty on his tongue. The consommé was followed by roast beef with potatoes and carrots, fresh fruit, and a piece of pineapple cake. The train rocked them gently from side to side as the lush green mountainsides slid past the window like a moving picture show.

Not long after, the train slowed, the wheels grinding against the tracks as the car lurched, glasses clinking against one another. When they rolled to a complete stop, Daniel saw the confusion on Maile's face as the other passengers began to stand, mumbling excitedly as they looked out the window to see that the car was perched atop one of the steel trestles built over a canyon below.

"Is there something wrong?" she asked.

"No, nothing's wrong," he reassured her. Daniel stood and reached for Maile's hand. "Come with me," he said. "It's part of the surprise."

Maile hesitated and then reached out.

They followed the other passengers to the front of the car, where Daniel helped her to step down onto a walkway built to the side of the trestle, bordered by an iron railing. They stood more than 150 feet above the valley below, surrounded by the massive cliffs, lush green trees, and tangles of overgrown tropical vegetation untouched by civilization. A waterfall cascaded down the mountainside in the distance. The air felt cooler, lighter, as if they were standing in the midst of another world, suspended in midair, trusting the steel trestle that ran across the enormous gulch below. The passengers stood clutching the railing, marveling excitedly at the sight from so high up. Daniel stepped back as eager voices filled the air around them. The wind suddenly picked up, quickly followed by the surprised squeal of a passenger as her straw hat blew away and glided down toward the valley floor like a pale bird.

He was with Maile. It was a small break from the real world and Pele's wrath. The beauty and brilliance of the lush valley below were heart-stopping. In that moment, Daniel realized why so many of the locals had never left the island; it was part of their lifeblood, a rare gift, even if nature's hand could be punishing. He and Maile remained side by side, pressed closely together in silence, the warm wind whistling through the valley below, wrapping itself around them until it was time to board the train again.

Daniel dipped yet closer to Maile and said, "I've missed this."

"I have too," she said.

"Look!" someone yelled.

Daniel turned toward the direction of Hilo and the mountains above to see a column of black smoke rising toward the sky.

Something else was burning, and he had no doubt Pele was behind it.

~

It wasn't until they returned to Hilo station and he walked her back to her cousin's house in silence that she seemed anxious again, the dream-like world of the train ride left behind. To his surprise, Maile spoke first, her voice low and tentative as she began to tell him the story of her years in Honolulu. "I was so naive," she began, and he saw the young, shy, fiercely intelligent girl he'd first seen in his freshman class who always kept to herself. As he listened, Daniel felt a host of emotions. It upset him to hear about her other life with another man until he looked into her eyes and saw her fear. When Maile finished talking, Daniel knew he would do whatever it took to keep that monster away from her.

"I won't ever let him come near you again."

"I should have been smarter," she began.

Daniel shook his head. "Don't say that," his voice louder than he intended. He saw Mariko flinch and added softly, "It wasn't your fault. He knew what he was doing. He used your love and trust to frighten and take advantage of you."

Daniel had learned firsthand when a young woman was rushed to the emergency room beaten beyond recognition. She had blamed herself, said it wasn't her husband's fault, that she shouldn't have made him angry. She'd been beaten so badly she died later that night from a brain hemorrhage.

Daniel shook the memory away and reached for Mariko's hand, only to have her jerk quickly away, as if his touch burned.

"I'm sorry," she said, her eyes tearing.

He shook his head and tried to smile, though her rejection did sting after their pleasant day on the train. "There's nothing to be sorry for," he said.

"I can't—"

"There's no hurry," he said.

They walked the rest of the way, with Daniel making small talk about the work he needed to do on the green bungalow, hoping to put her at ease again, hoping to drown out the woman's anguished voice pleading with him not to blame her husband.

GHOST VOICES

MARIKO, 1915

Koji and I are riding a passenger train toward the village of Mountain View when the noisy, rumbling railcar scrapes along the tracks with a sudden shriek, jarring my attention away from the window. I'm embarrassed to think that it's the first time I've been this far away from Hilo town. The fifteen miles seem a world away, yeah. Even my honeymoon was spent at the green bungalow because Franklin didn't have money to take us farther. Every year he promised we'd go away the following year. In the end, he was the only one who went away.

The train car is spare and practical, wooden benches and dirt-covered gray floors. It begins to rain, drops whipping against the window, leaving thin lines of snail trails. Still, I'm awestruck by it all. I can't take my eyes away from the fleeting coastline as the train carries us toward the mountains in the direction of the Kilauea volcano. And just as quickly the view shifts and we're suddenly bordered on both sides by a wall of tall eucalyptus and ohi'a trees. I can't help but think of how thrilled Daniel would be on this train with us. The trip was completely unexpected, something Koji had offered when he was at the house this past Sunday.

"There's a place I'd like to show you," he'd said as he stood to leave.

"Where?" I ask.

"Not so far. Near Mountain View."

"What about Daniel?"

We've done everything with Daniel since Franklin disappeared almost two years ago. At eight years old, he's beginning to look so much like Franklin it sometimes hurts to see him, a sharp, prickling stab in the middle of my chest.

"He'll be in school," Koji says. He gave no other explanation.

"Okay," I say, agreeing, and a warm flush rises to my cheeks.

"Good then," Koji says. "We'll take the train over on Tuesday, yeah." He wouldn't tell me where we're going, only to bring a sweater and wear some sturdy shoes.

≈

I turn away from the window and settle back on the bench seat, suddenly aware of how close I'm sitting to Koji and how little we've spoken. I wonder how he feels riding the train as a passenger, but nothing in his face gives him away. When we first boarded, Koji told me we would be getting off near the small town of Mountain View, before the train continues on to Glenwood, where the rail line ends. The passengers who want to see Kilauea volcano will have to go the last eight miles by horse and wagon. I look around the railcar, guessing that most of the warmly dressed passengers are going up to see the volcano, and part of me wishes we were going up to Kilauea too, which would be a real adventure. I wonder if we can do it another time with Daniel. I'm brought out of my thoughts when the train slows and stops in Mountain View to let us off. Koji waves to the engineer, who makes the unexpected stop for us. We're to be waiting at the same spot when the train returns in the afternoon. We stand at the side of the tracks like two orphans, yeah, and I still have no idea where Koji is taking me.

"You won't tell me where we're going?" I ask.

Koji grins and his face remains unreadable while he plays with the hat in his hands. He's dressed in jeans and his work boots, a rucksack slung across his shoulder. "You'll see soon enough," he says. "We have to walk the rest of the way from here, yeah." He points toward a path through the trees. "It's along that trail for about a mile."

I don't know what to think, but I do know that Koji is familiar with all the old roads in and around Hilo town. I'm thankful it has stopped raining. In no time, the hazy, warm sun is blocked out and we're surrounded by tall trees and the dripping green foliage of the rain forest. The path through the forest becomes steep and slick with moss-covered rocks and I'm mindful to watch my steps. The air smells of wet, dank earth. I slip more than once, but catch myself. When Koji takes hold of my hand and guides me down a steep, narrow path slowly, I'm only too happy. My thumb absently sweeps over the hard calluses on his thumb. Half an hour later, I'm hot and sweaty and have no idea why he has taken me out into the rain forest. I'm just about to ask again when he slows and then stops.

"We're here," Koji says.

"Where are we?" I ask. Buzzing mosquitoes fill the air as I swat them away.

"It's a special place, yeah," he says. "You'll see." Koji shifts his rucksack from one shoulder to the other. "It's just down there." He points toward a ravine covered in vegetation and vines.

When we finally climb down, I can see the entrance of what looks like a cave underneath all the overgrown foliage. I look at him and can't fathom why Koji would take me here.

"Just wait," he says, as if he knows what I'm thinking. He takes out two kerosene lamps from his rucksack and lights each one. "It's dark in there. Be careful where you step, yeah," he says. "It's a lava cave made from an old flow. The rocks are uneven and so sharp it can split open your side like a knife, yeah," he warns. "I used to come here when I was young."

I pause and remember Franklin once telling me about the lava cave when I asked him about the scar on his side that traveled to his back. As teenagers, he and Koji and Razor had discovered a cave in the rain forest that no one knew about. They'd spent all the summer weekends exploring it. It was where Franklin had fallen, slicing his side open, leaving the scar my fingers had lovingly traced. Why has Koji taken me here?

I step cautiously into the mouth of the cave, and a cold breath of stale air sends shivers down my back. It smells musty and damp and moldy. We're suddenly enveloped by darkness so black and thick our lanterns only provide a foggy light a few feet in front of us. In the distance the sound of dripping water echoes.

"There's a maze of tunnels in here," he says. "If you take the wrong one, you could be lost in here for the rest of your life, yeah," he teases.

"You're not making this any easier," I respond, my stomach in knots, my patience wearing thin.

He laughs. "I would never let anything happen to you. Leave your lantern here, yeah," he says. "We only need one."

I hesitate leaving the light behind, but Koji takes my hand again and leads the way through a low and narrow tunnel that we have to bend over to squeeze through. The light is murky and I feel trapped and frightened. "I can't," I whisper, and try not to panic as I pull at Koji's arm, wanting to back out. Stooped over, it's hard to walk on the jagged rocks, and I can hardly breathe in the humid, closed space. I begin to feel dizzy and nauseous and think I might faint.

Koji stops and strokes my hand to calm me before saying, "Trust me, yeah, it's only a little farther."

I do. I realize I trust Koji more than I'd ever trusted Franklin. I try to relax then and allow him to pull me forward, small, careful steps until we suddenly emerge into a large, open cavern in which we can stand straight again. It feels like we've stepped into the stomach of some beast.

"We're here," Koji says.

Where is here? I think, though I'm just relieved to be standing again.

"Now watch, yeah," he says.

Koji raises the lantern toward the ceiling, and the cave illuminates with a constellation of silver and gold patterns, setting the rocks overhead ablaze. I inhale at the sight, taking it in and breathing it out slowly. I've never seen anything like it, a small universe in the middle of a dark, dank lava cave that sends another shiver through me. I feel Koji move closer and take my hand again, warm and reassuring. And for just a moment, everything else disappears and we're standing in a world all our own.

AND THEN . . .

DECEMBER 11—16, 1935

25

RESTLESS

The morning had gotten away from Daniel. He lay in bed and couldn't stop thinking about Maile. Their day had gone so well on the Scenic Express until they returned to Hilo. It saddened him to hear she'd been so traumatized during her time in Honolulu, and he couldn't help but feel partly to blame. If they hadn't broken up, none of this would ever have happened. A moment later he sat up, tamping down his thoughts. You couldn't change the past. Hadn't he learned that from his own mistakes? You simply learned to live with them. It would take time for Maile, he knew, but they were seeing Mano and Kailani at the end of the week, and just being home again with people who cared about her would settle some of her fears. All that mattered was Maile had confided in him. It was a good start.

By the time Daniel walked to the fish market to borrow Uncle Samuel's truck to run some errands, it was already early afternoon. The sky was thick and gray, the heat held in by the clouds. He expected rain at any time as he drove to the Natua house, first to check on Mama, hoping the wheelchair had been helpful. He didn't expect great strides in such a short time, but just being mobile would get her out of her room, remind her that there was still an outside world around her. Part of him was also hoping to jog her memory about his father so he could piece together some answers, only to be disappointed when he arrived to find she was napping.

Auntie Leia ushered him in. "She'll be up soon, yeah. Stay," she said. "Just made some papaya juice."

"How is Mama? Is the wheelchair helping?"

"Like a dream, yeah," Auntie Leia said, and smiled. "She's much happier to be out of her room, even eating better."

He thought that Auntie Leia also looked happier.

"That's good to hear," Daniel said. It was what he hoped for. "I'll come by again tomorrow." He was feeling too restless to sit and wait, another reminder of his father and something he hadn't realized he inherited. "I need to stop by the hospital with some paperwork for Mama's file."

"Shame, yeah, you having to make another trip," Auntie Leia said.

"I'll come by earlier tomorrow," he said. "There are some exercises I'd like Mama to start doing."

Auntie Leia nodded. "We'll be here," she said.

Daniel walked back to the truck, sunlight streaming through the parted clouds.

⸎

From the Natuas, Daniel dropped off some paperwork at the hospital before driving back to the market. The day felt unfinished. The crowds thickened the closer he came to the wharf and Hilo Bay. From the way the locals were going about their business as usual, it was hard to believe that Pele was still erupting in the mountains above them. He observed a flock of day workers hovering like birds on the sidewalk and imagined his father among them. He slowed down to study their passing faces, watching for his familiar lean body, the high, straight nose; envisioning his time-weathered good looks, the deeper lines and grayer hair. Daniel shook away his foolishness. He knew there was little chance that Franklin Abe could ever have returned to the tightly knit Hilo community for long without someone knowing. They always watched out for and protected their own.

Daniel wasn't ready to go home. He glanced at his watch and stepped on the gas, making a quick turn at the next corner, driving away from the wharf. If he drove directly up to Puli Plantation he could talk to Uncle Koji and still return Uncle Samuel's truck before dark.

26

COLLECTING

Mama woke with a start. She heard voices outside, followed by a truck rattling down the road. Moments later, Leia peered into her room to see that she was awake. "You're up, yeah, you just missed Daniel."

Who was Daniel? The name settled on her tongue but she didn't say it aloud. Instead she raised her arms and reached toward her daughter like a child. In one quick swoop she was lifted into Leia's arms and gently placed into the chair with wheels. It was her favorite time of each day, being pushed out to the porch, or if it wasn't too hot or too wet or too windy, outside to the front yard.

"Good of Wilson to build the ramp, yeah," Leia said as she rolled her slowly down the wooden ramp and onto a shady, bald spot of dirt and grass in the front yard.

Mama smiled when she looked up at the cloud-spotted sky.

"Let me get you something to drink," Leia said. "Be right back, yeah."

Mama was joyous. She gazed across the yard at the full canopy of the monkey pod tree and the familiar road beyond, breathing in deeply to find Pele lingering in the air, yet overpowered by the scent of damp earth and seaweed, the smell of the ocean carried to her by the wind. As a child, she always loved the ocean, the roar of the waves, swimming in the push and pull of the salty sea, the sand collected between her toes, something Nestor, born an island boy, never liked. He thought the ocean was dangerous and unreliable. "Like a wild animal, yeah," he'd always say. "Can't be trusted. Can't be tamed."

That was exactly what attracted her to it.

Mama laughed and leaned into the memory it reawakened, quietly sneaking out of the house those early mornings while her family slept. It was still dark as the moon lit her way along the same road she'd been walking down since she first married. The sun wouldn't rise for another hour or more, and Mama loved this time just before dawn when night slowly lightened into day and secrets were revealed. During her early morning foraging, the air was still cool and moist. Mama swung her hips and moved down the road with the same urgent sway of the trees to the incessant music of *pomfret, pomfret* from the coqui frogs and the steady chorus of cicadas.

Mama loved the freedom of venturing out without the girls, who always wanted to tag along and help her collect what she needed for the leis. For Leia and Noelani, along with little Nori, who was always waiting to join them, it was all fun and games, a scavenger hunt. They gathered mounds of flowers, kukui nuts, and ti leaves before going down to the beach and running into and out of the waves, collecting whatever they thought was pretty, whether Mama could use them for her leis or not—seaweed, stones, pieces of driftwood, fallen leaves, broken pieces of glass.

"Yes, no, no, yes," Mama said, pointing to their hands filled with their sandy, damp treasures, which were just as quickly discarded.

She smiled at the memory.

Without the girls pulling her in every direction, Mama took her time collecting only the best shells and flowers for stringing her special orders. Even when it rained, the beach was always her first stop. She walked out toward the water and stepped onto the damp, cool sand as the cold rush of waves dashed in and out, erasing her footprints and washing over her bare feet. Mama crouched down and began collecting shells that had been half buried in the wet sand. The sharp *ping* of the first shells dropping into the pail always brought her such joy. It wasn't until she walked back up from the water toward the trees that she heard the raised voices.

The words were spit out harsh and angry, making Mama slow down and stop, surprised to recognize Koji Sanada's voice. She wasn't sure who the other man was at first, though he sounded familiar.

"You'll never have them!"

"You abandoned them years ago."

"They're still my family!"

"Do you even know what the word 'family' means?"

The voices escalated above the waves, roaring and crashing into each other. Mama stayed hidden among the trees, conscious even then that something bad was about to happen. It didn't take long for her to recognize that the other man's voice belonged to Franklin Abe.

≈

Mama opened her eyes when she heard the screen door spring open and clap shut. A clinking of glasses and Leia's humming led her right back home again. Mama's gaze wandered back to the monkey pod tree, where she saw Nestor leaning against its thick trunk, a sudden spark of energy making her sit up straight.

She blinked and he was gone.

27

SUGARCANE

Daniel hadn't been to Puli Plantation in years. He drove up the mountain on the paved blacktop, which soon gave way to rutted, dirt roads. He slowed as the truck bounced over the uneven tracks, past dense foliage surrounded by ohi'a, hau, and hala trees, cooler and darker, until he reached the summit and turned onto a wide dirt road bordered by eucalyptus trees that soon opened up to acres and acres of sugarcane fields as far as he could see. It was late afternoon and Daniel hoped Uncle Koji had returned from his last sugar train run and was back at his cottage by now. He felt guilty not having seen his uncle since the community meeting at the market two weeks ago when the lava began pooling. He was chasing after Maile before he even had a chance to say a real hello.

Daniel drove through the gates of Puli Plantation toward a cluster of long wooden buildings less than a quarter mile away—flat-roofed, two-storied structures resembling army barracks arranged in a U shape, a far cry from the small, run-down buildings he visited as a boy. The plantation structures had not only grown in size, but also had expanded in acreage since he'd been away on the mainland. According to the sign, the offices and plantation store were in the building to the left, the school and community center were in the middle building, and the hospital and dispensary were in the building to the right. Daniel was both surprised and delighted to see a hospital and dispensary. At least the cane workers no longer had to be taken all the way down to Hilo whenever there was a medical emergency. He couldn't imagine the number of accidents, the suffering and deaths caused by the rough two-hour journey by horse and wagon in the past. Koji's father had lost his hand because of the lack of medical care back then. By the looks of the growing plantation, it was obvious that sugar remained the reigning king on the island. Even amid hard times and the eruption, Puli appeared abuzz with activity, workers still toiling in the fields as the harvest continued in full swing.

Daniel stopped at the plantation store to buy some beer. The new store was larger, but no less crowded with goods and customers as the small store Koji had taken him to when he'd visited as a boy. Twenty years ago. He remembered the day was hot and still. His uncle had given him a tour of the train barn and sugar mill, introduced him to other workers whose leathery, rough hands had swallowed up his own in their handshakes. When he asked to see where Koji lived, his uncle walked him through a cane field instead, rows of tall stalks shadowing him on both sides, taller than grown men were. Uncle Koji had stopped. "Stand back, yeah. Don't want you to get hurt," he'd said. He squatted down beside a stalk, grabbed it higher up with one hand and swung his big cane knife with his other, severing the stalk clean through near the ground, dirt and dust rising into the warm air. "That's how we cut the cane, yeah, all the way down the row. Always pay attention, or you might cut more than you want, eh," Koji warned, and winked.

Daniel nodded. He could barely hold the knife straight with two hands, and was thrilled to see Koji cut cane, even if he couldn't imagine working in the hot field all day, sweaty and parched as he already felt in just the short time he stood watching his uncle. Afterward Koji had taken him to the plantation store run by a Chinese couple. "Go ahead, but don't break the bank, eh," Koji had teased.

Daniel had been relieved to step into the cool, dark, crowded store, away from the hot and humid heat. The store smelled sweet and vinegary.

The counter was cluttered with jars filled with hard candy, licorice, gumballs, and a big jar of what looked like cabbage fermenting in something murky and potent. He wrinkled his nose at the smell. Against one wall were wooden crates with sweet potatoes, Chinese cabbage, turnips, long beans, bananas, and lychee. On the other side were large barrels of rice and flour and sugar, and toward the back of the store stood a big icebox that held soda pop, beer, eggs, and rice balls. Daniel hesitated, walking slowly around the crowded store to the back, where he finally opened the door to the icebox and reached for a grape soda pop.

Daniel put the bottles of beer he bought on the passenger seat and sat in the truck watching the slow march of the tired, dusty men and women walking along the dirt road back to their villages after work. They carried tin pails and burlap bags, shedding layers of clothes. He wondered how many of them ever left the plantation, which was a world in itself, a map of crisscrossing dirt roads leading from their villages to the fields to these buildings, which provided everything they needed and were all Puli Plantation owned and run. Just over the hill on the far side of the fields, the plantation manager and his family lived in a big, sprawling house, surrounded by smaller houses where all the haole supervisors, lunas, and staff lived, adequately separated by several miles from all the cane workers.

A few years after his first visit, Daniel learned that what little wages the cane workers earned every week was spent at the small plantation store. "Most on the plantation have no choice, yeah, but to sign their lives away," Uncle Koji said. "Their credit keeps on growing until the owners have the families collared and tied from one generation to the next. Always been like that, yeah."

"Why?" he had asked.

"They have to feed their families."

"Why can't they pay the workers more?"

"Good question," Uncle Koji huffed, without giving him an answer.

Daniel thought of all the Sundays Koji came down to visit them after his father left, usually to help his mother fix things around the house. His uncle always seemed happiest when they sat down for dinner together. He looked at the home-cooked meal in front of him as if surprised at his good fortune. "Lucky, yeah," he said to Daniel on more than one occasion. Daniel had simply nodded, not quite understanding what it all meant back then.

"Do you have to sign for credit too?" he had asked.

Uncle Koji shook his head. "Easier for me, yeah," he'd said. "I don't have a big family to feed. Most of the families have their own small gardens and grow their own vegetables, taro, beans, sweet potatoes, and carrots to help keep costs down."

"We'll take care of you," Daniel said. It came from him spontaneously, serious and matter-of-fact.

It was the first time ten-year-old Daniel realized that working at Puli, even running the sugar train, was not the charmed life he had imagined it to be. Uncle Koji had turned away from him. Had he said something wrong? They could take care of him; his mother was the best seamstress in town. Lots of the locals wanted his mother to sew and mend their clothing. He stood there, waiting. When his uncle turned back to him, his eyes were watery.

Later, when Daniel was a teenager and no longer wanted to visit Koji at Puli, his mother had reminded him of how generous Koji had been. "If it wasn't for your uncle, where would we be now?" she asked him. He didn't know what made him feel worse, that she was disappointed in him, or that he'd so easily forgotten how much Koji had done for them.

Daniel started the truck and followed the dirt road that led past the train barn and mill up to Uncle Koji's cottage, perched at the top of the hill. He never did see where his uncle used to live with his family. Daniel pulled into the driveway of the small cottage as the truck's brakes squeaked to a stop.

28

A Visitor

Koji sat down on his front porch, lit a cigarette, and poured himself a glass of whiskey. A sudden fit of coughing racked through his chest, leaving him helpless but to see it through, eased along with the quick burn of whiskey. He'd just gotten comfortable when the dull crunch of tires along the dirt road made him stop and squint through the screen to see a truck driving up toward his cottage, kicking up a cloud of dust. There were very few visitors who came up to Puli this late in the afternoon, and even fewer who came to see him. Koji wondered if it was one of the Puli managers and stood to get a better look. He didn't recognize the green truck at first, not until it drove up the slope and he could see OKAWA FISH MARKET in black block letters on the side door just as it turned into his driveway. He was even more surprised to see that it was Daniel driving.

Koji stood by the screen door watching Daniel get out of the truck and was reminded of the first time eight-year-old Daniel had asked him if he could visit the plantation to see where he and Uncle Razor worked. Between watching the sugar train being unloaded at the station and discovering Koji's cane knife one day in the back of his truck, young Daniel had become fascinated with everything about the sugar plantation. Koji hesitated and cleared his throat, suddenly fearful. He tried to keep his two worlds separate: one was work, the other family. The real truth was a constant thorn pricking at him; he was embarrassed by and unsure of what Daniel would think of him when he saw the crowded, run-down cottage where he lived, the hard, dirty, grueling work he and Razor did in the fields that made up their daily lives.

"It's not a place for little boys," Koji had explained.

"Why?" Daniel asked.

"It's just fields and workers doing hard work with sharp knives, yeah."

"But it's where sugar comes from," he insisted. "I'll be careful, I will."

Koji looked to Mariko, who had smiled at him and nodded. If she didn't mind, how could he? It warmed him to be reminded that she never saw him as just a cane cutter.

≈

Koji pushed open the screen door and watched Daniel walk toward the house.

"What brings you all the way up here?" he asked. "Everything okay?"

"You bring me all the way here," Daniel said, lifting the bag in his hand. "Everything's fine. Everyone's still waiting for Pele to make up her mind which way she's going to flow, so I thought it was about time we sat down and had a beer together."

Koji smiled, happy to see him. "Come in." He led him through the porch and into the house.

"I see nothing's changed," Daniel said, stopping at the doorway and looking around his spare living room.

Mariko and Daniel had visited a few times after he moved to the sugar train cottage in 1919. By then Daniel was twelve and no longer captivated by plantation life. The cottage was still small and spare, but it was all his and meant more than he could say.

"I do have a radio now," Koji said. "Thought it about time to step into the modern world, eh."

Daniel laughed and handed him the bag. Koji walked to the kitchen, opened the bottles, and returned.

"Let's go sit on the porch where it's cooler," Koji said, handing him an opened beer. When they settled, he continued, "How's Maile? I caught a glimpse of her at the meeting before you shot out after her."

"She's fine," he said.

"Is she back for good?"

Daniel nodded and smiled.

"Good for you."

"Very good." Daniel sipped his beer in thought before he finally said, "She had a bad relationship in Honolulu. Still getting over it. We're going to take it slow and get to know each other again."

"That's part of the fun, yeah," Koji said. "Just don't mess it up this time."

"I'll try not to," he said, and laughed.

"I hear you're also taking good care of Mama Natua," he said. "How she doing?"

Daniel sat back in his chair. "Other than her senility, her health appears stable. She still needs to take a few tests to see how everything else is faring."

Koji sighed. "Fancy name for old age, yeah?"

"Afraid so," he said. "We will all walk down that road one day; some of us just lose more along the way."

"No need to tell me." Koji swallowed a mouthful of beer.

"Mama doesn't remember much of what's happening in the present. Her memories of people and events are from the past, but they've also become confused, mixed up. Time takes on a life of its own." Daniel paused and took another swig of beer. "Actually, it's one of the reasons I wanted to talk to you."

"Why is that?"

"While I was examining her, Mama mistook me for my father. She talked about seeing you and him together," Daniel said, his eyes on Koji. "It sounded like she might have seen you and my father after he'd left us." He smiled. "I'm not sure if it's just another one of her confused memories, but I've wanted to ask you about it ever since. Do you have any idea what she's talking about?" He paused to take another drink from his bottle. "Did my father ever return to Hilo after he left us?"

Koji breathed in slowly, sat back, and ran his hand over his head. He heard a scratching on the screen door and knew it was Hula, the feral cat who always came by in the late afternoon for dinner. "Just a minute," Koji said. He stood to let the cat in, watching her dart straight for the kitchen. Some things were simple: all Hula wanted was to be fed and she was happy. Koji returned to the conversation he'd been holding at arm's length.

"So, Mama said that?" Koji said, sitting back down. He drank some beer. *It's time,* he heard Mariko telling him. "She thought you were Franklin, eh?"

Daniel nodded. "I guess the resemblance between us brought up something she remembered from the past. She also could have been confusing an event that happened when you were young."

Daniel had always been methodical, weighing one thing against the other. Koji put down his bottle of beer and picked up his glass of whiskey before leaning forward. "She wasn't confused," he said.

A brief look of surprise crossed Daniel's face before it clicked and settled. "My father did return?"

This time Koji didn't hesitate to answer.

"Yes."

"When?"

Koji was sweating now, his shirt sticking to his back. "Almost five years after he left."

Daniel sat silent for a moment. The look of surprise on his face shifted to a darker, angrier gaze as he rubbed his cheek. Koji could see the questions percolating in his mind, just like when he was a boy waiting for him at the train station.

"Did my mother see him?" he asked.

Koji shook his head. "No."

"Why not?"

"He surprised me one night leaving your house."

"Did she know?"

"Yes."

Daniel coughed to clear his throat and asked, "Why didn't either of you ever tell me?"

"You were young and we didn't want to disturb your life," he said. "Your mother didn't know right away."

"Why? Was it because . . ." Daniel didn't finish his sentence.

Koji felt the blood rushing to his head. "You were settled and happy, and he was here and gone so quickly, yeah, it would only have upset you and your mother to see him." And then he added, "He wasn't here to stay."

"Why did he come back then?"

"He was in trouble," Koji said. "I was trying to protect you."

Koji saw a flash of resentment in Daniel's eyes. "You sure you weren't trying to protect yourself?"

Daniel's words felt like a slap. Koji gripped the glass in his hand and sat forward in the chair. "I wish it were that simple," he said flatly. "You want to hear the truth; your father was always a selfish son of a . . ." He paused to collect himself. "He came back because he needed money. He didn't come back for you, or for your mother." Koji stopped. He hadn't meant to be so brusque, but he was tired of carrying the burden.

Daniel sat still. Too still. Koji saw a thin layer of sweat on his forehead, felt his own stomach clench.

Then Daniel abruptly stood. "I have to go," he said.

"Daniel, don't," Koji said urgently. "I was going to tell you."

"But you never did tell me, did you?" Daniel snapped back.

"Daniel," Koji repeated.

He watched him leave and wanted to grab his arm, but knew to let him go. Daniel pushed through the screen door and hurried back to the truck. The engine roared to life as it backed up and raced down the dirt road, lost in the veil of dust. Daniel just needed time, Koji reasoned; it was his nature to think everything through. It must have felt like Franklin was leaving him all over again. Even as a boy when he was angry at Mariko, he went into his room, closed the door, and figured it all out in his head before talking to her again. Some things didn't change with age.

It's only the beginning of the story, Koji thought, *the hardest part I have yet to tell*. He absently touched his stomach, felt the pain again. That night Franklin had become someone he no longer knew. So had he. If he were honest, there was truth in what Daniel had accused him of; he was trying to protect himself, protect what he had with Mariko, and why shouldn't he? He was only too happy to be there after Franklin abandoned them. He'd done everything for Mariko. He had grieved for his lost boyhood friend, but the Franklin who returned was someone else. Was it so bad for Koji to be selfish for a change? Daniel deserved to know who his father was, both the good and the bad, even at the risk of Koji losing the only son he would ever have.

Koji sat out on his porch until his whiskey glass was long empty and the light began to fade to a dull gray. He heard the buzz of mosquitoes, the cicadas just beginning their nightly song. On the other side of the mountain the lava continued its relentless flow. Koji sat on the porch until it was almost dark and the persistent scratching against the screen door forced him to stand and let Hula back out.

29

RUN

The truck bounced and rattled across the rutted road as Daniel drove back down to Hilo. He rolled down the window and gripped the steering wheel, angry and hurt that not only Koji but also his mother had kept his father's return a secret from him. Over the years, she knew he yearned to know where his father was and why he never returned, and still she'd kept it from him. He couldn't get over the feeling that she'd somehow betrayed him.

"Where did Daddy go?" Daniel recalled asking his mother many months after his father hadn't returned.

"I don't know," she answered.

"Is he lost?"

"Yes," she said, tears in her eyes.

Daniel hated to see her cry and rarely asked again. But deep down there was a part of him that always hoped his father would return to them. He patiently waited year after year, only to realize now, when his father finally did, it had been kept a secret from him. Daniel swallowed down his anger, not only at Koji and his mother, but also at himself for not staying and listening to what his uncle had to say. Instead, he ran. When had running become so natural to him?

The truck picked up speed on the downslope and suddenly he was going too fast. Daniel pumped the brakes to slow down just as his right front tire caught a rut in the road, the truck skidding and fishtailing, sliding sideways directly toward a grove of trees that led down to a steep ravine. Heart in his throat, he shifted down and turned into the slide like Koji taught him, finally coming to a stop, the truck stalling. Daniel sat for a moment, hot and sweaty, breathing heavy with relief. He caught his breath before he swung open the door to see if there was any damage to Uncle Samuel's truck, grateful it hadn't tumbled down the side of the ravine. By the time he was back in the truck he had calmed down a little. He knew better than to be driving so fast. Daniel counted himself lucky when he turned the key in the ignition, and after a few tries, the engine caught and roared to life.

Daniel drove slowly the rest of the way back to town, his fury at being left in the dark all these years turning to a slower burn. The two people he trusted most in the world had kept his father away from him. The thought stung like an open wound, bringing tears to his eyes. As much as he wanted to hear the entire story of his father's return, right now he needed distance.

≈

By the time Daniel passed Yamamoto's Gas Station and Oshima's Grocery Store, it was nearly dark and the wind had shifted, carrying with it a heavier scent of sulfur. He parked Uncle Samuel's truck in front of the market. As soon as Daniel walked in, he knew something was wrong. There were no voices, no locals greeting him as he stepped through the screen doorway, no bursts of laughter from the yard, or low drone of music coming from the radio. The OPEN sign still dangled in the front window, but Jelly wasn't behind the counter, and the market felt bleak and eerily empty. Most of the time, Auntie Nori had to shoo away the last of the remaining stragglers at closing.

Daniel paused when he heard voices coming from the kitchen. By their quiet tones, Auntie Nori and Uncle Samuel were in the midst of a serious conversation.

Daniel stood in the kitchen doorway. "Is everything all right?" he asked, knowing it wasn't.

Uncle Samuel looked his way. "Daniel," he said, with a quick smile, which disappeared as soon as he began to speak, "word come from the volcano center: the lava above Saddle Road has begun to flow."

Daniel's throat went dry. He shouldn't have been surprised, but he'd been distracted the past two weeks, first by Mama and Maile, then by the news of his father's return. Meanwhile the lava flow had edged ahead of everything else. Hadn't he learned by now that life was a race you never could really win?

"Which direction?" he asked, already knowing it wasn't good with the market empty. Everyone must have hurried home after the news.

Auntie Nori answered this time. "The geologists at the volcano center say it's following the natural drainage down the mountain."

"Threatening our water, yeah," Uncle Samuel added.

"Not just our water," Auntie Nori added, a quiet and steady dread in her voice. "The lava is flowing directly toward *us*."

"Have the geologists said anything about what they're going to do?" Daniel asked. "There must be something?"

"They're not saying much right now," Auntie Nori said. "Until they do, there's nothing any of us can do, yeah, except wait again, and hope Pele will change direction, or stop the flow before it reaches town."

Daniel shook his head at the irony of it; modern science would always be at odds with the island's ancient beliefs. He didn't care which side won as long as the lava flow stopped. What Daniel hated most was the helpless waiting. If he were still working in the hospital's emergency room, he'd be calling out for vital stats, saline drips, blood transfusions to a rush of people in motion, trying to find ways to save the patient. Instead they stood there powerless and silent while the lava flow continued to destroy everything in its way.

Auntie Nori moved them out of the kitchen. On a piece of white butcher paper, she wrote the latest news to be tacked up on the bulletin board: WORD FROM THE VOLCANO OBSERVATORY CENTER . . .

He knew word had already spread through the community. They would quickly gather again at the fish market for another meeting, even if there was little they could do other than be together. Daniel's first thought was to go see Maile, relieved to know Uncle Koji was safe up at Puli. The resentment he felt now seemed small and insignificant. He should have been reassuring Auntie Nori and Uncle Samuel, but his head was spinning, and all that came to mind were the lines from the children's story his father had once read to him that afternoon years ago.

"Run, run," cried the snake.
"To where, to where?" asked the rabbit.
"As far away as you can go."

30

Nightmares

"Run, Nori, run!"

Leia's voice woke her. It was still dark outside and Nori couldn't tell how long she'd been asleep. The news of the lava flowing toward Hilo had shaken her more than she wanted to admit. It kept her up for a good part of the night until she finally fell asleep, only to be jarred awake by the nightmare in the early hours of the morning. Samuel slept soundly beside her. Until he retired, Samuel would be getting up early, going down to the wharf, and readying the fishing boat to head out like clockwork every morning, six days a week. In shadow, his boots stood by a chair draped with his clothing waiting to be filled with the warmth of his body. It was something he still did now out of habit, just like she occasionally paused to listen for any sounds of the boys, even with them long gone.

Nori lay still and couldn't shake the uneasy feeling that stayed with her even as the nightmare receded into the darkness. It felt so real, as if it were happening all over again. They were young, so full of life, she and Mariko were thirteen and Leia just fifteen, already tall for her age. They'd been down at the beach all day, Mariko rushing them to leave because she promised her mother she'd be home before sunset. They packed up and began walking home. After parting with Mariko, who took another road back to the green bungalow, she and Leia scurried toward their secret path, a shortcut down a cool and quiet strip lined with palm and banyan trees that cut through to the main road. Everything happened so quickly after that. She looked up and a man had suddenly stepped out from behind some trees. He was smiling when he saw them, a toothless grin, dressed in dirty clothing, his hair long to his shoulders. He stopped to ask them for directions, a small scar over his left eye rising and falling as he spoke. Nori knew the minute she saw him that something wasn't right, the way he looked at them as if he wanted to swallow them whole.

"What you girls doing out here alone?" he asked. It was a low, foreign voice. There'd been so many outsiders coming to Hilo to work on the sugar and pineapple plantations.

"We aren't alone," Leia quickly answered. "Our parents are just over by the road waiting for us."

Nori was tongue-tied, not knowing how Leia could speak up so quickly. She had always been the quietest of them all.

He looked toward the empty trail and laughed. "I don't think so."

Nori's hand found her way to Leia's. She held on tightly. They took a step forward but he blocked their path.

"Get out of our way," Leia hissed. Her voice rose in anger and confidence.

The man laughed, then pulled a knife out from behind his back. "And what if I don't?" he said, waving it in front of them.

Leia pulled Nori back quickly, stumbling one, two, three steps. Nori shuddered when she felt Leia's hand slip from hers. In the next moment, Leia pushed her back and had rushed toward the man, catching him off guard with the force of her body and knocking him to the ground.

"Run, Nori, run!" she yelled.

Nori remembered her heart pounding in her chest, the sourness in the pit of her stomach rising to her mouth. There was a split second when she didn't know what to do before a violent surge of fear rushed through her body. She turned and ran along the trail overgrown with shrubs and foliage, her eyes focused on the damp, uneven ground so she wouldn't trip over the slippery rocks and protruding roots, thinking Leia would be following close behind her. Nori ran so fast and hard she thought her lungs would explode by the time, sticky with sweat, she finally reached the main road. Only then did she stop to take a breath, and realized Leia wasn't behind her. A thick, dark fear filled her. *Where is Leia? Where is she?* Nori's heart hammered in her chest. "Leia!" she called out once, frightened that the man might hear her. Terrified, she quietly backtracked down the trail, halfway back to the spot where the nightmare began, but there was no sign of Leia.

She heard something, the snap of a twig.

She heard something, the wind in the trees.

She heard something, a distant voice.

"Run, Nori, run!"

≈

Nori ran toward town, frightened, hoping to flag down someone, but the road was quiet. Why was no one there? All Nori could think about was saving Leia the way Leia saved her. It felt like a long time before she stopped running, doubled over and out of breath, her lungs burning as she swallowed large breaths of air, not knowing what to do. She was drenched in sweat and it was still a few miles to town and then back. What would happen to Leia by then? Nori paused for just a moment before she turned around, thinking it would be faster to run back to the Natua house to tell Mama. Maybe Leia had gotten away, maybe she was already home waiting for her.

By the time Nori turned onto their street, her legs ached. She hurried past her house without looking, hoping her parents weren't home. It was just then that she heard her name called out. Nori paused to listen and heard her name fill the air again. It was Leia. She was hiding in the tear-down shed in their yard. *It's Leia*, she thought, heart racing with happiness. But when the door of the shed cracked open, it took only a moment for Nori to realize that her freedom had come at a price. Even in the hot, small space, Leia was shivering. Nori couldn't stop staring at her torn clothes, the thin, spidery cut on the side of her neck, her legs and arms scraped and bruised; the redness across her cheek where he must have hit her. Nori smelled the sack of pig shit her father had stored in the shed, hoping to grow taro, and thought she would be sick.

"Leia!" She willed herself to reach out and hug her. "It's over, it's over," Nori repeated, hugging her closer until she calmed. "Let's go tell Mama," she whispered. Mama would know what to do.

Leia shook her head, her face a mask of anguish. "No, no, please no," she said. "I just want it all to go away."

"We can't—"

"No!"

"What if it happens again to someone else?" Nori said. Nori breathed in the smelly, stagnant air. She kept her voice low and calm. "He deserves to be punished. He needs to be put in jail."

Leia refused to listen. "Promise me, Nori!" she said, her voice tight and shrill, like a thread about to snap. "You won't tell anyone about what happened. Promise me! Promise me!"

Nori had pulled away from her. *He is still out there*, Nori thought, swallowing down her disgust. Her stomach turned. A sudden, strangled cry came from Leia, followed by a whispered litany of "promise me, promise me, promise me, promise me—"

"Stop!" Nori screamed.

Leia stopped.

Nori leaned closer and whispered, "I promise."

Thankfully, her parents weren't home. Nori took Leia to her room, where she washed her face, drank some water, and changed into one of her clean shirts.

Then they walked back to the Natua house pretending nothing ever happened.

≈

It didn't go away. Two months later Leia realized she was pregnant. Through a girl they knew in school whose older sister was rumored to have been pregnant twice, yet never delivered, Nori was given the name and address of a woman who lived just outside of Hilo town "who could get rid of it," the girl said. *It is still an "it,"* Nori thought, trying to stay calm. She pooled her savings, along with Leia and Mariko, only to have three dollars and twenty-three cents of the five dollars they needed.

Nori suggested they ask one of the boys that they'd met down at the beach a few months earlier for help. It was taking a big risk: they hadn't known them long, but Mariko and Franklin were already smitten, and Nori instinctively knew that Koji was the one they could trust. He was calm and attentive. He always stood still, while the other two boys moved around in whirling circles.

"What about Franklin?" Mariko had asked.

"Franklin has too much going on," she said, hoping to appease Mariko.

Nori didn't want to hurt her feelings and it seemed to work, although deep down, she wondered if Mariko knew, even then, that Koji was the reliable one of the two. They needed someone they could trust. Nori hoped it wasn't a mistake. Fortunately, she'd been proven right. Nori watched Koji's eyes when she asked him the following weekend and saw his care and understanding. He not only helped them with the rest of the money, but also insisted on going along with them when the time came. "Don't know who you can trust, yeah," he'd said. Nori was more than grateful to have him along.

In the end, Leia wouldn't have made it back home without Koji carrying her to the truck he borrowed from someone at the plantation. Only years later did Nori ask Leia what had happened that long-ago afternoon.

≈

Leia had just turned sixteen at the time, too young and scared to know that the decision she was making out of shame and fear would haunt her through the years. She'd never forgotten the dampness of the dark room, stinking of mildew and rot, thinly masked by the sharp, medicinal edge of rubbing alcohol. "Lay still." She heard the older woman's monotone voice, and felt the hands of another, younger woman pushing her down, holding her, pinning her arms hard against the table covered in newspaper, legs spread open, something cold entering her. She remembered screaming, like it was happening all over again, his awful smell as they fell to the ground, the weight of his body rolling over and pinning her, a rock pressing against her back, his dirty, rough hand smothering her breath as she gagged, vomit rising, trying to fight as he forced her legs apart, slapping her hard and pressing the blade against her neck. "*Shut up! Shut up!*" he'd told her. He wouldn't hurt her if she'd just shut up and be still. All she could think then was that Nori was safe. It would be all right, it would be all right. Should she have fought harder, should she have screamed louder?

Leia opened her eyes to a blinding light from above, and a woman's hand, half covering her mouth and smelling of eucalyptus, on her cheek. "Quiet, quiet now, don't make trouble, yeah. It'll all be over soon."

More than thirty years later, Leia still occasionally felt a twinge where the baby had been scraped away, raw and tender. They'd given her something to numb the pain, and in her weakened state she was no longer frightened. She'd lost all feeling and just wanted to close her eyes and sleep. Leia had lost so much blood that afternoon she'd felt light-headed and wondered if she were dying. She knew it wasn't just the baby, but a part of her that had seeped away too. When it was over, the older woman said, "Let her rest here while you clean up." The younger woman had long ago let go of her arms, but Leia still couldn't move. She wondered if they had wrapped the baby up in newspaper like a dead fish. Tears came slowly. If Nori, Mariko, and Koji hadn't been there waiting for her, helping her home with what they told Mama was the stomach flu, Leia never would have made it back from that cold, dank cabin, but for the longest time she wished they had left her there too.

~

Nori still shook every time she thought of that day. Years later, Mama had said to her, "Did you think I didn't know? *Stomach flu*," she spit out the words in disgust. "Did you think I didn't look into the eyes of my daughter and know all that was lost?"

The past flickered and was gone again.

Nori slipped out of bed, careful not to wake Samuel, and began to dress. She was wide awake and might as well make herself useful down in the kitchen. The lava flow hadn't reached Hilo yet, and until it did, she still had a community to take care of.

31

PACKING

Koji fiddled with the radio knob through static until a voice caught and came clearly through. He listened every night for the past week, following the lava's steady flow toward Hilo, with no signs of slowing. He knew Nori was worried, not for herself, but for Mama and all those in the community who couldn't help themselves. She tried not to show it, but he saw her fear as she waited anxiously for Pele to shift her flow in another direction, or grow bored and simply stop, just as she had so many times before.

Koji learned early on just how protective Nori could be for those she cared for. A few months after they'd met the girls, they were all gathered on Onekahakaha beach again. He and Razor had almost missed the sugar train down to Hilo trying to clean up and look presentable. He wanted to make a good impression on Mariko, only for her to spend most of her time with Franklin. There'd been an anxious hum in the air, and Koji noticed that Leia sat quiet most of the afternoon, uncomfortably fidgeting with a piece of fishing line he later learned she used to string leis.

"Who wants to go swimming?" Franklin asked, with a sly grin Koji would later come to hate.

The girls stayed seated on the blanket as Franklin and Razor stood, already taking off their shirts.

"Not me," Leia said, her voice distant, just above a whisper. It was the first time she'd spoken since they'd said their hellos.

"What's wrong?" Franklin asked. "Water's calm, yeah, nothing to be afraid of."

"She doesn't want to swim," Nori said. "She isn't afraid."

"I'm not swimming either," Mariko chimed in.

Koji watched Leia grow more agitated. "Me neither," Koji said.

"Come on then," Franklin nudged Razor. "It's hot. We'll just cool off, yeah."

He and Razor laughed as they ran down to the water. Koji stayed sitting on the blanket, and it was then that Nori came over and sat by him, asking for his help with Leia. From that day on, they shared a trust that had never been broken.

≈

Now that the harvest was over, the plantation would be quiet through the next month, and Koji was finally taking up Nori and Samuel's offer to stay down in town with them. As the lava continued to flow toward Hilo, he knew the locals were growing more anxious with each passing day. This used to be his favorite time of the year, when he'd finish up the harvest and spend happy weeks with Mariko down in Hilo. With her gone, Koji had kept to himself the past two years, numb to everything. It had been much easier to hide away on the plantation, knowing Razor would come by. This year was different: not only did he want to wait out the lava flow along with the rest of the community, he also needed to clear the air with Daniel.

Koji looked around his spare living room, his leather rucksack sitting on his armchair. In it he had packed a change of clothes and a few belongings he wanted to take with him down to Hilo. He hadn't expected the memories of Mariko to return so sharply when he began sorting through his few things. Everything he valued was from her, the past everywhere, in everything. Koji checked his rucksack again to make sure the shirt was there, knowing it was: he had taken it from his closet, neatly folded it, and placed it right on top so it wouldn't get wrinkled.

"This is for you," he heard Mariko say again, handing him the gift-wrapped box. It was his birthday, a day he had long ago stopped celebrating. The last time was just after he'd started cutting cane, and his mother had baked him a small cake and surprised him when he came in from the fields. Even his father was happy that night as they sang and he blew out the one candle.

Koji was equally surprised by Mariko and wanted to know how she knew.

Mariko laughed. "Did you really think Razor could keep it to himself?" she said. "He was down in Hilo and came by last week."

Koji looked away, embarrassed. Razor always looked out for him. They'd grown apart the past few years, and the thought saddened him. He'd missed yet another of Razor's labor meetings, but his first priority was always Mariko and Daniel. Razor always understood, but he knew his friend's patience was wearing thin.

Koji was thirty years old and felt like an awkward kid when she handed him the present. "You didn't have to," he said.

"I wanted to. It's from the both of us."

Koji heard Daniel in the living room playing with his trains, delighted with the railroad tracks he'd bought him, the clickety-clack of the railcars moving endlessly in a circle around the living room. Koji smiled at her and carefully unwrapped and opened the box to see a white dress shirt. On the right cuff, Mariko had embroidered his initials, KS. She had bought it downtown and it looked expensive. She must have had to save for a year. It was the nicest present he had ever received. Koji felt different when he put the shirt on in the quiet of his room. He looked in the mirror and saw a town boy, not a cane boy. Koji had only worn it out twice, once when he and Mariko went out to dinner together at Chu's Chinese Café, where he sat nervously across from her and could barely eat for fear of dirtying his shirt; and the second time, at Mariko's funeral.

Koji drove slowly past the blackened sugarcane fields and back out through the gates of the plantation onto the main road. He hadn't seen Razor in weeks. All the while Mariko remained in his thoughts. Throughout their years together they'd never married. He had tossed around the idea a few times early on, finally asking her three years after Franklin left. Koji still felt that rejection lodged in the middle of his chest, like the hard bud of a flower that never bloomed. Even if she had been right, they were better than married. Still, he would have been happier if Mariko had divorced Franklin, relinquishing all claims on her, but Koji didn't want to risk losing her. He hoped time would change her mind, and had reluctantly honored her wish to simply close the door on that part of her life without any more worries or disruptions.

Just past the stripped cane fields along the main road, not more than a mile down the path, was the dirt track that led through the rain forest to the cabin where Razor's union meetings were once held. If Koji wasn't paying attention, he'd easily drive right by, as he usually did. Now he wondered if the cabin was still there, and had already slowed to turn down the tree-hidden lane toward the cabin. It was instantly darker and cooler as he bumped along the dirt road, branches whipping against his truck. Koji's thoughts had returned to the last time he'd been at the cabin, the handful of men sweating as they sat together, breathing in the same stale, thick air that tasted of . . . He suddenly slammed on the brakes and jerked to an abrupt stop to avoid hitting Razor, who was standing in the middle of the road. Heart pounding, when Koji looked again, Razor was gone. In his place was a rotted tree that had fallen, blocking the road just before the clearing, some thirty feet away from the cabin.

"Razor," Koji whispered.

He remembered that the meetings had been moved to the basement of a house farther down the road after Razor had died.

After Razor had been *killed*.

Koji sat in the idling truck. He wondered if he should walk the rest of the way to the cabin. From where he sat, he could see the forlorn structure. Part of the roof had caved in on the left side, the log walls swallowed up by a slick, green overgrowth as the front door gaped open like a dark mouth. He knew there was no point in going any farther; he was already years too late.

Koji swallowed the recurring ache and laid his forehead against the steering wheel. *You're not to blame, yeah.* It was as if Mariko were right there in the air surrounding him, and he suddenly couldn't breathe with the want of her. Koji sat up and reached for the rucksack next to him. He took out the shirt, needing to see it, feel it, the whiteness of the shirt against the darkness of the trees surrounding him that blocked out the daylight.

Only then did he feel better.

GHOST VOICES

MARIKO, 1917

It's Sunday morning and Koji is on his way down from Puli to see us. He keeps better time than a clock, and I'm expecting his truck to pull up to the house in thirty minutes. Ever since Franklin left, Koji has been a constant, helping us around the house, bringing Daniel more railcars and tracks, and answering all his questions. He even taught him how to play baseball a few years ago, which my son now loves even more than his trains. Who would have thought, yeah?

"How come you know so much about baseball?" I asked Koji back then.

He looked at me wide-eyed. "Nothing better to do on the plantation on weekends, not to mention the long afternoons after hoeing," he says. "We still had energy to burn, yeah. We played baseball till dark, mostly against the Chinese and the Sakata boys. Real leagues, eh. Sunday afternoon games still big highlights."

Now he spends every Sunday with us, watching Daniel at practice and playing on his school team. Coaching and strategizing during dinner. I feel at peace when we're together, something I always struggled to find with Franklin. Every time Franklin came home, it wouldn't be long before he was restless and edgy, as if he were just waiting for the next steamer to take him away from us again. It still leaves me uneasy thinking about it. I release a breath I didn't realize I was holding. I know now, I tell Nori, Franklin was always a hot spark, while Koji's a slow-burning fire.

≈

It's just another Sunday afternoon with Daniel away at baseball practice. Koji has replaced a few rotting boards on the front porch, and now sits at the kitchen table watching me pluck a chicken, gray down rising into the air and floating back into the sink. We're like an old married couple, and it feels safe and comfortable.

I remember once asking him, "Why haven't you married?" It was a few years after he'd begun helping me to pick the mangoes. It was back when Franklin and I had been married two, maybe three years and he was away again. Koji was perched high atop a ladder, reaching for a branch laden with mangoes.

He stopped working and looked down at me. With the sun in my eyes, I could only see him in outline.

"No one ever wanted me," he answered.

"I don't believe that," I said, and laughed.

Few are lucky enough to know Koji's dry sense of humor.

"Truth is," he says, "the only person I've ever wanted to marry was already married." Then he turned back and reached high, toward another branch.

≈

Standing at the sink, I can feel him watching me, even with my back to him.

"Want more coffee?" I ask, plucking the last of the chicken feathers.

Koji is tapping his fingers against the kitchen table. After a long pause he says, "No, I'm fine, yeah."

But he doesn't sound fine. There's something bothering him, I can feel it. He's quieter than usual, preoccupied. I rinse the stripped chicken with water, then lay it on the chopping board.

"Marry me," he says, serious and sudden. The abruptness of his words at first startle, then hover heavily in the air. Marry me.

I turn from the sink to face him, putting down the cleaver I'm holding. I wipe my hands on my apron and smile tenderly at him, but I don't mince words.

"I'm still married," I say. It's nothing but the truth, but I immediately realize how it must sound to him. "I just can't go through the process of divorcing Franklin, dredging it all up. As far as I'm concerned, I've already divorced him in my heart and mind.

"Just know, there's no need, yeah, we're just as good as," I add.

"But we're not," he answers, his fingers tapping faster against the table.

"I like what we have here and now," I say softly. But when I look at him, I see the hurt in his eyes. I don't know how to tell Koji that I can't bear the weight of marriage anymore. I married not long after graduating from high school, a girl who couldn't see the sky through the sunlight that was Franklin. Blinding, yeah. I've never lied to Koji. I like the lightness of what we have. I've always told him I was happy with the way things were.

I step closer to the table. "I'm more married to you than I ever was with Franklin, yeah," I say to him, reaching for his hand and watching him smile. "Please understand."

Koji stays quiet for a while. "I do . . ." he finally says, "understand. Too soon now, yeah, but later . . ." He looks away so I can't see the disappointment in his eyes.

I'm afraid to say anything else. Instead, I turn back to the chicken lying on the chopping board, to the comfort of doing something I'm completely in control of. I pick up my cleaver and quickly chop its head off, dissecting first the legs and then the thighs from the body. When Franklin first disappeared, I was always waiting for him to return, looking up when I thought I'd heard his voice, checking one more time before I locked the door at night. It was like a fever. I remove the chicken breasts and chop each into halves, then quarters. At every week's end I told myself he'd be back the following week, but he never was. It would have been easier if he were dead. I put down the cleaver and look over at Koji and smile again. No more, I just want my life to move forward. Koji is a good, hardworking man. No shame in cutting cane, I tell him. What we have now is a family, strong and solid. I gather up the vegetables to cut, potatoes, carrots, and onions that will later simmer along with the chicken in coconut milk and spices. But first I sprinkle salt and pepper over the chicken before dropping each piece into the hot skillet of oil to brown.

I hear Koji's chair push back, feel him standing behind me, watching. "Smells good," he says, breaking our silence.

I know how much he appreciates my home-cooked meals, having lived such a simple life. Early on, he told me his mother cooked over an open fire when they first arrived from Japan and lived in cane shacks. "One iron pot she carried with her from Japan," he said. "Root vegetables and tofu in shoyu, sugar, and a sake broth over rice. Couldn't afford meat most times, but after a day in the fields, yeah, nothing better."

Now his evening meals usually consist of rice and vegetables, a bit of meat, or fish from Nori, or something he has picked up from the plantation store. These Sunday dinners mean so much to him, so much to us. By early evening, a wonderful aroma will fill the house and we'll sit down to my Portuguese chicken and rice and listen to Daniel talk happily about his baseball practice, our words and laughter rising like steam through the kitchen.

SECRETS

DECEMBER 17–18, 1935

32

TOWN BOY

Koji lay in Mano's old twin bed and couldn't sleep. The night was hot and sticky, the room above the market still, with a quiet heaviness. He'd left the window open hoping for a breeze, watching the thin cotton curtain waver with a sudden whisper of wind as he lay sweaty and motionless on the damp sheets. When he was young, Koji couldn't wait to get down to Hilo town, wanting more than anything to be part of the bustling world Franklin lived in, and away from the heat and stench of the fields. Along with Razor, the three of them played ball or gathered sea urchins or had shave ice eating contests. After they met Nori, Mariko, and Leia, everything changed, and Franklin began to skip out on them when he began dating Mariko. By then, Koji was heartsick and preferred to stay on the plantation. Over time Koji came to learn that the only difference between being a town boy and a cane boy was where you lived, not who you were.

Koji hadn't stayed down in town for more than a day since Mariko's death, keeping the memories at bay. Now they returned to prick at him. When she told him her cancer had spread and there wasn't anything the doctors could do anymore, Koji had stood there speechless, letting her words quietly shatter the world around him. He and Nori had taken turns staying with her then, while Mariko made him promise her two things: not to tell Daniel how bad she was until he finished his residency in a few weeks' time, and to make sure she would stay at home. "I refuse to die in a hospital room," she told him. Koji felt a dry tightness in his throat recalling those fleeting months. He used to equate the passing of time with the seasons, the planting, growing, and harvesting of sugarcane. Suddenly life was moving too fast, and a matter of months meant the difference between life and death. When Daniel returned, he and Mariko had two good months together, followed by a handful of weeks that weren't.

Koji finally drifted off, only to be awakened in the dusty, dark light of morning filtering in through the curtains. It took him a moment to remember where he was. He heard footsteps on the creaking floorboards, knew they belonged to Nori making her way down the hall and downstairs to the market's kitchen to begin her day. She kept cane worker hours. Koji wondered if she needed any help, and then thought the better of it—he would only be in her way. He stretched out and closed his eyes for just a little longer.

33

NORI

Nori loved these early morning hours best. She began rolling out the dough for the sweetbread, pausing only to take down a jar of mango jam from the cupboard. Nothing made her think of Mariko more than the sweet floral scent of ripe mango every time she cut up the fruit to make jam. It always felt like Mariko was there in the kitchen with her, young again, urging her to finish up so they could take the boys across the road to the bay. "Let me help, yeah, the boys are anxious to go." Nori could hear their shrieks and laughter out in the market. Nori urged her not to wait for her, but she refused. "Together, yeah," she said. "Like always."

Mariko had been married to Franklin for seven years, of which he'd been away working for more than half the time, leaving her and Daniel alone. Nori wondered how she had put up with it. "The Hilo Aunties and Hearts, yeah," Mariko once told her. "You all saved me."

In the end they hadn't been able to save her. Mariko was gone now, leaving them all behind. Nori couldn't recall how she'd gotten through the first year after Mariko's death. It was a struggle, like having lost a limb and relearning how to live without it. Mariko was always there, from the time they were young girls in elementary school. She was Nori's first real friend who didn't ridicule her about wearing the same old clothes all the time, or going barefoot when she outgrew her shoes, and who didn't care where she lived and who her parents were. When her parents eventually died, first her mother, and then thirteen months later her father, it was from drinking enough ti root alcohol to leave a big hole in their stomachs. She was fifteen and felt nothing but relief. Mariko and the Natuas were the ones who had always taken care of her. Nori fingered the faint scar on the back of her right hand, the burn mark left there by her mother when she was ten years old and dared to hide a bottle of ti root from her. Nori wanted her lucid for one night. "Just for tonight, Momma," she begged, thinking she could still help them. Her mother had smiled, pulled on the cigarette she was smoking until it burned a bright orange full moon before walking over to her and snuffing it out on the back of her hand. Nori couldn't remember if she had screamed, couldn't remember feeling anything at the time. Only later did she recall the sharp, stinging pain and awful char smell of her burning flesh. The discolored scar would remain a constant reminder; if she couldn't save them then she had to save herself.

～

Nori paused when she heard movement from upstairs and glanced at the clock to see it was nearly 6:00 a.m. Samuel would still be in a deep sleep for another hour, catching up for all the years he'd awakened at 3:00 a.m. to fish. It must be Koji. He'd driven down from Puli the day before yesterday, his rucksack slung across his shoulder when he walked into the market smiling and asked, "Is the room still available?" She and Samuel were more than happy to have him finally come down to stay with them after the harvest.

In the two years since Mariko passed, Koji had kept mostly to himself up at the plantation. Nori wondered if she would have seen him at all if he didn't run the sugar train down to Hilo every day. Still now, Nori could tell he wasn't himself. He looked thin, tired, as if something were weighing on him, an air of sadness sitting on his shoulders, in the spray of lines around his eyes. She hadn't seen him like this since Mariko died. She placed the sweetbread in the oven and hoped Daniel's return would help to bring the change Koji needed.

Moments later, she heard his heavy footsteps coming down the stairs, stopping at the kitchen doorway.

"You're up early," she said. She scooped some mango jam into a bowl.

"Never needed much sleep."

"Coffee?"

Koji nodded. "That I need, yeah."

Nori poured him a cup of coffee and gestured for him to sit down at the battered kitchen table. She cut some papaya. From the icebox she pulled out a slab of butter and cut a quarter onto a plate, putting it on the table along with the bowl of jam. The warm air of the kitchen quickly filled with the sweet aroma of the baking bread.

Nori poured herself a cup of coffee and took the chair across from him. They sat quietly for a moment before she asked, "You look tired. Everything all right?"

Koji took a sip of coffee. "Daniel knows about Franklin," he said.

It took Nori a moment to understand what he was talking about, before the clouds in her head cleared. Daniel had found out about Franklin's return.

"Did you tell him?"

"Mama thought Daniel was Franklin when he gave her the exam, told him to go home where he belonged."

Nori shook her head. It sounded just like Mama. "How's he holding up?"

"He wasn't happy to hear some of the truth. Ran out, yeah, before I could tell him everything."

"Part of growing up, eh."

"Not sure who needs to grow up," he said. "Should have told him long ago."

"It was a decision you made with Mariko," she reminded.

"It feels like a part of her has returned with him."

"A blessing, yeah." They sat in the quiet. "You know life doesn't stop moving forward," Nori added. "Time for you, too. Mariko would want you to."

Nori watched him in thought. She'd known him for thirty-five years and still couldn't judge what he was thinking. With Samuel and her boys, everything was always out in the open in every movement they made.

"I don't know how," he finally said.

"You do," Nori said, and smiled. "Talking to Daniel and being here, back down in Hilo, you've already taken the first steps."

They sat in silence again. Daylight began to seep in. Nori pushed her chair back and stood to check on the sweetbread. "Just about ready," she said, pulling the two loaves out. "What you planning to do next?" she asked.

"Tell him the rest of the story. Part of the reason I came down, yeah," Koji said. "The other part to hold your hand during the flow." She heard the smile in his voice as he lifted the cup to his lips and drank the rest of his coffee.

"Like I need you to hold my hand," she countered.

They both laughed, only to pause when they heard creaks and footsteps coming from the apartment above.

Samuel was up early, and the day was about to begin.

34

NAUPAKA

By the time Maile and Daniel arrived at Mama Natua's house, the rain had stopped. Maile stepped out of Uncle Samuel's truck into the sticky, warm air that smelled of the sharp, wet earth. Mama's house looked nothing like she remembered. It was smaller, more disheveled, though she hardly paid much attention back then. She came by with Daniel once or twice to pick up Auntie Mariko years ago when they were still in high school. At the time, she knew and admired the Hilo Aunties, while Mama already seemed old.

"Ready?" Daniel asked.

Maile watched him approach and nodded.

Daniel had asked if she would stay with Mama for a short time this morning while he took Auntie Leia to the hospital to sign some papers. Auntie Nori and Auntie Noelani were both working, and Mama would most likely be dozing in her chair after breakfast, he'd said. Ever since their afternoon on the Scenic Express, they were slowly getting reacquainted, finding hints of their old selves again along with all the changes. What Maile hadn't expected was that she wasn't the only one returning to Hilo with scrapes and scars from their time away. She knew it was wrong, but it somehow made her feel better to know she wasn't alone.

A few nights earlier, she and Daniel had been walking back from Mano and Kailani's place. A moonless darkness blanketed them, along with the distant sounds of the cicadas and the wind gusting through the trees. She felt comforted, shielded by the shadows. All night they had talked and laughed together, like when they were young and Maile dared to hope. Daniel's voice suddenly filled the quiet again, telling her about studying and working in Chicago, including some of the patients he encountered at the hospital, and how it was Auntie Nori who asked him to check on Mama Natua when he returned.

"Mama's lucky to have such a good doctor," she'd said, still impressed that he had fulfilled his dreams.

Daniel remained quiet, and it seemed that her words had simply floated away. Maile was mystified by his sudden silence when he finally said, "Sometimes good isn't enough."

"Try telling that to the aunties after all you've done for Mama," she'd said, hoping to lighten his mood, which had shifted so quickly. "Auntie Nori can't stop talking about—"

"Mama's suffering from senility," Daniel interrupted. "It doesn't take a genius to treat her."

Maile stopped walking. The darkness suddenly felt suffocating; his sharp words hung heavily in the air. She felt the blood rush to her head. "Maybe not," she said, "but it still takes a doctor whom Mama trusts enough to treat her, and that says a lot."

Daniel stopped, too, and turned to her. "I'm sorry," he said. "I didn't mean to sound so arrogant."

Maile saw him clearer as the clouds shifted and moonlight seeped through, saw the anguish and apology in his gaze. She never would have spoken up in Honolulu, held back by fear, but she was home now, and with Daniel. She'd forgotten how good it was to simply say what she felt. She looked at him and saw that there was something she'd missed, too wrapped up in her own anxieties. Whatever was upsetting him lay just beneath the surface.

"Is everything all right?" she asked.

"I'm fine," Daniel answered, and smiled. "I should get you home."

She stepped closer and inhaled the sweet, dark air, changing the subject as they began to walk again. "Uncle Koji must be happy you're back," she said.

"Right now, I don't think he's too happy with me," he said.

"Why?"

"We had a disagreement last week," Daniel said quietly. "I left before hearing his side of it."

Maile couldn't remember a time when they'd ever fought over anything in all the years she'd known them. "About what?" she asked.

Again Daniel paused. She watched him weigh whether to tell her or not.

"He lied to me . . . kept the fact from me that my father returned when I was a boy. He and my mom both did."

Maile heard the young Daniel again in his voice. She'd heard scant bits and pieces about his father when they were in high school, but he was long gone by then.

"Would Uncle Koji forgive you if it were the other way around?" she asked.

She couldn't imagine that Uncle Koji would deliberately hurt him. He loved Daniel like a son.

"Probably," Daniel finally said. "But it isn't the other way around." His words were laced with a quiet disappointment.

Maile wondered if he was upset with just Uncle Koji, or also with himself. She leaned closer and reached for his hand.

≈

When they stepped into the kitchen, Mama sat in her wheelchair, her eyes closed, her head resting to the side. "Barely finished eating, yeah, before she nodded off again," Auntie Leia whispered to Maile. "Can't thank you enough for watching her; best thing if she sleeps until we're back, yeah. If she does wake, there's papaya for her in the icebox, for you too," Auntie Leia added. In the next hurried moments, Daniel and Auntie Leia were in the truck and driving off, leaving Maile with Mama.

While Mama slept, Maile looked around the porch. The wind had picked up, rattling through the screen door as the clouds veiled the sun and the porch darkened. She wondered if it was going to rain again as she looked at all the flowers and leaves collected on the wooden table where Mama and now Auntie Leia strung their leis. Maile picked up an orchid, soft as skin to the touch, when she heard Mama talking aloud in the kitchen and quickly let go of the flower.

Maile stood in the kitchen doorway, anxious, as she listened to Mama mumbling something she couldn't understand. What if Mama caused a fuss that she couldn't handle? What would Daniel and Auntie Leia think of her? Mama hardly knew her, having met her only once or twice, years ago; she most likely had no memory of who Maile was.

When Maile looked over at her again, Mama was staring calmly back.

"You come to pick up the leis?" Mama asked.

Maile moved slowly toward Mama, not wanting to upset her. She knelt in front of her at eye level. "Mama," she said, "I'm Maile, Daniel's friend. I'm here to spend some time with you."

Mama looked at her. "You come home, yeah."

"Yes. How did you know?"

Mama smiled. "Naupaka bloom whole again, eh," she said.

Maile wasn't sure what Mama was talking about, but was relieved she seemed comfortable and in good spirits, whether she knew her or not. She recalled Daniel saying it was important to keep Mama engaged.

"Tell me about the naupaka blossom," Maile said.

Mama's eyes focused. "Naupaka, a beautiful princess, yeah, fell in love with a poor boy she could never marry, eh, so Naupaka vowed to stay in the mountains, and Kaua'i, he remained near the ocean. Last time together," Mama said, as her hand rose to her hair, "Naupaka took the flower from her hair and gave half to Kaua'i. All the nearby plants so upset, yeah, the next day they bloom only half flowers in honor of the parted lovers." Mama paused, then said, "You back now, eh?"

Maile nodded. "Yes, I'm back."

Afterward, Maile pushed her wheelchair back out to the porch for some air and Mama pointed to her work table. She was surprised when Mama leaned over and grabbed a piece of fishing line. "Sit, yeah," Mama said, her eyes darting back and forth as her face lit up and she began to teach her how to string a lei with the plumeria flowers on the table. The sweet fragrance was calming as Maile pushed the needle and line through the stem and out through the eye of the flower, one after another, while Mama watched, rolling and unrolling a ti leaf between her fingers.

"Ti leaf brings good luck, yeah," Mama said, looking down at the green leaf. "Wards off the evil spirits," she added. She stared at Maile longer than she was comfortable. "Nothing to worry about now, eh, the ti leaf will keep you safe."

Maile listened as Mama continued with her conversation. "Good luck, yeah," she said, while Maile continued to string the plumeria lei. She breathed in and out slowly, the first time she'd felt completely comfortable since returning to Hilo.

Not long after she finished stringing her lei, Daniel and Auntie Leia returned.

"She didn't give you too much trouble, yeah?" Auntie Leia asked.

"No trouble at all," Maile answered. "Mama taught me how to string a lei." She held it up for them to see, thrilled at the accomplishment.

"You did a fine job, yeah," Auntie Leia said, inspecting her work. "Could always use an extra pair of hands," she added.

Maile felt light-headed at the thought. "Just call any time you need help," she said.

≈

Later, as Daniel drove her back to the green bungalow, Maile remained quiet, looking out the window with hopes of glimpsing a naupaka flower.

"Everything okay?" Daniel asked as the truck slowed and bounced over dips in the road.

"Yes, everything's fine," Maile said, and smiled. In her hand was the ti leaf Mama had given her for luck.

GHOST VOICES

MARIKO, 1912

It's Saturday morning and Franklin is back home for a few weeks. Tonight he's taking us out to dinner. This afternoon he and Daniel are going to the Wailuku River, while I go to the market to play Hearts with the aunties. It's our second anniversary and a welcome tradition I love, being together every Saturday after the lunch rush to play Hearts, a deck of cards waiting on the back table, along with a bowl of rice crackers and plates of sliced papaya or pineapple or mango, our voices tumbling over each other. It makes it easier moving through the week, yeah, knowing I'll see the aunties at the end of it, like the pot at the end of a rainbow. It's become my mainstay.

When I arrive this afternoon, the aunties are excited. We sit at our back table like schoolgirls again because a photographer from the Hilo Registry has come by, wanting to take a photo of us for the newspaper.

"Why us?" Nori asks.

"Human interest story," the photographer says. "Good to have, yeah, when it's a slow news day and we need fillers." He holds up the folding pocket camera with red bellows and stands back. "Act natural, yeah, and don't look at the camera."

I hear the camera click followed by a bright flash as we all look down seriously at our cards. We rarely look serious when we're together. It's only when we look up and laugh that the flash explodes again. The photographer talks to Nori for a moment, and I'm relieved when he leaves and we get down to the business of playing Hearts.

I grab the deck and shuffle the cards.

In the past two years, we've each developed our own small habits and superstitions when handling our cards—Nori likes to wait until all the cards are dealt to her before she picks them up, immediately ordering them according to suit: spades, clubs, diamonds, and hearts. Leia stacks hers into a neat pile before fanning them out, one by one, yeah, while Noelani never keeps to one way of doing things, just like the way she lives life. If I wasn't dealing, I'd immediately pick up my cards as they're dealt to me. I look down at my growing pile. And there it is again, that small jab, the feeling that there's no time to waste.

I listen to Nori and Leia talking about the new Hawaii Volcano Observatory Center being built by two mainlanders, wondering how they'd gotten all the financing, and if it will bring more tourism to Hilo. Along with the railroad and the burgeoning sugar industry, Hilo town seems to be expanding each week.

"More people, just what we need," Leia says.

"Good for business yeah," Nori adds. "You remember when it was so quiet here, a sneeze brought excitement!"

We all laugh.

"Franklin applying for a job?" Noelani asks.

I deal out the last round of cards. "He was turned down," I say, wishing he was hired for the observatory crew so he could stay home for a while.

As if Nori knows what I'm thinking, she says, "Not using our local boys doesn't make sense, yeah; instead they bring in workers from the mainland. Doesn't sound like good business to me."

Nori glances over at me and smiles, knowing how much I hate it every time he leaves. I quickly gather up my cards, only to realize it isn't that Franklin didn't get the job that's bothering me, it's that he seemed almost happy to have been turned down.

ANSWERS

DECEMBER 18–20, 1935

35

LAVA

Koji pulled his truck into the driveway of the green bungalow. He'd spent the morning with Samuel and the boys out on the boat, and had planned on driving back to the market, but Daniel was again lingering heavily in his thoughts. Koji had been down in Hilo for the past two days and hadn't seen him yet. He turned off the engine and sat in his truck, staring at the house. He could almost convince himself that Mariko would step out onto the porch at any minute, her apron hanging loosely around her neck as she smiled and waved him in. He remembered the warmth of her body pressed against his, how hard it was to leave her in the early hours of the mornings to return to Puli. No matter how hard he willed Mariko to return, the porch remained empty and he couldn't bring himself to get out of the truck.

Koji gazed at the fruitless mango tree and imagined its branches once again heavy with mangoes. He loved the tree almost as much as she did. Wasn't it what had finally brought them together?

It had been the most auspicious day of his life. Koji was supposed to meet Franklin at Mariko's house, and he arrived to find her picking mangoes off the lower branches of the tree, which stood more than fifteen feet tall. His throat tightened at the sight of her. She had already filled a basket full of mangoes and was looking hot and sweaty on that muggy day in late July when he walked up the driveway. At the time, Mariko and Franklin had been going steady for almost a year, so she must have known that Franklin was late to everything, stopping to talk to friends or getting pulled into card games or dice games, and later making it up to her with his sweet talk and flowers that he'd most likely picked from someone's yard. Koji had lost count of all the times Franklin had shown up late, or not at all, while he and Razor waited for him at the train station. He could see it plain as day. Why couldn't she?

"You're late again!" Mariko yelled, standing up and turning around only to see that it wasn't Franklin walking up the drive, but him. Koji was wearing pants cut off below the knees and carried a bat and glove. He saw the glint of disappointment in her eyes, which quickly turned to recognition and a smile.

"I'm supposed to meet Franklin here for a game," Koji said, looking down at the stack of baskets next to her.

"Franklin said he'd help me pick mangoes this morning, so where is he?" Mariko asked, an edge of anger pushing through.

Koji was startled for a moment but then caught himself. She wasn't mad at him. "He sent me instead," he teased. He didn't quite know where the words had come from, but she simply shook her head.

"You'll do," she finally said with a smile. Mariko pointed to a wood ladder lying on the ground. "Can you pick the mangoes that are higher up?"

"I can manage, yeah," he said.

Koji raised the ladder and propped it against the tree. He quickly climbed up and began picking the mangoes, placing them gently into a waiting basket. He reached to the left and felt her gazing up at him.

"When did you see Franklin?" she asked.

"Last weekend," Koji answered. "He told me to meet him here."

Mariko paused. "I guess I'm lucky, eh, the mangoes will be picked after all," she said.

"You *are* lucky," Koji said, smiling down at her. "Don't worry," he added. "Franklin will show up soon."

At seventeen, Koji wondered where this new boldness came from; he was always the quietest of the three. Franklin was the smooth talker, and Razor just the talker. Mariko remained silent, and he wondered if he'd said something wrong. There was only the rustling of leaves, the soft pluck of the mangoes as he pulled them from their stems.

"You know, this mango tree is special," Mariko suddenly said, breaking the silence. He carried a filled basket down the ladder and placed the basket to the side. "It was grown from one of the seeds my grandfather brought over on the ship with him from Japan, from a tree that gave mangoes to generations of our family back in our ancestral village. When my grandfather arrived in Hilo and found out that all of his possessions stored on the ship had been sitting in seawater, he thought the seeds had been ruined. But he dried them and planted them anyway. And now, all these years later, the tree still gives us baskets of sweet mangoes every year."

Koji pulled another mango off the branch. "Everyone knows your tree produces the sweetest mangoes on the island," he agreed.

"I don't know about that," she'd said.

"Just speaking the truth, yeah," Koji added. He leaned over and shook the branches. "The branches are still healthy and strong, eh, it should produce mangoes for years to come."

She looked up at him and smiled. "That's what Franklin says about you, that you're strong and dependable."

Koji hadn't realized Frank talked to her about him, and he looked away flushed with embarrassment. He wondered then what else she knew.

"Don't believe everything Franklin tells you," he finally said. Koji cleared his throat and reached up to pull a few more mangoes off the tree, placing them carefully into the basket.

He had returned to pick mangoes with her every year since.

≈

Koji rolled down the truck window and leaned back against the seat. The warm wind carried the sweet scent of wild *kahili* ginger from the yard. He looked up, heart jumping when he heard the door of the bungalow open, only this time it was Maile who stepped out onto the porch, followed by Daniel. *Sweet Maile*, he thought, *she'll save them both*. Koji was lifted from his thoughts by the sight of her. The first time he met her, she was a thin, shy girl who could barely look him in the eyes. Now she was all grown up, looking straight at him with a welcoming gaze. Mariko had always liked her. *She's a smart girl, yeah, won't let Daniel always have his way*. She knew the pitfalls of being an only child. When the young couple broke up, Koji knew Mariko was equally as heartbroken, though she never showed it.

"You coming in, or are you going to bake in your truck all afternoon?" Maile called out, a smile on her face.

Koji sat up and ignored her teasing. He pulled the key out of the ignition, but instead of getting out of the truck, he leaned out of the window and said, "Good to see you, Maile girl, do you think I can borrow Daniel for a short time?"

"Just as long as you promise to return for dinner," she said, not missing a beat.

"It's a deal," Koji said. He was glad Maile was home and happy to see them together again. It was what Daniel needed—grounding. Koji turned his gaze toward him and said, "Let's go for a ride, yeah."

"Where to?" Daniel asked.

"You'll see."

≈

They were back together in Koji's old gray truck for the first time since Daniel had returned to the mainland. They both remained quiet, the air thick with uneasiness as he drove slowly back out to the main road, the squeaking springs of the front seat loud and insistent. Koji grimaced, never having noticed it when he was by himself. The old woolen blanket covering the front seat did little to hide the coils that sprang through the worn leather and pressed against the back of his thighs. Once they were back out on the main road, Koji turned right and away from town. He wasn't certain where he was going until that very moment. The truck bucked and the gears ground as he shifted and headed uphill toward Saddle Road and the lava flow.

"Let's go see what all the fuss is about," he said.

Daniel cleared his throat and relaxed back in his seat. "The other morning Wilson and Mano were talking about driving up to the flow."

Koji heard the relief in his voice. They weren't quite back to normal but they were heading in that direction.

"We'll beat them to it, eh," he said.

Daniel nodded and turned to him. "I'm sorry," he said. "I'm sorry for running out on you last week."

He glanced at Daniel and glimpsed a slight twitching under his left eye. It was something he'd brought back from Chicago.

"I wanted to tell you about your father. I should have," Koji said, staring straight ahead, the truck bouncing along the uneven road. "And then time slipped by, yeah. You were in high school studying so hard, and then you left for college and medical school in Chicago. By the time you returned, your mother was sick." He turned onto a smaller road and remained quiet in thought, finally adding, "You were right, too, yeah. I didn't want to lose you both."

Daniel inhaled and let out a quick breath. "You took care of us, you could never lose us."

Koji stayed quiet. It was always his greatest fear. They were all he ever had.

"Seems foolish now," Daniel continued, "but I waited so long for him to come back. When I was young, I used to tell the other kids at school that my father had an accident at work and had lost his memory, and that's why he never came back. It was because he didn't remember where we lived. I was afraid I was the reason he left, that I was in the way."

Koji didn't know what to say. He knew Franklin's leaving had to have affected him, but he never knew to what extent. Daniel was so young, and he tried to step in for his father in whatever way he could. Koji realized now that he never really could have taken Franklin's place.

"You were never in the way. You and your mother were the best things to ever happen to Franklin, yeah. Don't ever think otherwise. Your father had his own problems."

"Why didn't she tell me? Why keep it from me then?"

"It wasn't so simple; you were still a boy and she didn't want you to hate him."

"So you both lied to me."

Daniel pursed his lips and Koji glimpsed his greatest weakness, his shortsightedness when he felt left out. He wondered if it would have eased his fears if Franklin hadn't left them.

"It was never about lying to you. We just wanted to save you from the hurt, yeah."

Daniel remained quiet in thought. "I shouldn't have run off."

"I should have told you sooner," Koji said. He turned to him with a smile. "Time to stay put, yeah. I've found running only makes you tired in the end."

"Exhausted," Daniel said.

We are talking again, Koji thought. *It's a step in the right direction.*

～

The farther they drove away from Hilo, the thicker and fuller the vegetation grew, the enormous trees, shrubs, and foliage overgrown and unmanageable, the lingering scents of night-blooming jasmine, white ginger, and wild orchids spilling onto the road. The island never failed to surprise Koji, how a raw and wild rain forest teeming with life could suddenly open up to miles of black, barren landscape, leveled by large swaths of smooth *pāhoehoe* or jagged *'a'ā* lava. As they drove farther up the mountain, Daniel leaned out of the open window and Koji knew they were nearing the lava flow by the bitter smell of burning in the air.

"Getting closer, yeah," Koji said, and pointed. "Just beyond the trees there, eh."

Smoke rose and drifted into the sky. Koji slowed to turn down a narrow dirt road to avoid any roadblocks set up to stop the locals from getting too close to the flow. They were quickly enveloped by a tunnel of trees and shrubs to both sides of the truck, the *thwack thwack* of the branches hitting against their windows as muted daylight entered slantwise through the branches. Koji stopped the truck when the road narrowed and became too tight for them to drive down any farther.

"We'll walk the rest of the way, yeah," he said.

"Ever been up this close?" Daniel asked.

Koji shook his head. "First time," he said.

They pushed through tree branches and foliage for another half mile up a slippery, rocky trail when Koji felt the heat rise considerably, along with the smoky, stink-filled air. They held bandanas over their mouths, keeping the acrid smoke at bay, even as their eyes stung and their throats felt raw and irritated. Koji began coughing.

"Okay?" Daniel asked, stopping. "Should we turn back?"

Koji shook his head and cleared his throat. "Let's go a little farther," he said.

They continued along the trail as the trees began to thin and the air thickened, making it harder to breathe. Between bare branches they glimpsed a dark and smoldering world, bleak and barren, the hot, molten lava flowing like a river not thirty feet from them. They walked farther still until the trail narrowed and Koji stopped them from going any farther. From where they stood among the trees, they watched the molten lava surging down the mountainside, hot and alive, waves of orange-red seething with the gurgling and burping of methane gas. Anything in its way was quickly consumed with the explosive crackle and pop of flames. Koji heard a cacophony of sounds, the air so alive it felt as if it would swallow them up. He didn't know how long they stood there sweating, mesmerized by the lava's relentless migration, when he heard a crackling sound, which grew louder before it was quickly followed by an explosive burst of a new eruption from a fissure not fifteen feet from where they stood. The lava shot up like fireworks, sending out steam and smoke, followed by the red-hot beast oozing from the new vent and heading in their direction.

"Let's go!" Koji yelled. He turned and grabbed Daniel's arm, pushing him toward the trail as lava showered down nearby. "Go now!"

Daniel nodded and quickly ran back down the trail.

Koji couldn't help but turn back for one moment, hypnotized by the scene, a world in which only Pele had control. In that instant, he wondered what it would feel like to just let go, to give himself up to the goddess. A righteous sacrifice if it would stop the flow from reaching Hilo. Would Mariko be waiting for him? A loud, crackling sound quickly pulled Koji back as raining lava set a shrub next to him ablaze. He felt the advancing heat, knew he had to leave right away. He turned and quickly followed Daniel down the path.

Koji moved cautiously down the damp, uneven ground of the slippery trail. He was careful not to trip over the snakelike roots, the overgrown vegetation, and the moss-covered rocks when he heard a loud splintering, followed by the crash of a tree that pushed him faster forward. In no time this part of the rain forest would be gone, reduced to black lava. At the turn in the path he slowed and lost sight of Daniel. All they needed to do was get back to the truck and they would be out of there. What was Koji thinking? He knew better than to get so close to a flow. He could already hear Nori chastising him. How could he explain to her that he needed to feel the blistering heat close up, needed to *feel* again?

Koji began to cough and stopped to catch his breath, sweaty and suddenly nauseous, his heart racing. He looked down the trail to see Daniel, but he was nowhere in sight. Koji just needed a moment and he'd be on his way again. He bent over, taking small, calming breaths, a reminder of his younger days during the cane burning when nothing stopped him, especially not the heat and smoke. He had cut through hundreds of pounds of cane in air so smoke-filled from the burn, it was like swallowing coal.

When did he become old?

Koji stood straight, having regained enough breath to continue down the trail again, his legs lighter and moving faster. *Everything will be all right*, Koji thought, feeling like his old self again. But even before he could digest the thought his foot caught on a tree root and he tripped, falling forward, his forehead striking a tree stump before he landed hard on the ground. It felt as if someone had sucker-punched him with a shovel. Koji stayed on the ground. His head throbbed. A thin trail of sweat trickled from his forehead and down the side of his face. Only when he wiped it away with his sleeve did he see it was blood.

Koji slowly tried to get up.

Stay still, old man, he heard Mariko tell him.

"Just a bump," he said aloud.

Just like you said about that night, she reminded him.

"Just a cut," he'd said then. How he missed her.

It had been much more than a cut, though. He and Franklin had fought, years of anger filtered down to that early morning on the beach. Hadn't Mariko suffered long enough because of him? When Koji saw the knife, something had snapped in him. He fought for his life, hitting Franklin with a strength that had sprung up from deep within. He still couldn't remember what happened to Franklin after that. Koji was bleeding and knew he had to get away. A crackling sound followed by a crash of something falling quickly snatched away the memory.

Koji pushed himself back up and stood, legs shaky and weak, head throbbing. He grabbed for branches and moved slowly down the trail again. All he had to do was get to Daniel and the truck. He counted each step—one, two, three, four—before his legs gave out and he collapsed to the ground. He just needed to rest a minute more.

Koji closed his eyes and everything went dark.

36

UNCLE KOJI

The smoke grew heavier, dimming the sunlight. Daniel finally slowed and turned around, expecting to see Uncle Koji right behind him. Instead there was only a cloud of smoke wafting down the empty trail. The truck was just up ahead. Daniel waited, catching his breath, his throat dry and scratchy, dread rising as he stood there expecting to see Uncle Koji coming around the bend at any moment. Instead there were only shadows playing tricks, the air moving around him growing warmer and darker.

Where was he?

Daniel quickly backtracked up the trail. It felt like he was walking into a cave, leaving the daylight behind. Why hadn't he waited? He should have waited. Instead he took off like a shot and ran when Koji told him to. Daniel knew how dangerous it was so close to the flow. The air hissed and crackled as trees caught fire. Uncle Koji was no longer the young man who had somehow made it down the mountain amid a typhoon to get to them. That night he'd brought him his first railcar. His once invincible uncle was as vulnerable as they all were now. Daniel shook away the thought and hurried back up the trail, calling out, "Uncle Koji!"

He ran faster, careful not to fall.

"Uncle Koji!"

Still there was no answer. Daniel looked up to see the smoke rising over the trees, the new lava breakout consuming everything in its path. He hurried up the trail. The smoke thickened and he began to cough, his eyes burning, his bandana lost somewhere along the path. What was he thinking? He held his breath through the cloudy smoke. Why didn't he wait instead of running again? Did he let his anger rule his judgment? *Why did you both lie to me?* he thought. He felt sick knowing that Koji never would have left him, not in a million years. What was Daniel thinking? All his uncle and his mother ever did was protect him.

Stupid. He was stupid.

"Uncle Koji!"

Daniel was afraid of what the silence meant. He ran farther up the empty trail where a sputtering, crackling, whistling noise filled the hot air, blowing like the beginnings of a typhoon. He imagined the trees engulfed, catching fire and falling over like dominoes, worried that his uncle might be trapped underneath one of them. Koji had always been the one who saved them, never asking for anything in return. Where was his father all those times?

"Uncle Koji!"

Daniel's heart pounded against his chest. If something were to happen to Koji he would never forgive himself. He couldn't help but think of his mother and how distraught she would be. In all the years she and Koji were together, Daniel had rarely seen his uncle unable to manage any situation, fix what was broken, or calm their fears. All except for the one Sunday evening when Koji's low, anguished cry moved through the house. Daniel had just turned ten, only interested in baseball and being with his friends, but the sudden and unexpected cry from Koji was startling. Was he hurt? Daniel was hit with a quick jolt of fear and was off his bed and at his room door in a flash, quietly opening it and stepping into the hallway. From the living room, he listened to Koji and his mother talking in the kitchen. Koji was sitting at the table with his head bowed low. He watched as his mother knelt by him, her hand on his knee.

"Mama said there must have been something wrong, yeah."

Koji moaned softly. Daniel had been shocked to see Koji so upset.

His mother closed her eyes. "Something that had caused the miscarriage," she continued. "It would have been more difficult if the baby had gone full term and had problems, yeah." Her voice caught and she didn't say anything else.

Koji looked up at her and slowly stood, helping her to stand. He wrapped his arms around her and pulled her close. "Doesn't mean there won't be another chance, eh," he said.

His mother nodded.

Daniel stepped back and knew something big had happened. There was a baby and then there wasn't. A brother or sister. As far as he knew, another chance never came. Whatever anger Daniel felt, whatever childish resentment he held against his mother and Koji, only left him embarrassed now. He looked toward the smoke-filled, suffocating darkness. He had to find Koji.

"Uncle Koji!"

Daniel paused and coughed, his throat parched and raw. He was scared and wasn't sure how much farther he could go before the path was completely engulfed in smoke. Where was Koji? He could hardly see two feet in front of him. Just after he rounded the next bend, the smoke thinned and he saw Koji's dark shadow lying on the ground. Daniel rushed to him, his instincts kicking in. He gently turned him over. There was a gash bleeding profusely below his hairline. He felt for a pulse on his neck, then quickly took off his own shirt to stanch the flow of blood from Koji's forehead.

"Uncle Koji," he said, patting his cheek. "Uncle Koji." He heard a soft moan and saw movement. "It's okay," Daniel said. "I'm here."

Koji tried to sit up but slumped back down.

"Stay still," Daniel said. He put more pressure on his forehead.

"Tripped."

"Looks like your forehead took the brunt of it. Are you feeling pain anywhere else?"

"No," Koji said. He began to cough, his hand rising to his forehead.

Daniel waited until his coughing subsided. "Can you stand up?" he asked.

Koji nodded.

"We need to get out of here!" Daniel said. "Come on."

He helped to lift Koji to his feet, his uncle leaning heavily against Daniel as he half dragged him back down the smoked-filled trail toward the truck. The spitting, crackling noise felt closer and louder, as if the fire were chasing them down the path. Koji's foot slipped and they almost fell when Daniel found his balance and managed to heave his uncle back up.

"Leave me," he heard Koji tell him.

"Never! We just have to move faster," Daniel said, raising his voice against the hot wind of the firestorm. "Just a little farther," he encouraged.

Koji grunted, and seemed to understand as he began to push forward. They picked up their pace until they finally glimpsed the truck through the murky air up ahead.

"There's the truck," Daniel said.

"The truck," Koji said, squeezing his shoulder, coughing.

Daniel breathed a sigh of relief when Koji was finally in the truck, leaning heavily against the passenger-side window, his eyes closed. Daniel quickly backed the truck, completely engulfed in smoke now, out of the narrow dirt track and onto the main road. From there it was an easy drive down the mountain to Hilo Hospital.

"Hold on," Daniel said. "You're going to be all right."

Koji lifted his hand in response but didn't say a word.

〜

It took nine stitches to close the gash on Koji's forehead. Even in his groggy state, he refused to spend the night in the hospital to be monitored, so Daniel took responsibility of watching over him. By the time he drove home, it was long after dinner. He was surprised to see that Maile had stayed at the house and came outside as soon as she heard the truck. He saw the worry and relief on her face as they helped Uncle Koji inside.

37

THE TRUTH OF IT

Koji woke to darkness, his head throbbing, and a bitter taste on his tongue. He must still be in the hospital. His eyes adjusted to the dimness in the room, focusing on the shadows that slowly took shape. He reached over to turn on the lamp on the bedside table, knocking over a glass instead and causing a small ruckus. A cool wetness spread across his pillow. The one movement had sapped all his strength, and Koji slowly lay back down on the damp pillow to rest for a moment. He gently touched the bandage that spread halfway across his forehead. His body ached along with the pulsing wound. He heard the sudden burst of rain pebbling against the windows, creaks, and then footsteps before the door opened. Everything felt heightened. When the light clicked on, Koji squinted against the painful brightness to see Daniel standing there.

Koji was confused to see him there in the middle of the night. "Where am I?" he asked hoarsely. His mouth felt like cotton.

Daniel moved closer and picked up the glass that had fallen. "You're at the house with me. How are you feeling? You hit your forehead hard up at the flow. Nine stitches."

Koji remembered. He had tripped on the trail. "A tree root got in my way, yeah," he said, and coughed, pain shooting to the top of his head.

Daniel smiled. "Do you have a headache? Any nausea?"

"Head's pounding," he whispered. He'd felt more sensations in the past ten minutes than in the past two years.

Daniel reached down and checked his pulse, then carefully switched his damp pillow for a dry one on the bed. "We need to see about that cough, too."

"It's nothing."

Daniel shook his head. "We'll see." He paused and then said, "Uncle Koji, I'm sorry. I should have waited for you on the trail, I don't know what I was thinking."

"You were doing what I told you to do," Koji said. "Nothing to be sorry about."

Daniel looked as if he might say something else, but didn't. "I'll be right back," he said, taking the empty glass with him. "Don't go anywhere."

Koji smiled and didn't move. He closed his eyes. It took a moment for it to flicker through his brain before his eyes opened wide. He was in Mariko's room and lying in her bed again.

~~

Three days later, Koji was up, sitting on the edge of Mariko's bed. He'd slept most of the first two days, realizing he hadn't slept that much since he was a baby. When he woke this morning, his headache was all but gone and the sunlight no longer bothered him. The bandage across his forehead made things look much worse than he felt. Koji stood and slowly dressed, still a bit unsteady as he stopped to take a good look around the room now that he was upright. It was just as he remembered it, warm and comfortable, uncluttered except for the top of Mariko's dresser, which was covered with small objects she'd collected over the years, stones and shells and carved kukui nut shells. "I'm leaving a trail of my life," she once told him. "Tells folks where I've been and what meant something to me." He could see her once again holding each small prize, delight radiating across her face. Then, from the corner of his eye, he saw a small black lava rock that she must have taken the day they visited the lava cave so many years ago. He had reminded her it was bad luck to take any lava rocks. "No bad omens," she said, "as long as the lava doesn't leave the island, yeah." But when he looked closer, he was relieved to see it was a piece of black obsidian glass instead.

Koji stared at her collection, his throat dry. There was so little he had collected along the way, so little to show for except for Mariko and Daniel. All the other surfaces in his life were empty.

≈

Koji heard voices from the kitchen and knew Nori had arrived. She and Maile had come by each day bringing food, making sure he was eating and comfortable. "Don't know how you're going back up to Puli after being so pampered," Daniel teased. Koji had seen the worry in Nori's eyes when she'd visited the morning after he'd fallen. Each day since, he lay in bed waiting for her to scold him for being so foolish, for going so close to the lava flow, but she still hadn't said a word.

Koji knew Nori wouldn't be happy to see him out of bed and dressed. If she had her way, he would rest for a few days more, a full week preferably, but he couldn't; he was already going stir-crazy lying in bed the past few days.

Koji paused in the living room, listening.

"Lava's been flowing for ten days now, folks don't know whether to stay or leave," Nori said. "Uncle Samuel wants to wait it out."

"And you?" Daniel asked.

"Same."

"Me too," Daniel said. "This house is all I have left of her. I'm not abandoning it."

Koji cleared his throat and walked into the kitchen.

As he expected, it was Nori who spoke first. "What are you doing out of bed?"

"Feeling fine," he said. "Time to get going again, yeah, before these bones get too stiff to move anymore."

Nori watched him for a moment. "What were you thinking?" she asked sternly. To his great surprise, she didn't say anything else about it. "At least sit down and eat some breakfast," she then said, glancing at Daniel as if they shared some secret.

After they'd eaten and Nori returned to the market, Koji looked across the table at Daniel and said, "Be nice to get some fresh air, eh. Let's go for a ride."

Daniel smiled. "You do remember what happened the last time we went for a ride," he reminded him.

≈

Koji leaned back in the passenger seat, happy to be outside for the first time in days as Daniel backed the truck out of the driveway and drove toward town. When they reached downtown, Koji turned to him and said, "Let's go to Onekahakaha Beach."

Onekahakaha Beach was four miles down the coastal road from Hilo. He, Razor, and Franklin used to walk the distance from the train station to the beach and back as if it were nothing. Koji hadn't been back to the beach since Mariko died. He paid close attention to the coastal road, lined with waving palm trees, a sprinkling of sand rising in the wind and dancing along the blacktop. Everything appeared to come alive. He felt different, too, as if the numbness in him were finally beginning to thaw. He looked for the words to explain what he was feeling, but it was Daniel who spoke first.

"I made a mistake," Daniel said. His voice rose above the rumbling of the truck. "A little girl will never be the same because of me."

Koji glanced over to see Daniel's hands, white-knuckled on the steering wheel. He saw the boy again first learning to drive, who always tried so hard to get everything right. He knew now what had brought him home from Chicago.

"Life doesn't always work out the way we want it to, yeah," Koji finally said.

Daniel remained silent. Koji didn't know what else to say. If only he could heal his own wounds so easily.

"Tell me, would you have done anything different?" Koji asked. It was something he'd asked himself over and over since Razor's death.

Daniel licked his lips, deep in thought. Koji imagined him reliving every step, every decision he'd made concerning the little girl. Minutes passed. "No," he finally said. "Given the circumstances, no." He said it softly, shaking his head as if to convince himself.

"Things happen beyond our control, yeah," he said. "No fault in doing your best," he added, wondering who he was trying to convince.

Daniel looked at him. "Only the guilt," he said.

It was something Koji knew well.

~

The last time Koji saw Razor alive; he'd made him a promise he couldn't keep. He ran into Razor coming out of the plantation store. Koji was all cleaned up and there was an extra lightness in his step knowing he was on his way down to Hilo to see Mariko and Daniel. Razor knew how important they were to him, how long he'd waited to be with Mariko, so he always nudged but never pushed him to attend the union meetings held once or twice a month. It was the first time Razor was serious and insistent.

"Just the man I wanted to see, eh," Razor said, pulling Koji to the side. He lowered his voice. "There's a meeting tomorrow night. I need you to be there. It's important, yeah. We're voting to strike."

As soon as Koji heard the word "strike," he grabbed his friend's arm, worried. "You saw what happened to the workers over at Kailua. The plantation police have been like rabid dogs since that strike was put down. You know what will happen, yeah, if the lunas and owners get wind of it," he said. His voice rose and he quickly reined it in. "You could lose your job, even worse, be labeled an agitator and blacklisted from working at any other plantation on the Big Island. On any of the islands, dammit! Then what will you do?"

Razor smiled at him. "More words than you've said to me in a long time, yeah."

Koji felt guilty hearing the truth. He worked cutting cane, then spent as much time as he could down in Hilo with Mariko and Daniel. It was the first time in a long while that he'd actually had a conversation with Razor, who was his oldest friend, the one person on the plantation he'd trust with his life. He was about to apologize when Razor continued talking.

"You know what I'll do if they dare to run me off the plantation? Keep fighting, that's what I'll do," he said. "You can't keep thinking that I'm standing under a teetering mountain of cane just waiting to come crashing down on me. We've learned over the years. We're always careful, yeah. We won't make the same mistakes others have."

Koji stopped resisting. Razor was right: Koji still saw him as that antsy, funny, impetuous kid, always leaping before looking. During the years in between, Razor had grown up, settled down to become a passionate and strong organizer.

"That's why I want you there, to keep me careful, yeah, like always," Razor added. "You can't keep standing on the sidelines. I won't take no for an answer this time."

Koji looked away before Razor saw the quick flicker of guilt he felt. He was right: Koji had run out of excuses.

"What time?" Koji asked.

"Seven p.m. At the cabin."

"I'll be there," he said.

"Promise me."

And there was young Razor again, that kid always trying to coerce him to play one more game of baseball, even when it was almost dark and the lunas would eventually come out and chase them back to Kazoku village.

"I promise," he said.

Razor smiled. Only then did he let him go.

≈

They drove down the road in silence until Daniel braked to slow down as they turned off the main road.

"When did you tell my mother that my father had returned?" Daniel asked, his voice calm.

Koji inhaled and took his time. He was going to tell the story only once. What Daniel did with it was up to him. He didn't need to protect either of them any longer.

"When I came back down to visit the following Sunday," Koji answered.

"What did she say?"

"She was hurt, yeah. And angry, but not as surprised as I thought she would be. As if she knew he'd be back one day." Koji glanced at him, adding, "Your father came back because he was in trouble."

"What kind of trouble?" Daniel asked. He slowed down as they bounced over the rutted dirt road.

"He'd been gambling in Honolulu, owed a lot of money. He came back because he needed money from your mother."

Daniel looked over at him, surprised. "She didn't have any money," he said, quiet and filled with emotion.

Koji paused, swallowed, and kept talking. "I told him I'd get him the money if he would leave you and your mother alone, yeah. We agreed to meet again down at the beach early the next morning. That was when Mama saw us, when she was out early collecting shells."

"You had the money?"

"Most. I've never needed much. Borrowed the rest."

Daniel turned down another road that led directly to the beach, and Koji rolled down his window. It was windier down by the water, the air cooler, smelling briny and reminding him of the sea urchins they used to catch when they were young on the rougher, wilder north side of the beach, where the currents ran stronger.

"He never asked about my mother?" Daniel asked.

The truck bumped and squeaked.

"No."

The word fell flat and hard, like a rock hitting water.

"Did he ask about me?"

"No," Koji said again.

"You never saw him again?"

Koji shook his head. "No."

The roar of the waves filled the truck. Daniel stared straight ahead. There was another moment of silence as he gathered his thoughts and then asked, "What about all the blood Mama mentioned?"

Koji ran his hand over his short hair. "We got into a fight the morning I brought him the money."

"Were either of you hurt?"

Koji nodded. "We both took a licking. Nothing that didn't heal, yeah, we're tough old suckers," he said.

Daniel parked and turned off the engine. Onekahakaha Beach was right across the road, the rush and roar of the waves as they rose and fell. Koji leaned out the window and breathed in deeply, a dull ache pulsing across his forehead. He looked up at the clouds pushing in, muting the sunlight for just a moment, as if someone had abruptly pulled the curtains closed. Koji turned back to find Daniel watching him.

"Tell me," Daniel said. "Tell me everything."

≈

It was late March. Koji moved quietly through the darkened house, already missing the warmth of Mariko's body next to his. It was not quite 3:00 a.m. He was careful not to step on eleven-year-old Daniel's baseball glove and bat lying on the living room floor. In the past year the boy lived and breathed baseball. Koji quietly pulled the front door of the green bungalow closed. He hadn't planned to stay so late, but it was hard to leave once he'd settled in. At thirty-three, he relished the thought of having a family, but he still had to be back up at the plantation before the cane cutters were out in the fields. He rubbed the stubble on his cheek. Little chance he'd be catching up on sleep. Koji had promised

Razor he would attend his union meeting the following evening. He had already missed so many.

It was warm out. The only light came from the moon overhead, a watery glow dulled by the clouds. Koji heard the trees rustling, the cicadas in their nightly chorus. When his family first arrived in Hawai'i from Japan, he couldn't sleep with all the noise at night. Now he couldn't sleep without it.

Just as he opened the door to the truck, Koji heard something move from behind the toolshed. *A cat or dog*, he thought. But when he turned, he saw a shadow walking toward him, the ghostly orange glow of a cigarette dancing up and down in the darkness. Koji couldn't imagine who would be out so early in the morning. He reached for the crowbar under the driver's seat and waited.

"I should have known. You were always panting after her."

Almost five years had passed, and Franklin's voice remained unmistakable. Koji turned as he stepped out from the shadows.

"I was wondering if you'd ever come crawling back." Koji kept his voice a low whisper, hoping not to wake Mariko or Daniel.

"Not crawling, returning on my own two feet to see *my* wife and *my* son."

Even in the shadows, Franklin looked older and thinner, rougher around the edges. "You lost that privilege when you walked out on them."

"Well, I'm back now."

Koji's heart pounded. He wanted nothing more than to make Franklin disappear once and for all. The thought was unsettling. He breathed in slowly and said, "Get in the truck. Let's go for a ride." He wanted Franklin away from the house.

Franklin watched him for a moment. "And what if I don't?"

"Then you'll lose them for sure making a scene out here," he said, getting into his truck. A moment later the passenger door opened and Franklin climbed in, bringing with him the ripe stinks of alcohol, tobacco, and sweat.

"You do understand that they're still my family," Franklin said. "It's my blood that runs through Daniel's veins, yeah, and no one, especially not you, will ever take my place."

Koji lit a cigarette. "You gave up your place years ago."

Koji drove toward Onekahakaha Beach, knowing the road would be empty and quiet so early in the morning. Franklin lit another cigarette and relaxed when he saw where Koji was driving them to, the place of their boyhood adventures, the beach where they'd first met Mariko.

"Just like old times," he said.

"Why are you back?" Koji asked.

"I'm here to visit my family," Franklin said, smiling.

Koji knew better. "Why are you really back?" he asked again.

Franklin was quiet for a while, staring at the dark road illuminated by the headlamps. "I ran into some trouble in Honolulu," he finally said, blowing out smoke.

Koji turned down a dirt road and then another before he stopped the truck at the edge of the beach. He turned to face Franklin. "You better not have brought your troubles back with you."

Franklin smiled and said, "'With this ring I thee wed, and all my worldly goods I thee endow. In sickness and in health, in poverty and in wealth, till death do us part.' I think those are the words Mariko and I recited."

"Mariko doesn't have anything," Koji said, hating that he was taking the defensive.

"She has the house."

The house. Koji swallowed the words like a bitter tea. His anger rose so quickly he didn't have time to think. His fist struck Franklin hard several times in the close confines of the truck before he stopped, leaving Frank with a bloody nose, a split lip. *Who's the pretty boy now?* Koji thought. He was breathing hard as he watched Frank open the door and stumble out of the truck. His knuckles stung.

The next thing Koji heard was Franklin laughing.

"You'll never have her," Franklin said, slamming the door shut, wiping the blood from his nose with his sleeve. "You can pretend all you want."

"Neither will you," Koji said, jumping out his truck and following him down to the beach. There was a briny and decaying smell in the air, as if something had died and washed up with the surf. When he was within striking distance, Frank had turned and swung at him but missed. Koji stepped forward, hitting Franklin in the face again. He was ashamed at how good it felt when Frank stumbled and fell on the sand. "How much?"

"Too much," Franklin said, staying seated.

"How much?"

"Three hundred."

Koji always knew Franklin's luck would change. He couldn't always win, but Koji was willing to pay him to save the house, and for him to stay out of Mariko and Daniel's lives.

"Meet me back here tomorrow night, same time, yeah. I'll have the money for you," Koji spit out. "Then you leave them alone. I want you gone for good."

Franklin stood shakily. "A ready-made family, yeah. Not a bad deal for three hundred," he said.

Koji ignored him. "Tomorrow night," he said, walking back to his truck.

≈

When Koji returned to the beach the following night, the ocean was rough and restless, mirroring his own emotions. He turned, sensing movement, and saw Franklin walking out from a grove of trees toward him. Everything moved quickly as soon as Franklin demanded more money for the price of his family.

"I need more," he said. There was a smirk on his face.

Koji had nothing more. He'd depleted his savings and borrowed the rest of it. Even if he did have it, he wasn't going to give one more penny to Franklin. He threw the envelope of money at him. "That's it. No more," he said. They argued, their rising voices lost in the roar of the ocean, their angry words carried down the empty beach. Somewhere along the way it wasn't about the money anymore. This time Franklin swung a hard right and connected with his cheek. Koji didn't hesitate after that. His strength came from years of working in the fields. He hit Franklin several times before Koji saw him reach toward his back, returning with the glint of the knife he suddenly held in his hand.

"Go ahead, come again!" Franklin yelled. "I've killed pigs bigger than you!"

Before Koji righted himself, Franklin lunged at him, the sharp sting of the knife slicing across his stomach. He saw a flicker of surprise on Franklin's face before it turned to anger and determination. The knife came at him again, but this time Koji stepped back and grabbed Franklin's wrist with one hand while throwing a punch and hitting him hard in the face with the other. Koji pulled back and threw another one-two punch with all the strength he had, hitting him hard in the ribs and watching him fall heavily to the sand, the bloodied knife still in his hand.

Koji's pain quickly took over. He pressed firmly against the wound to try and stop the bleeding. His shirt turned crimson. How did it all get out of hand so fast? He stumbled backward, the pain suddenly crippling. Franklin was still down. Koji's legs felt like lead moving across the sand and back toward his truck. *All I need is to get sewn up and I'll be just fine, yeah,* he thought. He looked back toward Franklin, who hadn't moved. Koji stumbled farther, falling to his knees, his stomach on fire. There was so much blood. He lay down on the sand. It was becoming hard for him to concentrate, so he focused on the lightening sky and the sound of the waves, which offered comfort. He knew someone would eventually find him. *What a fucking foolish way to die,* he thought.

They were all so young when they met for the first time, not ten feet away from where he lay on the sand, the day he couldn't stop looking at Mariko. He saw her again. And Razor. He hoped his friend would forgive him for missing another union meeting. He hoped Razor would understand that he couldn't let Mariko lose her house. Koji closed his eyes, thinking he heard someone running toward him, hoping it wasn't Franklin. His stomach burned, his body reeling from the loss of blood as he felt himself slowly disappearing, moving farther and farther away from everyone and everything he loved.

≈

Koji touched his stomach, the wound long healed. He'd been lucky the knife missed puncturing anything important. Once in a long while, he still felt a twinge of pain if he overdid things. The scar had faded to a pale white still visible across his midsection. It had taken him almost six weeks to heal and six more before he could be out in the fields and cutting again. He worked through the pain, slowly building back his strength. It was nothing compared to the pain he'd felt learning Razor had been killed after the meeting that night on his way back to the plantation. He would have died, too, if it wasn't for Mama Natua.

≈

"He stabbed you?" Daniel asked. He was stunned at first, and then angry.

Koji cleared his throat. "I lived."

Daniel raked his fingers through his hair. "What kind of person would do that, stab an old friend?"

"A desperate one."

They sat in the warm silence of the truck and Koji turned to see Daniel lost in the enormity of it all.

"You could have died," Daniel finally said. His voice was tight with disbelief.

"Wasn't my time yet," Koji said quietly.

"What happened to him?"

Koji shook his head. "Gone," he said.

He had wondered for weeks after if Franklin had really left, worried that he might return asking for more money from Mariko. The fear followed him like a shadow, but weeks led to months and the dimness finally cleared. Franklin may have thought he killed him that night. Either way, he was unlikely to ever return.

"The Sunday you came to the house all beat up, it was during that time, wasn't it?" Daniel remembered. "You were moving so slow that day. You couldn't play catch with me that afternoon like you always did." Daniel sat quiet for a moment before he said, "I should have known something was wrong, I was old enough."

Koji looked at Daniel. "You were just a kid, yeah."

"I *was* just a kid in so many ways. When I was younger, I some-times wondered why my mother was with you and not with my father anymore.

Koji hesitated a moment. "A fair question." He then said,

"I couldn't ask my mother; I didn't want to make her sad, so I kept quiet. There was a small part of me that always thought when I went to the mainland for college that I might see him there again. That's one of the reasons I studied so hard. Foolish, right?"

"No more than any of us," Koji said. "Your mother meant the world to me. She always did."

"I know," Daniel said.

Koji looked away and out the window. "We're wasting a nice morn-ing, yeah. Let's get some air, eh."

He opened the door to the truck and gingerly stepped down. The clouds had cleared as he squinted against the bright sunlight.

GHOST VOICES

MARIKO, 1918

Koji usually stops by during the week when the sugar train is being unloaded, but I haven't seen him since last Sunday, when he returned to Puli in the early hours. The night he left I was awakened by a voice in the wind that sounded so much like Franklin's I got up from bed to look out the window just as Koji's truck drove off. It's funny how the mind can play tricks, yeah. And still I've had this nagging feeling follow me for the past week.

It's Sunday morning again. I take the eggs out of the icebox, along with a slab of bacon and a loaf of sweetbread to make breakfast for Koji and Daniel. The rain suddenly splatters against the kitchen window and I hope it passes quickly so that we can work outside later. We often spend the morning after breakfast cutting branches and pulling weeds, taming the wildness that's my yard. I smile at the thought. I slice the bacon and lay the strips down sizzling across the hot cast iron skillet. A moment later, the savory aroma of frying bacon fills the kitchen. For years now, ever since Nori found out Koji came down from Puli on Sunday mornings, she insists on giving me more bacon than I need. "Fair trade for the mangoes, yeah," she says.

Nori's generosity is boundless. I know a basket or two of mangoes isn't a fair exchange, since I give her mangoes from the tree every year, anyway. Little has changed between us since we were young girls. And maybe that's what she means, we give and take, finding balance through the years. We've always taken care of each other, from her stormy childhood through Franklin's disappearance to raising our boys together. We're closer than sisters. Not born to be, yeah, Nori likes to say, but chosen to be.

≈

The kitchen hums with activity, the crackling and sizzling, percolating sounds of breakfast being made. It's something I've done a thousand times, but this morning it feels new. I wipe my hands on my apron and begin slicing a papaya. Daniel sleeps through it all, the hard sleep of a growing boy. He's almost eleven and already tall and thin like his father. The table is set, three plates, and a bowl for Daniel's cereal. I lay the crisp strips of bacon on a plate and crack the eggs into a bowl. As soon as Koji arrives, I'll scramble them the way he likes, thickened but still runny.

I don't hear a sound from Daniel's room so I take a moment to sit down and savor a cup of coffee. Not long after that I hear Koji's truck pull into the driveway. I immediately stand, smoothing my apron. It's become a habit for me to walk out to the front porch to meet him. When I open the door, I'm greeted by a gust of fresh air smelling of wet earth, ginger, and plumeria now that the rain has stopped. In a few hours it'll be hot and muggy again.

Koji takes his time getting out of his truck. Usually by now he's already making his way toward the porch. I watch him sitting there, wondering if I should walk down to see if everything's all right, when the door to his truck finally swings open. I already know something's wrong, seeing his slow, deliberate movements. I hurry down the steps to meet him, and that's when I see the angry greenish-yellow bruise on his cheek, the stiff and awkward way he's walking, his bandaged hand hovering over his stomach.

"What happened?" I ask, reaching out to touch his cheek. "Are you okay?"

"Razor's dead," he says softly.

"What?" I see his eyes tearing. He suddenly looks older, tired. "How?" I ask.

"He was run down last Monday night. They've been trying to keep it hush-hush, yeah. No one was allowed to leave the plantation until today."

My stomach drops. No wonder I hadn't heard anything. "After a meeting?" I ask.

How many times did Nori and I warn him to be careful? "You're not invincible," I'd said, the last time he came to visit. Razor smiled, flexed his muscles. "Am, yeah," he said, ever endearing before adding, "Promise I'll watch out." I can't imagine no longer hearing his easy laughter and his bad jokes that filled any room he walked into.

Koji's face is pale with grief and he nods and winces in pain.

"Were you there?" I ask, seeing how hurt he is.

Koji shakes his head. "I ran into an old friend."

All of this makes no sense. Razor, dear Razor is dead, and Koji wasn't there, but he shows up looking as if he's been on the losing end of a fight. "I don't understand. Did you get into a fight with this friend?" I ask.

I look up and see Koji hesitate before he says, "It was Franklin."

It takes me a moment to register what he says, and when I do, just the sound of his name is like a punch that knocks the air from me. I stop in the middle of the walkway, my mouth suddenly dry, my stomach churning, and I feel like I want to throw up. Then I remember the voice I heard last week. It was Franklin's. "Where is he now?" I ask.

I look up to see a flicker of sadness in Koji's eyes. I suddenly realize he must think I want to see Franklin, that I might want him back. "Why did he come back?" I quickly add. "I know he wants something." I feel my anger rising, hard and complicated. He wasn't even man enough to see me.

"Found trouble in Honolulu, yeah. He needed money."

"You gave it to him?"

Koji nods. "He didn't get it easy."

"How badly did he hurt you?"

"It's nothing," Koji says, "just a cut, yeah." His hand still hovers over his stomach.

"He's gone?"

Koji nods again, grimaces.

What has Franklin done? The blood rushes to my head. How dare him, I think, even if a part of me does want to see him again. I bite my lip against the desire. At the same time, I'm relieved he's gone. He has always been too selfish to see beyond himself. "I'll pay you back," I say, angry and embarrassed. "Did he remember he has a son?"

Koji pauses, as if he's deciding what to tell me.

"Tell me!" I say, angrier than I mean to be. Koji has done everything for us.

"He remembers, but he was more concerned about the money," he finally says.

We both turn when we hear the front door swing open. Daniel is standing there in his pajamas and smiles wide when he sees Koji. "I'm hungry," he says. "Are we going to eat breakfast soon?"

I take a breath, find a smile for Daniel. "Right now," I say, "go pour a glass of milk. And be careful, yeah."

"Okay," he says. And then, "Uncle Koji, you okay? You don't look so good."

Koji smiles, lifts his hand in a wave, and grimaces. "Just a small accident," he says.

"Come on then!" Daniel says.

"A minute, yeah," Koji says, and glances over at me.

"Not now," I say softly. "Tell me later. You need to sit down and rest." I gently take hold of his arm to help him up the steps.

He won't ruin our day, I tell myself. I watch Daniel disappear back into the house and wonder if Franklin has any idea just how much he has really lost.

WAITING

DECEMBER 22–26, 1935

38

REVELATIONS

The day after Daniel and Uncle Koji had gone to Onekahakaha Beach, Daniel was still shaken by what Koji had told him about his father. For the first time, Daniel felt the father he'd conjured up in his head through the years was simply a figment of his imagination, a variation of the game they'd once played, Who Is He? Where Is He? He no longer cared.

Daniel left his uncle at the house to rest, walking to the fish market to see Auntie Nori. According to Koji, other than Mama, Nori was the only other person who knew of his father's return. Daniel intended to check on Mama Natua afterward, carrying his medical bag with him. As he rounded the corner toward the bay, the winds had risen and the ocean was rough, whitecaps rippling across the surface. Boats bobbed and creaked in their berths down at the wharf. It began to rain lightly. He looked up to see a plume of smoke hovering over Mauna Loa, still smoking and steaming as the lava continued to flow, Pele watching, ready to make Hilo all hers.

It was just after the morning rush and the market was quiet. Daniel was greeted by Jelly clearing the trays from the counter. "Thought you were another one of those skinny geologists coming in again," she said, happy to see him. She shook her ample hips.

Daniel laughed. "Just came by to see Auntie Nori," he said. "What did the geologist have to say?"

Jelly's voice turned serious. "Came to tell us the lava flow had picked up, flowing down the mountain at the rate of a mile a day now, yeah. If it keeps up, it'll reach the Wailuku River in two weeks."

Daniel flinched at the news. It felt like a bad dream, like the old bed-time stories the aunties and uncles used to tell them as children about the awakening gods causing havoc.

"There's still time, anything can happen," Daniel said reassuringly.

"Last straw for some folks," Jelly said quietly, stacking the last empty tray on top of the others. "I'll wait until after Christmas. Things can change at any time, yeah."

Christmas was three days away. It was the first time Daniel heard Jelly mention leaving and felt her fear. "Let me know if there's anything I can do to help," he said.

"Thank you," Jelly said. "Nobu can be a handful, yeah."

"How's he doing?"

Ever since Jelly's son, Nobu's, accident nine years ago, she'd had her hands full caring for her middle-aged son, who had never been the same after nearly drowning at Ke'aloha Beach. He'd been caught in a rip current while swimming and wasn't breathing when they pulled him from the ocean. When he was finally revived and brought back to life, the Nobu they knew had died. Once easygoing and athletic, he could hardly walk now without help, and was prone to angry outbursts when he couldn't form a sentence or express himself.

"Good as can be, yeah."

"Just let me know if I can help in any way," Daniel repeated.

"Thought I heard your voice," Nori said, walking out from the kitchen carrying a tray of Inari sushi for the lunch crowd.

Daniel smiled. "You're just the person I was hoping to see," he said.

≈

They sat down at the back table where the Hilo Aunties still played Hearts every Saturday, close to where he and Mano shot marbles in the back corner of the market when they were boys. He could still hear the marbles rolling across the wooden planks, the *click click* of one hitting another, followed by their joyful shouts as the victor collected his marbles, remaining oblivious to their mothers and aunties talking and laughing nearby.

Auntie Nori put a plate of Inari sushi and cups of green tea within reach. The sushi rice wrapped inside sweet soy-marinated tofu was always one of his favorites. Up front, Jelly had switched on the radio, and the market filled with the low hum of an orchestra playing.

"Koji all right?" Nori asked, a look of concern darkening her gaze.

"He's fine," Daniel said. "We went for a walk on Onekahakaha Beach yesterday. He should be completely back on his feet in a day or two."

Nori shook her head. "Just wait until he gets better. He's going to hear an earful."

"It was an accident, just as much my fault," Daniel said. "He'll be fine," he added, and then changed the subject. "We had a long talk at the beach. I asked him about my father's return."

Nori looked up at him knowingly. "He told me you knew."

"It was Mama who first mentioned seeing him," Daniel said. "She thought I was my father the day I gave her the checkup. She said Koji was there on the beach with him, kept asking why I didn't return to my family."

"Mama," she whispered, "always rescuing strays." She sighed and began to talk. "Franklin always caused drama, yeah, even when he didn't try. It was in his nature, eh, so different from Koji."

Daniel nodded; he couldn't agree more. He wrapped his hands around the clay teacup. "I need to know," he said. "What did my mother tell you about the night my father returned? How did she react? Uncle Koji said she never saw him. Did she want to?"

All of a sudden it was as if Daniel couldn't stop; he wanted to know everything. He must have been ten or eleven back then, and he'd been clueless. How had his mother dealt with the loss all over again?

Nori picked up an old union meeting flyer on the table and folded the sheet in half. "You were young when he left, but you remember how difficult it was for your mother after your father disappeared."

Daniel sighed. He saw his mother again; how thin she'd become and how she couldn't stop moving. Sometimes he heard her in the middle of the night walking back and forth from one end of the house to the other.

"The fool left her without a word, yeah, leaving nothing but an empty place in her heart, the terrible kind of missing that comes from not knowing. All the questions left unanswered. I don't think she ever let go of that feeling. Who could blame her, eh?" Auntie Nori asked. "But you kept her going, and time, yeah. And later there was Koji, who'd been waiting for her since the first day they'd met. In the end he filled a good deal of the emptiness she felt."

Daniel leaned forward and sipped his tea. "Uncle Koji was devoted to her all those years?"

"From the beginning," Auntie Nori said. "Even after she married your father, he stayed loyal to her."

"I can't imagine our life without him."

Nori smiled in thought. "When we were young, Koji was always the one we turned to when there was trouble."

"Trouble?" Daniel asked, and smiled. "What kind of trouble would you and the Hilo Aunties get into? You were always keeping the three of us *out of* trouble," he said, thinking of Wilson and Mano.

"We were young once too," Nori said, pausing in thought. "But those are other stories for other times, yeah." She poured more tea and continued, "I know that after your father returned, it was hard on your mother and Koji. It took time for Koji to get over the insecurities Franklin brought back in him. He was always afraid Franklin would return and take your mother away again. But something did change in your mother after your father returned. She realized how important Koji was to her. When she saw him hurt, the thought of losing him, yeah, hit home."

Auntie Nori paused to sip her tea. "Your mother never said much about your father afterward; she seemed relieved that she never saw him when he returned. "For the best" was all she told me, but I know he was still in her thoughts. Seeing him would only have been more difficult. She loved your father but she didn't always like him. Takes the two to make a good marriage, yeah," Auntie Nori said.

Daniel watched her gaze move to the yellowed photo of the Hilo Aunties on the bulletin board, so young and happy together.

"Franklin never should have married," Auntie Nori continued, "not to say that he didn't love your mother as much as he could love anyone, yeah. He was taken with her from the moment he saw her on Onekahakaha Beach. Trouble was, Koji felt the same—you could just see it in his eyes, a longing, yeah. Both of those boys loved her, but Franklin claimed her from the start." Nori paused. "In the beginning, we were all taken by your father, such a good-looking boy, a real smooth talker, until he began disappearing, only to return with one excuse after another. 'Got caught up, yeah,' he'd always say."

Daniel ran his fingers through his hair. "How did he get caught up?"

"Playing basketball, or in a card game, at the beach or upcountry, and later, your mother suspected other women when he worked on the other islands. He never kept time, always kept your mother waiting, or just never showed up. Shame, yeah, Franklin had everything, things always came easy to him. But in time you saw there was something, something always missing inside." Nori cleared her throat. "Never knew how lucky he was to have your mother. For years Koji watched on the sidelines, helped her when Franklin was away and he wasn't cutting cane. Right until that night your father returned, yeah, when he carelessly took so much away from Koji."

"What do you mean?" Daniel asked. "I know he was hurt in the fight."

Nori turned back to him. "Koji didn't tell you everything then?"

He looked at her confused. "What didn't he tell me?"

Nori fingered the rim of her teacup. "Razor died the same night Koji was knifed by your father. Koji was supposed to be at that union meeting; he had promised Razor. That night, Koji not only lost his best friend, he was never able to get his cane cutting swing back after being cut. Not long after, he quit cane cutting for good. That's when the Puli manager asked him to run the sugar train."

Daniel sat back in the chair, stunned. His father's return had irrevocably changed Koji's life forever, and he never said anything. He'd never really known how Uncle Razor died. The last time he'd seen him, Razor, a strong, stocky man who always made his mother laugh, had come by the house to see Mariko. Daniel was in the yard, bat in hand, practicing his swing. It was windy that day, and on his way back out, Razor had stopped to watch his swing before changing Daniel's grip on the bat. "You'll hit farther now, guarantee, yeah," Uncle Razor said, and winked. "Just don't tell your Uncle Koji I showed you my secret; he's wanted to know since we were kids, yeah." Daniel never did tell, and never saw him again.

"He never told me," he said.

Auntie Nori reached across the table and covered his hand with hers. He looked down at the small, round scar on the back of her hand, the dark brown of a kukui nut. He'd always meant to ask her how she'd gotten it.

"The cane work would have ended given time, yeah, but Razor was a hard loss, the guilt runs through his blood," she said. "You and your mother kept him going."

He'd known his uncle all his life, but he never knew the man. "So my father took everything away from Koji," Daniel said.

"Not everything," Nori said. "Koji will never forgive himself for Razor's death, but running the sugar train was the best thing that could have happened; he was given his own place to live, and the train brought him down to Hilo every day to see your mother. Ironic, yeah, Koji was always the family man, while for Franklin, it became an anchor around his neck. Best thing to come out of the marriage was you," Nori said. "I once told your mother that your father was a no-good lazy ass all his life, but worth it, if only for you. The other good thing in her life was Koji."

Auntie Nori stopped talking, sipped her tea, and looked back at the photo on the bulletin board.

Daniel closed his eyes for just a moment and thought of his father, but it was Koji's face that he saw.

≈

By the time Daniel left the market, the wind had died down, the sky gray and overcast. The heat remained trapped by the low clouds that wrapped around Daniel as he walked up the road to Mama's house, a sweaty grip on his medical bag, the prickly dampness of his shirt pressed against his back. The faint buzz of mosquitoes circled around him. He should have borrowed Uncle Samuel's truck. Instead he turned the corner and began walking up the hill to the Natua house.

Daniel knocked several times on the screen door, and for the first time there was no answer. He stepped inside to find the house empty, fearful that something might have happened to Mama until he realized her wheelchair was also gone. They couldn't have gone far with Auntie Leia pushing Mama's wheelchair in the humid heat. Daniel sat down on the porch and waited. It wasn't long before he saw them moving slowly up the road and hurried to meet them.

"Let me help you," he said.

Auntie Leia quickly relinquished control of the wheelchair to him and wiped her neck with a handkerchief. Mama's head lolled to the side, her eyes closed in sleep.

"Sticky today, yeah, going down the road was easy, back up not so much, eh," she said. "I took Mama to visit the neighbors down the road. They're packing a few things just in case Pele switches direction. I told them all I need is right here," she said, looking down at Mama. Auntie Leia wiped her own brow and took a breath.

"I'll get her back to the house," Daniel said.

Auntie Leia smiled. "Thank you, I'll go ahead, yeah, have some papaya juice waiting," she said, and quickly walked toward the house.

Daniel watched her go and pushed Mama along the rutted dirt road, avoiding the rocks and potholes. He didn't stop until they reached the shade of the monkey pod tree in front of the Natua house. When he looked down, Mama was awake and looking up at him.

"Did you have a nice visit with the neighbors?" Daniel asked.

Mama looked at him as if he were a stranger at first before something clicked and she found recognition. "Mariko's boy," she said.

Daniel stepped to the front of the chair and crouched before her. "That's right, I'm Mariko's boy," he said, surprised. "You remembered—" he began when he heard a truck driving up the road and stood to see who it was. He looked down when Mama's hand reached for his wrist, gripping it with surprising strength.

"Good, you back home, yeah," she said.

Daniel smiled. "I'm happy to be home," he said.

Mama let go of his wrist.

As the truck grew closer and slowed to a stop, Daniel saw Uncle Samuel driving. Uncle Koji sat next to him in the passenger seat.

"Everything all right?" Daniel asked. He stepped closer to Uncle Koji's open window.

"Drove by the house to see you," Uncle Samuel said. "Found him instead. After you left the market, news came from the volcano center."

Uncle Koji leaned out the window, touching the bandage across his forehead. "They've asked the US Army on Oahu for help to stop the lava flow, yeah, hoping to at least divert it from reaching the watershed and Hilo."

"How are they planning to do that?" Daniel asked.

Uncle Samuel pulled out a piece of paper from his pocket. "They want to bring in the army flyboys, drop bombs to control the flow. Says here a Lieutenant Colonel George S. Patton is the one in charge, yeah."

"Think it'll work?"

"At least it's something," Uncle Koji said. "Folks getting anxious waiting around. Everyone's ready to leave at a moment's notice."

Before Uncle Samuel could say anything more, the screen door whined open and Auntie Leia called out to them. "Come in, yeah, before you all wilt out there."

39

SAFE PLACES

Two days had passed since they received word of the bombing and then nothing. There was a strange hush in the air, a quiet restlessness that made Nori nervous. Talking to Daniel had brought Mariko and Razor back to the forefront of her thoughts. She missed them, and felt foolish wishing they were still with her to help cut through the dread of waiting. The uncertainty was taking its toll, making everyone anxious. Nori felt something shift within the community as their thin edge of hope turned into anxiety. Many of the older locals kept up with their daily routines, stopping in to listen to radio broadcasts, or checking the bulletin board for any news, everyone looking for ways to manage.

One look at the bulletin board—heavy with slips of paper dangling like *o-mikuji* fortunes at a Shinto shrine—conveyed the community's confusion and turmoil. Every day Nori saw more and more slips of paper pinned desperately on the board—locals selling off family heirlooms and furniture, chickens and pigs, while others were looking for rides to other parts of the island, or for a safe place to stay and shelter for their animals. And still others looked for tents or tarps, blankets, shovels, and buckets; someone needed extra shotgun shells, another needed a tire for a 1930

Ford truck. The list grew. In the past week, long lines of packed cars and trucks waited down the street from Yamamoto's Gas Station filling up their tanks, while all the canned and jarred foods, bags of rice and beans, and anything preserved or dried quickly flew off the shelves.

Some locals had already left town, while others were preparing to leave, and a handful stubbornly refused to go. They were adamant in not abandoning their property for looters to come swooping in, and vowed to stay even if the molten lava oozed right up to their front door. Uncle Akamai, whom Nori had known since she was a little girl, was staying, repeating over and over, "When the lava comes, yeah, I'll open the door and invite it right in."

Nori sighed and walked back to the bulletin board to pin up a new list of evacuation steps brought in that morning by a young, earnest geologist. He also told her it was "time to make plans about leaving in the event the army's bombs don't divert or stop the flow." While they waited, each day brought them closer to the reality of Hilo being abandoned and completely devoured by the lava's fire. It would be as if Hilo never existed. It took all Nori's effort to pin the list up. She re-arranged the flyers on the board until she found a spot just to the right of center to tack up the list of evacuation steps.

TRANSPORT

EVACUATION ROUTES

SAFETY ZONES

ASSEMBLY STATIONS

SHELTER

COMMUNICATION PROCEDURES

The words filled her mouth until she couldn't swallow. Didn't they know? The locals knew all the roads out of Hilo, including the back-road shortcuts outsiders never knew existed. Wilson and Mano also had the fishing boat ready in case of a last-minute departure by sea. They didn't need directions on how to leave Hilo town; they needed to know what they could do to stay.

～

As the lava continued to flow toward Hilo, Nori and Samuel retreated to their own safe places, both becoming sentimental, mindful of all they had to lose. A few days earlier, Nori noticed some items in their apartment missing, a family photo when the boys were young, a few kitchen utensils, and a small needlepoint cushion Samuel's mother had given them. She later found that Samuel had quietly packed them away in a box in their bedroom closet. Without a word, Nori added to the box—a comfortable pair of shoes, her favorite wooden rolling pin, and her father's ukulele. It was the one good memory she had of him, her father playing his ukulele and singing, "Oh my darlin', oh my darlin', oh my darlin' Clementine." His runny eyes focused just long enough to really see Nori, until the song was over and she quickly lost him again to the stink and haze of the ti root alcohol. Try as she did, she couldn't find one good memory left of her mother.

They established other habits. Each evening after the market closed, Samuel went down to the docks to check on the Okawa fishing boat and see the boys. Nori knew her husband enjoyed the distraction of having a beer with Wilson or Mano and his old fishing buddies at Hoku's Bar down at the wharf. The two-story building, with its faded wood exterior and slumping corrugated overhang, had always looked like a structure on its last legs. It had survived the corrosive sea-salt air, howling typhoons, and drunken fist fights for the past fifty years and was beloved by the fishermen. Inside the dark and cool interior, it smelled of fried fish and stale beer, while the ceiling fans turned too slowly to generate any real relief. "More beer sold that way," Wilson had once explained to her. Now they hoped it would survive Mauna Loa.

"Be back soon, yeah," Samuel said, pausing at the door.

Nori smiled at his reassurance. "Tell the boys I love them," she said before locking up behind him.

After Samuel left, Nori went directly to the market's kitchen. It was where she always felt safest, where wonderful things bloomed from her measuring and mixing, kneading and baking. She kept busy cleaning

up, breathing in all that was calm and familiar, finding comfort in
the years of old stains on the scuffed floorboards, the worn furniture,
the lingering sweetness in the air. Nori filled the empty containers
with precious flour and sugar, and made sure there was enough lard
in the icebox. She took down two jars of mango and papaya jam
from the pantry and relished these moments when she cleared the
large wooden table to make room for rolling and cutting the dough
out for the morning's sweetbread and rolls. Every morning felt like
a new beginning, like anything was possible, seeing her empty table
waiting, knowing that she was going to cover every inch of it with
her sweet comforts. Nori breathed deeply. She would leave the rest
for tomorrow. She took one more look around the readied room before
turning out the lights.

≈

By Christmas Eve, word still hadn't come from the army as to when they
would bomb the lava flow. Nori was fed up waiting. It was Samuel who
provided a calming voice. "Not so simple, yeah, the winds and tempera-
ture play a big part," he said, explaining all the planning and logistics
the army had to consider. "Planes aren't like birds, yeah."

Nori couldn't be appeased. "Aren't planes man-made birds?" she
asked. "With all the money spent on the military, they should be able to
fly at a moment's notice."

It was up to her to look for other distractions. Nori walked back
to the kitchen when an idea came to her. She returned with her largest
mixing bowl and a big glass jar that once held dill pickles. She placed
the bowl and jar on the counter next to the register, along with a pencil
and pad of paper. It was time she turned their anxiety into something
more productive.

"Five-cent buy-in! Winner takes all!" she announced to everyone in
the market. "The one coming the closest to picking the right date and
time of the bombing wins the entire pot, yeah. And don't forget your
name or I keep the pot!"

Maile and Kailani had come by while she was back in the kitchen and helped to keep everyone orderly and relaxed as they lined up to write down their predictions. Coins clinked into the jar, while slips of paper filled the mixing bowl. As Nori thought, the betting pool cheered everyone up. By the time she locked the door that evening, they were up to $1.65 and counting.

40

MELE KALIKIMAKA

"Nice, yeah," Nori said when Koji walked into the market, his eyes wide with surprise. The fish market had been transformed into a scene from a mainland Christmas card Daniel had sent to them one year when he had to work and was too busy to return.

In red block letters, MELE KALIKIMAKA, Merry Christmas, was tacked up on a long piece of paper behind the front counter, while Benny Goodman and his band's jazzy rendition of "Jingle Bells" played on the radio, and two large poinsettia wreaths, no doubt Leia's handiwork, hung from the front picture windows. On the koa bar were growing piles of papayas, lychee, and coconuts picked right from the trees, while Nori's sweetbread and tarts sat next to freshly sliced tuna Wilson and Mano had caught that morning, and the hulking centerpiece was a large kalua pig the Yamamotos' older son had shot and cooked all night in a fire pit.

"Thought it would be good to forget about the lava flow for a few hours, yeah," Nori explained. "Sent Samuel and Wilson out to cut down an island pine." She pointed to the large tree they'd decorated with flowers and colorful ribbons and put up next to the back tables. "Just like the movies, yeah."

The first time Koji had ever seen a real Christmas tree was when Daniel was still a toddler and Mariko had asked him to help cut down a small pine for the house. He was confused at first; didn't seem to make sense dragging a live tree into the living room, but when he saw the tree decorated, the sharp, woody tang of pine in the air, and Daniel running around it with such joy, he saw the sense of it.

"Went all out, eh," Koji said. He knew it had nothing to do with the haole religion. Nori's Christmas had to do with cheering up the community. If this was to be their last celebration together in Hilo, then Nori wanted it to be a memorable one.

"Also brought back this," Samuel said, sneaking up behind Nori and holding a sprig of mistletoe above her head, stealing a kiss.

"You are an old fool," Nori said, teasing.

Samuel leaned closer to Nori. "*Your* old fool, yeah."

Koji laughed. He stood among his old friends and glimpsed the almost full pickle jar of nickels next to the cash register. When he dropped his five cents into the jar yesterday, he'd predicted the planes would be bombing the lava flow the day after Christmas at midmorning, and he planned to stay the night with Nori and Samuel to collect his winnings tomorrow. He had bothered Daniel long enough.

The Christmas party had succeeded in not only cheering the locals, but also the restless dockworkers, the new young teacher and his wife from Texas who lived above the Kilauea café down the street, and all the other shop owners and their families in the surrounding blocks of Kamehameha. No one spoke of the flow, and when the dancing began, Koji watched from the sidelines, happy to see Daniel and Maile together most of the night. Whatever had happened to her in Honolulu had left her jumpy, always looking over her shoulder. He hoped that being home again would help her to relax, that Daniel would be able to see her through whatever trouble she was having. Koji touched the bandage that covered his forehead, his stitches itching more than anything else. He pressed against it gently, trying not to scratch.

"It means you're healing," Daniel said, walking over to him. "Just leave it alone," he scolded with a smile. "You'll be as good as new in a few days."

Koji lifted his beer in a toast, happy to get on with his life, and drank. He looked again to see Daniel's gaze lingering on him until he began to feel uncomfortable.

"You didn't tell me the knife wound was so bad you had to quit cutting cane," he said, his voice low and serious.

Koji didn't have to guess. "You talked to Nori."

Daniel nodded.

"It was time anyway, yeah," Koji said. "I was in my thirties, middle-aged. Most cutters already retired, finding easier work planting or milling or moving down to town to work as mechanics or knife sharpeners, like Uncle Chigo. Others just simplifying, yeah, living off the land, eh."

Daniel shook his head. "What about Uncle Razor?"

Koji swallowed. Suddenly the room seemed to shift and the Christmas music blared too loudly from the radio. "It wasn't his time."

"It wasn't your fault," Daniel said.

Koji steadied himself. No one would ever be able to convince him he couldn't have saved Razor's life had he been at the meeting that night. It would always be his burden to carry, something he sensed Daniel knew all about.

Koji leaned in closer. "It wasn't your fault either," he said.

≈

Koji lay in Mano's cramped twin bed; thankful he was so tired, he closed his eyes and fell immediately into a dream. He was back near his train cottage perched above the cane fields. It was windy as he stood outside looking down at the distant lights flickering from the other villages scattered around the plantation, each celebrating Christmas in their own way. As a boy, Christmas was simply a rare day off, while all the families at Kazoku village prepared and gathered for the New Year, bringing food to share. It was always his favorite time of the year.

As Koji walked back up the dirt slope to his cottage, he looked out at the wavering shadows of the uncut cane fields. The winds had picked up and he felt something or someone tugging on his sleeve. Koji paused when a rustling movement at the edge of the darkening field caught his eye and filled him with hope. Razor. He hadn't seen his old friend since the day he left for Hilo and stopped at the cabin. Koji stood and waited, his wound tingling until he saw the tall leaves part and Razor step out from the cane field.

Koji hurried back down the road to the field, happy to see his old friend. "I was wondering when I'd see you again," he said.

Razor stood, waiting. "You the one been gone, yeah," he said, and smiled.

"Lot's happening, eh. Back now," Koji said.

Razor pointed to his forehead. "Bumped your head?"

"Tripped."

Razor reached for the whiskey bottle in his shirt pocket. "Cures all," he said, offering it to him.

Koji declined.

"Like I told you, Pele's having her way, eh."

Koji nodded. "You were right, yeah. The army wants to bomb the vents, divert the flow away from Hilo."

Razor laughed. "Won't make any difference," he said, shaking his head.

Koji missed this, their simple conversations that set the world right, even if they were wrong. "I'm sorry," he suddenly said. "I've always wanted to tell you, yeah. I'm sorry I wasn't at the meeting that night," he said, the old ache rising again. "I was supposed to be there, I promised you. I would have, but Franklin—"

Razor inched forward. "No need," he said.

"It's important you know, yeah, I want you to know."

"I do," Razor said. He looked toward the field of cane and back again. "I do know. I wanted you to see that I was more than that crazy kid you grew up with, eh."

"Much more," Koji said.

The sky darkened. Last chance for daylight before the spirits came out, his father had said. He'd lost his oldest friend that night, while Franklin had lived. Razor's death would always haunt him. The years since had allowed him to bury that night until Daniel's return stirred everything back to the surface again.

Razor shook his head. "Franklin always put his needs ahead of everyone else's, yeah. Nothing would have changed; you couldn't have saved me. If not that night, would have been another."

Koji swallowed. "I should have been there for you."

Razor drank from his bottle. "You have been," he said. "Life doesn't boil down to one night, yeah. Remember the time Laki ran into the fields? You saved us both that day from that crazy luna. Don't know if he wanted to kill me or the dog more, eh."

Koji smiled at the memory.

Laki had suddenly showed up in Kazoku village one day and never left. The dog was as playful and tenacious as his size, and he and Razor had adopted each other almost immediately. His friend loved that dog in an easy way he'd never shown to anyone else before. Laki took to trailing Razor everywhere, and was especially eager to follow Razor into the cane fields every morning, even when his friend did everything he could to keep the dog away from the lunas. If Razor tied Laki up, he'd gnaw through the rope; if he closed him in a room, he'd find a way out. Nothing could keep him penned up without his breaking free. "A free spirit, yeah, can't keep Laki down for long," Razor boasted.

One morning, when Razor thought the dog was secured, Laki came running through the cane fields looking for him, loping across the tall shoots, panting wildly and crushing anything in his way. Just as they caught sight of Laki, so did a luna on his horse at the edge of the field. The foreman rode down the path toward them, dirt rising, whip in hand, and quickly brought the strip of stinging leather down on Razor's shoulders. "What the hell did I tell you about keeping that mutt out of the fields?!" he yelled. Just as quickly, Laki turned and charged, spooking and nipping at the horse as it rose on its haunches and came down hard before taking off down the path, the luna trying to calm the frightened animal. Razor quickly grabbed Laki and dragged him out of the field, while Koji began cutting not only his row of cane, but Razor's too. By the time the luna returned on foot, Laki was gone, and they were both down the field cutting another row of cane as if nothing happened.

Razor laughed before turning serious. "Best dog, yeah."

"Best."

Koji knew he was thinking of what had happened two nights later when they found Laki lying at the back door of the Takahashi's cottage, his stomach sliced open, his intestines dragged halfway out and being picked at by crows. Razor screamed and kicked the crows away and then went silent. He pushed Laki's intestines back in, his gray, matted fur stained a rusty red by the dry blood, then picked him up and walked toward the fields. It was one of the few times Koji had seen his friend cry. After Laki was killed, Razor was never the same. The fun-loving, carefree Razor he grew up with became more and more involved with the growing labor movement, a staunch fighter against the lunas and plantation owners whom he blamed for Laki's death. Koji was proud to see the fight Razor had helped to start continue to grow in numbers that could no longer be denied.

"You helped to start something big, yeah," Koji said. "The unions have grown tenfold, their voices louder than ever."

"Not for nothing, eh?"

Koji shook his head. "You did good."

Razor smiled and looked at him in the eyes. "You the only one blaming yourself all these years, you need to let me go, yeah."

"No, don't. Stay."

Razor suddenly appeared like the young boy Koji first met, mischievous and playful. "Got other business," he said.

He turned around and lifted his hand in a wave as he disappeared back into the fields. There was the sudden rustling of the leaves, and Koji could have sworn he heard Laki nipping and panting after him.

"Razor, wait!" Koji yelled, quickly following him into the row of cane, but Razor was already gone.

"Wait!" he said again into the darkness.

Koji's eyes snapped open in the breathless room. He was sweaty and his forehead itched. "Wait," he whispered one more time, though he knew Razor was already gone.

GHOST VOICES

RAZOR, *1918*

I'm early and peek out through the curtains from what was once the kitchen
to see the workers filing into the old, abandoned cabin tucked away in the rain
forest, mud-caked boots thumping in, bringing with them the stink of sweat and
the sour smell of damp, dirty clothing that quickly fills the small space, yeah.
The cabin is roughly a mile from the plantation. A loud splattering of rain slaps
the roof, which I hope won't leak too badly. Some arrive on foot, others in the
backs of trucks whose watery headlights approach slowly down the muddy road.
A crowded commotion fills the room. Benches scrape against the rough wooden
planks as voices rise and fall in waves and every seat quickly fills. Behind me
I hear a scratching sound and turn to see a rat scurrying along the wall and
quickly out of sight. My mouth is as dry as sand, yeah, my heart racing just like
it always does before one of our meetings. This looks to be one of the biggest
turnouts yet.

Growing up, it was all fun and games that kept me going through the long, hot
days working in the fields. Koji was always the hard worker, the serious one.
Not that I didn't have dreams, eh. No one wanted to cut cane more than I did. I
dreamed of the razor-sharp machete in my hand, slicing through the cane like
silk. But it wasn't a talent I had. It's grueling, exhausting work, yeah, and I was
a lousy cutter at best. Didn't have the speed or the swing that came naturally to

Koji, who thought nothing of helping me by throwing his cane stalks onto my pile when I fell behind.

What I did learn in the fields was to listen. Me listening, eh, what a surprise, but the workers' whispers don't stop, they keep growing louder, angrier, yeah. It doesn't take long for me to see my real talent is in recruiting for the unions, fighting for higher wages and better working hours for the workers. Who would have thought, eh? After I attended my first union meeting with a handful of other men, I found my inspiration. I began recruiting workers on the hush-hush to continue our fight against the owners. Over the years, I moved up in the ranks to being the right-hand man to Hideki Sato, our labor leader here at Puli. He's a smart guy, yeah, who reads and reads and always carries a book in his hands. He's from a family of scholars back in Japan and teaches at the plantation school. The owners have no idea he's our labor leader and we plan to keep it that way, on the hush-hush.

We've kept close track of earlier strikes on the other islands and why they've failed. I've begun to recruit from outside Kazoku village, hoping other plantations will do the same. "The only way we can make headway is to keep recruiting, yeah, and combining forces with our Chinese and Filipino brothers." Most of the workers assembled tonight are Japanese, but I look around the room to see two or three Chinese and double the Filipino men from our last meeting. I'm overjoyed, knowing it's a start, and I'm hopeful others will follow. We can only fight the owners as a collective. It seems so simple, yeah, but it's anything but. It's taken me a few months to recruit forty-eight new men, bringing us into the hundreds.

The room is hot and crowded. Just thankful the cloud of cigarette smoke covers up the foul odors. Workers squeeze in, standing two-deep against the walls, while still others spill into a smaller room in back and out the front door by the time I step from behind the curtain. We're all sweating, breathing the hot, smoky air. Up front are a wood table and three chairs. I sit down in the chair to the right of Hideki. To his left sits Aoki, our secretary and treasurer, who calls the meeting to order.

Hideki speaks up. "Thank you all for coming."

His teacher's voice is soft and calm, yet measured and forceful, and the room of rowdy men, like a schoolroom of children, immediately stops talking and fidgeting. It becomes so still I can hear the rat scurrying around in the kitchen. The cabin pulsates with a thick, raw energy. Looking among the faces, I don't see Koji, but it's still early. Everyone is in great spirits and it's a good turnout, and then there's the unanimous vote to strike right before the next harvest. We have five months to plan, to unite the workers from the Japanese, Chinese, and Filipino villages at Puli to strike together and eliminate the owners from using us against each other. For the first time, it doesn't feel like the mountain we're climbing is that steep.

≈

It's 9:00 in the evening by the time the meeting is adjourned, and the men rush back to the plantation. I tell Hideki to leave first, that I'll make sure nothing is left behind and then walk back to the plantation. No worries, yeah. I know how to slip back in undetected through the northern fields. Right now I need some fresh air after being cooped up in the hot, sweaty room for the past few hours.

"I'll see you tomorrow then," Hideki says.

He stuffs his papers back into a folder and looks around the rough cabin. We've come so far together trying to unionize the workers. I never thought I'd get along with a book-smart guy like him, but we work well together. My teenage years with Koji and Franklin are far away now, but it's the same kind of brotherhood. Even if I want to be angry at Koji for not showing up tonight, I'm feeling too good about how well the meeting went.

"Was a good meeting, yeah," I say.

"We couldn't have done it without you, brother," Hideki says. "You've done a good job getting the men to the meetings. I can't thank you enough."

I nod, a flush of embarrassment rising. It takes me a moment to grasp what he's said. I can't remember the last time someone as smart as Hideki thanked me for doing something right. If ever. He lifts the latch on the door and is gone before I can give a real response.

~~

There's a pale, silvery light from the moon when I leave the cabin, like someone has left a lamp on low. The trail ahead of me is otherwise dark. The air is warm and calm and my body's still buzzing with excitement from the meeting. I usually cut through the forest, stay away from the main road just in case a luna or the plantation police are out and about catching the late stragglers. Makes the mile back to Puli even longer with each careful step. Tonight I'm itching to take a chance but decide to stay careful, sticking to the hidden dirt paths. No use looking for trouble, not with all the work we have to do in the months ahead. Calm, yeah, and just bright enough that I can easily see through the trees if there's someone coming down the road but they can't see me.

The moonlight casts the main road in a whitish glow when I finally emerge from the dark forest path near the northern side of the plantation. There's only the last long stretch of empty, open road to walk down before jumping the fence and cutting across the fields. In the distance I can see the dark shadows of the plantation buildings. Not far now. I can already taste the sweet burn of whiskey from the bottle I keep under my mattress.

I walk quickly down the paved road when I hear the low rumble of a motor starting. I turn back to see nothing, darkness, the road empty until bright headlights flick on and a dark sedan roars out from behind some trees not far from the path I came out of. I start to run, thinking I'm fucked with this bum leg, thinking I can still make it back to the fence and into the fields before the car reaches me. There's nowhere else to hide now, the forest behind me, the fields ahead.

"Run! Run! Run!" I hear Franklin yelling at me again, like when we were young and caught stealing lychee from old man Pakua's backyard tree. He'd been waiting for us, and had come out of the house with his shotgun in hand, but we were too fast jumping over the fence, running down the road before he got to the gate.

"Run! Run! Run!" I see Laki running down the dirt road to greet me at the end of the day, good dog, best dog.

No such luck tonight. In no time, the car is so close behind me that I can hear the gears shift and grind, the engine roaring. No way I'll get off the road in time. I run zigzag until my lungs are about to burst, knowing they're just teasing me as they fall behind, only to speed up again. Run! Run! I think. The fence is just up ahead. I get cocky, believe I'm going to make it. A story to tell the grandkids, I think, when the car clips me the first time, a dull thud against my right hip, sending me hard to the ground. Hurts like hell, yeah. I try to get up but the pain shoots straight up my body to my teeth and I can hardly move. I reach down to my boot, the pain so bad I want to puke, relieved when I finally feel the solid weight of my father's razor in the palm of my hand. I swing it open. The car backs up, idling in the middle of the road. I slowly drag myself toward the side of the road. Not going to make it easy for the bastard, yeah. At least put him into a ditch so deep he can't get out of it. But the fucker knows what I'm thinking. I hear the car gun its engine and accelerate like a wild animal on the hunt coming straight for me.

I turn back toward the field to see Laki waiting for me just like always, big and gray and howling in the moonlight. Twelve years since I've seen him and my heart races at the sight. My eyes burn at the thought. "Almost there, boy. Good boy," I whisper.

SHOOTING THE MOON

DECEMBER 27–31, 1935

41

BLACKBIRDS

"The Alala!"

"The Alala are coming!"

Excited voices drifted into the market from the street. It didn't take long for the army planes to be nicknamed Alala by the old-timers after the blackbirds they resembled in the sky. "Cawing crows up to no good," someone added. Koji stopped when a young man paused to shout the news again through the screen door before he ran off down the street. He had just finished helping Samuel clean and filet a large ahi tuna the boys had brought back earlier that morning and was loading it into the icebox when all the commotion began outside.

Word had finally come the day after Christmas that the bombing would take place the following morning, on December 27. Koji touched the tender tracks across his forehead after Daniel had removed his stitches just yesterday under Nori's watchful eye. In a few more weeks the angry-looking marks would begin to fade, leaving a faint memory. Koji stopped a moment to listen. He finally heard a low drone in the far-off distance.

More locals swept by the front windows. Haoles from the hills made their way down, children and servants in toll, hurrying toward Hilo Bay, where others had already gathered, waiting since dawn for the planes, watching for any sign in the clear, bright sky. According to the radio bulletin, six US Army Keystone B-3A bombers and four LB-6 light bombers were scheduled to leave Luke Field on Oahu and fly to Hilo, where the pilots would be dropping twenty six-hundred-pound bombs on the lava tubes and channels near the vents, hoping to divert or disconnect the flow near its source and stop the lava from flowing toward the watershed and Hilo town.

It sounded simple enough. The older folks called it army talk, all show, like the starched creases of their uniforms. It would just be a pinprick against Pele, only enough to rile her up even more. Still, Koji heard whispers of curiosity within the entire community, wondering if the bombing could really stop the flow, fearful of what Pele would do in return.

Koji stepped outside to the street, the air warm and clear, the distant hum growing louder. All the locals in the market followed, Nori and Samuel the last to make their way across the railroad tracks to the bay. Whether the Hilo community believed the bombs would stop Pele or not, Koji felt their collective excitement just as the planes were sighted. He quickly looked around the growing crowd, happy to see Wilson, Mano, and Daniel there among them. Then all eyes stared toward the wide-open sky as the droning noise increased. In the distance the flock of blackbirds appeared. The first group of three planes flew in a V form-ation, with two others trailing alongside.

As the planes drew closer, the blackbirds grew in size as they flew low over Hilo, morphing into large winged biplanes, thundering and rumbling destruction overhead as windows rattled with the pass-over, shaking already anxious nerves as they headed toward Mauna Loa. And just as quickly, the planes flew off in the distance, whizzing away like insects. Koji still felt the vibrating hum through his body as they quickly faded from sight. Not long after came the second flock roaring above their heads, followed by the distant *thud thud thud* of the bombs exploding, smoke rising toward the sky, though no one could tell if it was the bombs, or Pele, responding in anger.

And all they could do was wait again.

~

It was strangely quiet after all the commotion. Hilo Bay remained as still as glass, while Koji wondered if the lava had shifted direction or stopped flowing after the bombs were dropped. It would be at least a day or two before they'd hear anything from the geologists at the Volcano Observatory Center. The island was always unpredictable, but at that moment the sky was clear and the bay was nothing but calm. Koji lingered longer down by the water after most of the crowd had wandered back to their lives. He was tired. The past five weeks had him reeling, no longer able to hide in Puli. "It's time." He heard Mariko's voice, only this time she was talking about him.

When he heard footsteps approaching, he turned to see Maile.

"Maile girl," he said, smiling at the sight of her. She was dressed in shorts and a shirt, looking like a high school girl again.

It was the first time since Maile returned weeks ago that they were alone together. She and Nori were often at the house during his recuperation at Daniel's, bringing food and helping to prepare his meals while he slept. He was both grateful and embarrassed by all the attention he received.

"Uncle Koji, I thought that was you. How are you feeling?" she asked.

"Doing well," he said, lightly touching the tender scar on his forehead out of habit. "I was hoping to catch you. Thank you for helping to take such good care of me," he added. "Spoiled me for life, yeah."

"You had us worried," she said and smiled, "but it did give me a chance to see Daniel as a doctor."

"My plan all along," he teased. "He's good, yeah?"

She nodded. "He always knew what he wanted to do, lucky one."

A slight wind began to blow, the bay beginning to stir.

"How are you?" Koji asked. "Seems you and Daniel stepped right back into the eye of a storm."

He watched her fidget, run her fingers through her hair. "Seems I left one storm for another," she said.

"Storms run their course, yeah."

She smiled. "Hope so," she said. "I'm happy to be back."

"Not as happy as we are, eh, back with family now."

Maile stared out at the bay for a long time. "I never should have left," she finally said.

Koji rubbed the stubble on his cheek. His life had been one of acceptance and fear, of never looking beyond Puli. He knew that now.

"You wouldn't have known unless you did," he said. Again, it was one of those times he didn't know where the words came from, just like the day he stumbled upon Mariko picking mangoes.

Maile paused for a moment in thought before she looked up at him, then reached out and took hold of his arm. "That's something Auntie Mariko would have said." She smiled again. "I miss her."

"Me too," Koji said, and cleared his throat. "Everything will be all right, Maile girl, just trust yourself."

"I'm trying."

"I'm sure Daniel wouldn't mind helping," Koji said, and smiled.

"He already has," Maile said quietly. "We're helping each other."

"The way it should be, yeah."

Koji paused to look out at the bay, the winds returning, rippling upon the surface. He could almost feel Mariko there with them, and the thought made him happy. Koji looked at Maile, and without saying a word they turned and began walking back to the market.

42

MOSQUITOES

Mama sat on the porch dozing, startled awake by a buzzing sound overhead. She yawned, her neck stiff. *The mosquitoes are back*, she thought. They were always whirring around Nestor, taunting and waiting for the right moment to strike. "Like honey to them, yeah," her husband used to say when he complained about the itching after being bitten. She would then send Leia or Noelani out to collect aloe vera leaves that would take care of the itching and keep the swelling away. She smiled. Her thoughts felt clearer again this morning. Mama leaned forward in her chair to listen. The buzzing intensified, too loud for mosquitoes. The sound was coming from outside, growing louder and more insistent. She peered through the dark screen, but after weeks of providing her an airy freedom from her bedroom, today the porch felt more like a cage.

Mama pushed forward, again and again, trying to move the chair toward the screen door, but the wheels were locked and wouldn't budge. She sat back, hot and frustrated. "Aya," she said aloud, before gripping the armrests and pushing herself up, dangling above the chair for an instant before her arms shook and she dropped back down on the cushioned seat with a frustrated cry. Her heart raced from the exertion. She heard Leia moving around in the kitchen, most likely to return any minute with a bowl of mashed something or other. The thought was enough to encourage Mama to try again. She gripped each side of the chair and rocked forward one, two, three times, gaining the momentum to push herself up until she was almost standing. No time to waste; if she sat down again she'd never get back up. Instead, Mama inhaled deeply and pushed with all her strength until she was completely standing. She smiled, eyes shining with accomplishment as the droning sound outside grew louder.

Mama moved one slow step at a time. Her legs felt like guava jelly as she teetered and grabbed onto the long, scuffed table to regain her balance. It was covered with flowers and leaves and shells. It all felt so familiar. She saw again all the colorful leis she and Leia had strung as they sat together for hours and hours to finish an order. How many times did she reach for another green ti leaf stacked in front of her, folding and twisting it with nimble fingers before she pushed the needle and thread through, pulling the rolled-up leaf tightly next to the others?

Mama looked across the table and saw Leia beside her as clear as day, each so much younger. She had finished stringing a lei and held it up to inspect her work. The garland and crown were made for a famous hula dancer who would wear them as part of the story she told in the sway of her grass skirt, the careful movements of her arms and hands, the quick, smooth turn of her hips. Mama suddenly wanted to put the lei lovingly over Leia's head and onto her shoulders so that she would finally tell Mama her story, the sorrow she held. Instead, she dangled it just in front of her daughter.

"Who was he?" Mama asked gently.

Leia looked up at her, surprised at the question, her eyes focused on the lei Mama held up high in front of her, an invitation to tell her story.

"No one," she whispered, "no one anymore." Leia pleaded with her eyes for Mama not to ask again.

Mama nodded and slowly lowered the lei. "Finished then," she said, knowing that so many stories didn't have happy endings.

~

Take a breath, old woman, Mama reminded herself before moving forward, balancing steady against the table, her hand running over the worn surface before she shuffled the next few steps to the screen door. When Mama finally pushed it open, it was as if a gray veil had been lifted from her eyes. She saw a clear wash of bright morning sky and noticed her beloved monkey pod tree across the yard as the sun's warmth stroked her face. Mama looked up as the droning noise grew louder still, squinting against the brightness of the sunlight in her eyes.

"Hurry, yeah!" she heard Nestor's voice call out to her.

Mama looked around but couldn't see him. "Where?" she asked, irritated.

Nestor was always playing games. "Look again, old woman." She thought she saw him by the monkey pod tree. The noise in the sky grew louder. Her legs inched forward down the ramp as she grasped the railing for support. With each step she seemed to gain her strength back, stand straighter, remember more. At the end of the ramp Mama no longer needed the railing, arms held out for balance like a toddler learning to walk as she slowly tottered across the grass toward the monkey pod tree on her own two feet.

"Where are you?" she called out.

One more step as the ground shook, the house rattled in protest, and the neighborhood dogs began to bark with the noise overhead. Mama looked up just as the roar of five large blackbirds thundered across the clear sky. "Not mosquitoes," she said as she watched the big birds fly toward Mauna Loa, two more trailing behind. She shook her head. Pele wouldn't be happy with whatever was going on. After they passed, her gaze returned to the tree where Nestor stood grinning at her.

Mama smiled. "There you are," she said, her heart beating at the sight of him. She moved faster, lighter, excited to see him, one step and then another before her legs suddenly buckled under her and she fell heavily to the ground.

43

FAITH

The day after Mama's collapse, Nori sat by her bed and waited for her to regain consciousness. Leia found Mama only moments after she'd fallen in the front yard, still breathing but unconscious. Suddenly nothing else mattered. Nori no longer cared that the bombs dropped onto the vents still hadn't stopped the flow. She didn't care about the half-filled box with their useless possessions sitting in the closet, or if the fish market was swallowed up by the lava, becoming nothing more than ashes and memory. All her fears had shifted to the woman lying in the bed in front of her. All that mattered was for Mama to wake up.

Nori watched her sleep, remembering the time she was eight or nine and had forgotten to take the laundry in before it began to rain. Her angry mother had shoved her against the kitchen wall, her head striking it hard and knocking down the picture she'd made from seashells at school. It crashed to the floor, the tiny shells clattering in all directions, as if they were running away. It only made her mother angrier, grabbing her roughly by the arm and pushing her down to pick them up. Later, Mama had soothed her, gently rubbing the bump on the back of Nori's head, telling her to lie down and rest.

"Sleep," she said, "will make you strong again, yeah."

She looked down at Mama now and wished the same for her, realizing how age hadn't taken away her beauty, only changed it to something deeper; weathered and blessed by the wind and rain.

According to Daniel, Mama's vital signs appeared stable but he was worried about all the underlying conditions that could be the causes. He wanted to take her immediately to Hilo Hospital, but Leia had firmly refused. She would do what she knew Mama wanted.

"When Mama wakes up, I want her to know she's home, yeah."

≈

Three days later, Mama still hadn't awakened. Nori was dizzy from the lack of sleep. She closed her eyes each night, serenaded by Samuel's intermittent snores, only to be up again before dawn, working in the sweet warmth of her kitchen. Business had slowed since the bombing, the market quieter. The lava flow hadn't stopped or been diverted. It continued to surge toward Hilo with no remorse. Many of the locals had left Hilo, while others began to pack with conviction. Nori couldn't begin to think of either. She carried a tray of sushi and another of red bean mochi to put into the display case before she started the coffee, only to glance at the clock to see that it was almost six and Jelly still hadn't arrived.

For the past twenty-five years, her cousin opened the market every morning, arriving at a quarter till to turn on the lights, set up the cash register, and make sure there was enough ice in the icebox for the fresh catch the boys returned with. Before the lava began to flow, the market remained busy from early morning until midafternoon. Nori waited now as a pale light slowly filled the market, bringing everything into focus, everything except for Jelly.

Outside, Nori heard voices. A handful of dockworkers stood in front, waiting for the market to open. She felt a quiet anxiousness creep up inside of her and stepped back, waiting in the shadows a few minutes longer. Nori knew it was silly, but they had a long-held tradition of Jelly opening and she closing the market every day. She wasn't about to break it this morning.

The voices outside picked up again, Jelly's rising above them. "Wait one more minute, yeah, just let me get settled, eh."

Nori sighed, her body relaxing. The screen door whined open, followed by the click of the front door unlocking before Jelly quickly stepped in and closed the door behind her.

"I was just about to send Samuel to check on you," Nori said, her voice light and steady. She walked toward the front window, reached up, and turned the sign to OPEN.

"Just in time, yeah," Jelly said, catching her breath.

"I was beginning to worry." Nori said. "Thought you might have left without telling us."

"Never," Jelly reassured her. "Decided to keep the faith that the flow will still stop. Overslept is all, yeah," she said. "How's Mama?"

"Same, last I heard."

"Nobody stronger than Mama, remember that, eh."

Nori nodded and watched her cousin reach for the change drawer under the counter and place it in the cash register. From her bag, Jelly took out her worn black Bible and slipped it under the counter. It was given to her when they were girls and both baptized by the same pompous, self-righteous missionary. One of the many who had swarmed to the islands like flies, clutching their Bibles and pamphlets, building churches, preaching and converting and saving. Nori never trusted those stern-faced men and women who seduced and cajoled and bribed the islanders to join their churches. They were the same "saviors" who also brought with them the diseases that had killed so many of the early Hawaiians they hoped to convert.

Jelly had taken to carrying the Bible around after Nobu's accident. "Calms me, yeah. I don't understand half of what I'm reading, but trying to keeps me busy, eh," she'd told Nori, placing the strip of red ribbon between the thin, wispy pages to hold her place.

≈

Nori walked back to the kitchen to finish up her coconut tarts, rolling out the dough and readying them for the oven. It hadn't taken her long to dismiss all those missionary folks, their long speeches and demanding God. She'd only been baptized because her mother realized she could get something from the haole missionaries who had come knocking on their door if she let them baptize her young daughter. So, with the promise of two hens and a rooster, along with a leather-bound Bible, Nori had been baptized. Religion in their house had lasted just long enough for her parents to sell the Bible to buy three bottles of ti root alcohol, eat the eggs the hens had laid, and eventually eat the hens too. She never did know what happened to the rooster.

When it came to her own boys, Nori declined all religion. Being baptized hadn't changed Nori's life in any way. And while Mariko hadn't been religious either, she had chosen to have Daniel baptized so he could start out in life with every advantage. She'd attended a handful of services before she stopped.

"Only a bit of water on his forehead," Mariko always said.

Still, Nori refused to baptize Mano and Wilson, leaving them heathens. "I'll take my chances, yeah," she'd said.

It was one of the few disagreements they'd had between them.

"Well, it didn't hurt him," Mariko said, adding, "and it might help."

She wasn't about to take any chances.

≈

Nori slipped the tray of tarts into the oven and began to clean up. She was older now and understood that the religion Mariko and Jelly sought had to do with hope. She couldn't blame them for leaning toward the side of faith. It was something she'd always hung on to when she was young, even if she didn't know it back then. The only difference was she hadn't found her faith in a thick black book with onionskin paper, or with a bit of water sprinkled on her head. Her savior had always been Mama.

44

THE RIVER

By late morning on New Year's Eve, Daniel borrowed Uncle Samuel's truck and drove directly to the Natua house to check on Mama again. Five days had passed since both the bombing and her sudden collapse. Mama remained in a comatose state, the world between the here and the there. Daniel thought again of the little girl back in Chicago, hoping she was at least home and happy. He'd carry the scar of it for the rest of his life. He didn't want Mama to be his second.

Auntie Leia led him to Mama's room, bright with daylight streaming in through the opened curtains. Mama lay on her bed half covered by a sheet, arms to each side of her, tentacles of white hair spread across the pillow. She looked as if she were floating. Daniel was reassured by the slow rise and fall of her chest, the fluttering of her eyelids. Leia hovered behind him as if he could magically awaken her. But after all his years of study, all he could do was check her vitals and wait along with everyone else.

"Mama needs more care than I can give her here," Daniel said, trying again to persuade Auntie Leia to move Mama. "She would be well cared for at the hospital."

Auntie Leia set her steely gaze upon him. "No better care than what I can give her here, yeah," she said, closing the door once more.

Later, when Auntie Leia left the room for a moment, Daniel leaned closer to Mama and whispered, "Wake up, Mama." Her wrinkled face in the harsh sunlight looked calm, almost childlike. He wondered for a moment if it was such a bad place to be, shaking away the thought as he bent still closer to her ear and whispered again, "Please wake up."

From the Natua house, it was a short drive to the Wailuku River. Daniel hadn't been back ever since he was in high school. Before then, his father would always take him to the river when he returned home after weeks working away. And for those few hours, he belonged to just Daniel. As a boy it made him happy to know he had all of his father's attention. Only now did he realize his father never belonged to anyone for long—he was always searching for something he could never hold onto and hurting so many along the way. "Oily hands" Koji once described him as having. Daniel wondered if his father ever thought of them after he left, only to catch himself; they'd slipped from his fingers a long time ago.

As the lava surged closer to the river's watershed, the scent of sulfur had grown more potent. Daniel walked along the main path down to the river, the one place he had avoided for years, and where he still felt his father's presence the strongest. He turned onto the small trail they had walked down so many years ago, immediately embraced by a forest of tall banyan trees. When he emerged at the river's edge, Daniel took off his shoes and rolled up his pants, remembering the five-year-old boy walking with his father, laughing when each step in the wet mud sucked and smacked and sounded like a kiss. The river had been rough that day so they couldn't swim, and instead they hiked along the embankment at the river's edge. Daniel followed after his tall, lean father, who always seemed hungry, but he was never sure for what. It was hot and muggy, the air filled with the sounds of the rushing river, the high shrill of the birds above, the mosquitoes that buzzed and taunted as he swiped them away from his sweaty, salty body. All he wanted to do was to jump into the river to cool off, but his father kept walking in the breathless heat. It was the afternoon Daniel wanted to know why it was always so noisy.

His father finally paused. "Island voices," he'd said, and very little else. He soon grew impatient with Daniel's questions and began walking again, the white scar on his side dancing up and down like a wiggling worm.

When his father finally stopped walking, he stood on the edge of the bank and looked down at the moving, churning river. Daniel slowed a few feet from him and wondered why they couldn't just step into the water near the river's edge, to cool off. He was so hot. All he wanted to do was touch the water, flick some across his chest and on the back of his sweaty neck. While his father was distracted, Daniel sat on the dirt embankment and scooted down slowly. He was just a few feet from the water when the loose dirt gave way and he suddenly slid the rest of the way down and into the river. Daniel cried out, dragged away by the currents, pushed and pulled down the river by the quick-moving water. His head bobbed up and he saw his father running along the bank beside him, pointing and yelling something he couldn't hear beyond the tumult of the river. Daniel's raised arms reached and grabbed, unable to hold on to a rock or a branch as he moved too fast with the rushing currents, swallowing water as he tried to keep his head up, his knee slamming into something hard.

It seemed like forever, but the river had carried him greedily for just minutes. It wasn't until the river narrowed and turned that the currents slowed. Daniel flailed and struggled to grab onto something when he was quickly plucked from the river by his father. He'd run ahead, beating the currents and waiting, half submerged, one hand clinging onto foliage by the side of the bank, the other reaching for him, grabbing his arm and pulling him back to shore, his grip so tight it was almost as painful as Daniel's throbbing knee. His father crouched over him, panting hard, a glint of fear in his eyes as he looked him over. Water dripped from Daniel's hair and nose, and it was the first time he had ever seen his father scared, the one time he'd held on to him so tightly. It was only then that Daniel started to tremble and cry.

"You're okay, you're okay, you're safe now, yeah," his father said, wrapping his shirt around him, wrapping his arm around him.

His father bought him a shave ice at Oshima's on the way home, and told his mother there was a small accident at the river but didn't explain in detail. Daniel had said he'd scraped his knee was all. It was his fault and he didn't want his mother to worry, or to get mad at his father when they were a family again. It was the one secret Daniel ever had with his father, his finger marks on his forearm remaining for days until they faded away.

≈

Back home that evening Daniel looked around the quiet kitchen, the last of the daylight disappearing through the window. He was edgy. Daniel hadn't seen Maile since the bombing five days ago, and was resigned to taking things slowly, aware that she needed time. One moment she was her old self and he felt like he could tell her anything; the next, she was distant and skittish. Daniel was suddenly unsure of what their future held.

Hilo's future felt just as uncertain. At the rate the lava was flowing, it was expected to reach the watershed and Hilo in less than a week's time. Daniel knew he should be packing, but the thought seemed unbearable. He'd just returned and was settling in. When he left Chicago, he was relieved to know he had a home to return to. The moment he stepped back on the island he felt its embrace. The mainland already felt a world away. Now, where would he go? Daniel couldn't imagine losing this house, the one lasting memory of his mother. He could almost see her standing by the sink, turning back to him, and saying, "It's a house, yeah, it isn't me. You won't forget me no matter how far away you go. I won't let you."

And yet . . .

Outside the winds had picked up, rushing through the trees. Daniel heard a splattering of rain against the roof. And still the rain could do nothing to stanch the lava flow, whose heat simmered and stoked from the volcano's core. A low roar of thunder boomed and shook. Daniel hoped it wasn't another eruption, Pele venting her anger at the bombing. The thunder boomed again, and just trailing it, Daniel thought he heard something else, footsteps. He listened intently, and a moment later, someone was knocking on the front door.

Daniel hurried to answer, hoping it wasn't bad news about Mama. Instead, he was surprised to see Maile standing at the door.

"Maile," he said, "is everything all right?"

"I could use some company," she said, her hair clinging to her cheeks from the rain.

Daniel smiled, happy to see her. The wind blew and he breathed in the salty spray from the ocean, the tinny tangs of wet earth and fallen leaves. It wouldn't be anything more than a passing rainstorm. For tonight, he could pretend everything was the way it should be. He didn't have to pack to leave. He still had the house, and Maile was standing right in front of him.

"I could too," he said. "There's something I've wanted to tell you, something that happened in Chicago."

Daniel took a step back and swung the door open for her.

Ghost Voices

Mariko, 1912

Franklin and Daniel return from the river just after I arrive home from playing Hearts with the Hilo Aunties. I don't know what it is, but I immediately sense something happened. My little boy is quieter than usual, while Franklin can't stop talking. Standing next to each other, I see the growing resemblance between them, the thin lips and the narrow shape of their faces now that Daniel has lost his baby fat, even in the way they move. I know I'm just being overprotective and swallow my concern. I don't want to waste the moment—they're home, and I'm just happy they spent the afternoon together. A boy needs to know his father, yeah.

Franklin pours a cup of coffee, lights a cigarette, and sits down at the kitchen table. "Had a little accident at the river. Daniel skinned his knee," he says.

Daniel nods.

"Are you all right?" I ask.

He looks up at me and nods again, eyes glassy.

"He's fine," Franklin says. "It's just a scrape—right, buddy?" He blows smoke upward.

"Yep," Daniel answers.

I reach for his hand. "Come on then, let's get you cleaned up before we go to dinner."

Before we make it down the hallway Franklin's chair scrapes back and he's standing in the kitchen doorway. "Forgot to tell you, I have to run a quick errand, be back in half an hour. Be ready to go then."

"What kind of errand?" I ask. I hate the sound of my voice.

"Nothing to worry about," he says. "Be back soon, yeah."

Franklin smiles at us and is gone. It isn't until I feel Daniel squeeze my hand tighter that I move again.

Daniel sits still on his bed while I clean the wound, cover it up. "There you go," I say, "good as new, yeah." And for the first time since he came home, he smiles.

"Did you have a good time with Daddy?"

"It was hot," he says. "We had shave ice."

"Did you swim?"

Daniel shakes his head. "Too rough," he says, sounding like Franklin.

"But it sounds like you still had a good time."

He nods. "Yep," he says, and smiles.

I leave him to play and go to change my clothes for dinner.

Two hours later, Franklin still hasn't returned. I'm so angry I can barely keep my emotions in check, but there's Daniel in the living room waiting and waiting. I swallow my anger, make him eggs and toast for dinner, and tell him Daddy had an unexpected meeting.

"Where'd he go?" he asks.

"A meeting," I repeat. "We'll go out for dinner another night."

"Aren't you eating?" he asks.

"I'll wait for Daddy," I say, knowing I wouldn't be able to keep anything down.

He simply nods and says, "I like eggs."

After I put him to bed, I clean up the kitchen and try not to think about where Franklin might be, what bar or card game he's fallen into. He just came home and he's already left us again. By the time I go to sleep, its past midnight and he still isn't home. By 2:00 a.m. I hear the front door open, his noisy shuffling through the house to the kitchen. He staggers down the hall and there's a short pause before our bedroom door opens.

"Baby?" he says. "Baby, I'm sorry, eh, I got caught up. We'll go out for dinner tomorrow, I promise."

But I turn away from him and his cigarette and alcohol stink, close my eyes tightly, no longer listening.

A New Year

January 1–2, 1936

45

THE BEATING HEART

By the time Koji drove back up to the plantation, the sun had set low across the mountains. He'd been gone for two weeks, though it felt longer. He touched the raised scar on his forehead and knew how lucky he was. He felt better, coughing less since Daniel urged him to quit smoking. Nori and Samuel had tried to convince him to stay in town until after the New Year, but Koji couldn't be swayed. There'd been something pulling at him to return to Puli since the bombing. "Be back soon, yeah. I promised I'd visit Kazoku village on New Year's Day," he'd told them. "A turnaround trip," he added, knowing the lava's flow toward Hilo was escalating and they were running out of time. Still, he needed a night back at the plantation to check on the cottage and to sleep in his own bed. Nori let him go with a promise that he'd be back down in the next day or two. Koji left shortly after, stopping by to see Mama, who remained in a state of deep sleep, Daniel called it. He saw it as straddling life and death.

When Koji finally pulled in front of the sugar train cottage, it was like returning home to an old friend.

Koji poured himself some cold green tea like his mother used to make and sat down on the steps outside of his front porch. There was still a warm, muted light. All the cane workers were back at their villages getting ready for the New Year. It was the most important day of the year for all the workers, and Koji looked forward to seeing his old friends. From the villages scattered across the plantation, the warm wind carried a fragrant aroma of cooking as they prepared for tomorrow's celebration. Koji's stomach growled. He hadn't eaten since breakfast, and the village fires brought back those boyhood days when he ate platefuls of his mother's *kiri kinton*, the plump dumplings made of mashed sweet potatoes and chestnuts, which represented good fortune in the year to come. He later felt the same gratifying New Year's spirit when he was down in Hilo with Mariko frying mochi to be dipped in soy sauce and sugar, Daniel watching, excited, and impatient to eat and begin celebrating. He smiled to think his two worlds weren't so far apart after all.

Koji turned when the old cat Hula stole around the corner of the cottage, leaped up the steps, and waited in front of the screen door to be let in. "Nine lives," he said, smiling.

He stood up to let the cat in.

≈

New Year's morning was cool and clear and rainless. It was still early when Koji cut across the fields. The sky slowly brightened, bringing everything into focus as he walked down the rutted dirt road that led to Kazoku village. Over the years, not much had changed since his family moved from the cane straw shacks and into one of the tin-roofed cottages. The village was its own community, crowded with families, dogs, cats, and chickens. Every empty patch of dirt in front or back of the cottages became small vegetable gardens, brimming with sweet potatoes, taro, turnips, beans, and pumpkins. Koji had walked down the same dirt road hundreds of times over the years. There were the faint sounds of the villagers just rising, but it was still quiet except for

Mrs. Takahashi grating carrots on her front stoop. He knew she'd be up and cooking before dawn.

"Koji-*chan*, that you!"

He smiled to see Razor's mother. Thin and gray-haired, her face was a myriad of wrinkles and furrows as she smiled to see him. Next to her was a bowl piled high with grated daikon in which she would add the carrots, along with sweetened vinegar, to make *namasu*, a New Year's salad that Razor had loved. After he died, she continued to make namasu every year, leaving a generous bowl for him at the table where he sat as a boy.

"I'm hungry," Koji teased, patting his stomach. She always loved to cook for all the children of Kazoku village.

"You come to the right place, eh. Come, come in," she said. "The *ozoni* should just be about ready."

He helped Mrs. Takahashi up and followed her into the house she shared with her daughter, son-in-law, and grandchildren, who were still asleep. She had lost Razor, and another daughter in childbirth. She seemed smaller every year, the top of her gray head barely reaching his chest, her clothes swallowing her up. Koji stepped into the small house, the air thick with the smells of ozoni simmering on the stove, the New Year's soup that was eaten in the morning and made of miso, dry kelp, dashi, and yuzu peel. She made it her own by adding chicken or fish, taro, spinach, and mushrooms, leaving the toasted round mochi rice cake to place in each bowl last. It had always been Koji's favorite way to start the New Year.

Koji paused at a photo of Razor as a young boy, sturdy and bull-like, holding up a cane knife with two hands pretending to cut. Even with her back turned to him, dishing up a bowl of soup, Mrs. Takahashi said, "He always had big dreams, eh, sometimes too big for his own good."

Koji sat down at the kitchen table. In the quiet moment before the others would be up, he asked her, "Have you seen him?" She was the only other one who saw his spirit.

Mrs. Takahashi turned around and placed the steaming bowl of soup in front of him. With chopsticks, she placed the mochi on top. She brought another bowl and sat down across from him. Only then did she shake her head. "Gone," she said. "I'll see him soon enough, yeah. It's time." She looked up at Koji and smiled. "For you, too."

"I never told him why I stayed with the cane work even after . . ." he said and then couldn't finish.

Mrs. Takahashi smiled. "We make our own lives, Koji-*chan*, right or wrong, we have to live with our choices. The rest is no one's business."

Koji still felt the need to say it aloud. "The cane work was all I'd known, the only thing I was good at doing."

"You never gave yourself a chance," she said.

He felt the tears push against his eyes and looked down at the table. With her, he felt like a boy again. Cutting cane was simply a means to an end. The only life he ever wanted were all the days and nights he had with Mariko and Daniel. He couldn't leave them to make the long trip back up the mountain to sit in a sweat-stink room of men whose fight he believed in, but not more than the life he was finally living in Hilo. He would never apologize for needing Mariko and Daniel. Still, it didn't make his grief any less for failing Razor.

Mrs. Takahashi reached out to him. "Koji-*chan*, don't be like your *okaasan*. After your father died, your mother felt as if her life was over; she was filled with anger and couldn't see beyond it. Is that what you want, to live with this sorrow? Not too late to let it go, eh," Mrs. Takahashi said. "Life's too short and too long for anything else."

She stood and refilled his bowl with the New Year's soup he hadn't realized he'd already finished. "Eat," she said. "A good start to the New Year, yeah. A new beginning."

Her words soothed, at least on the surface.

～

Koji turned back for one last look at the train cottage, his truck packed with all his worldly goods as he drove down the hill and away from the plantation. There was nothing left for him at Puli. He looked at the quiet fields and heard again the faint refrains of the *holehole bushi* work songs that once rose above the stalks and into the air. Even Razor, his last tie to the cane life, was gone. Koji had spent New Year's Day at the village catching up with old friends, seeing the wealth of all his years on the plantation. The sugar plantations were what brought them to the islands, but it wasn't what made them stay. It was the community they'd formed in spite of it, growing friendships and families as well as cane. Even in the hottest, cruelest days, filled with blisters and boils, itching bites and stinging whips, Koji knew, even if he hadn't fully realized it back then, that fate had brought them all so far from their homelands to their new lives at Puli Plantation. He heard his mother's voice rise again like on the first day they arrived, asking his father where the beating heart was. "There," Koji would tell her now, looking back across the fields and beyond to the villages that held the men and women who worked the sugarcane. "There is where the beating heart lies."

46

JANUARY 2, 1936

Mama was running, the muscles in her legs strong and taut. She couldn't remember the last time she'd felt such pure happiness or had covered so much ground. She ran down the wide-open streets crowded with vendors on market day, selling everything from fruits and vegetables to freshly caught fish and sushi, along with her favorite, mochi filled with sweet red beans. Dogs whined for scraps of food as people moved in thick throngs from one vendor to the next. Still, she ran down the dirt paths unhindered, wearing her favorite loose muumuu with the red hibiscus flowers, the crowds parting to let her through. Mama felt like a child of privilege, though her family had little. She was running toward her family home, a two-room shack near the beach, filled with beans and nuts they sold at the market. Her mother made a soup with them, which was the best thing she'd ever tasted. At one point, it felt as if she were soaring above the town, looking down and seeing her lithe body weaving in and out without a care in the world, so young and daring.

Mama could have gone on running forever, but for Nestor's voice calling out to her. She strained to hear what he was saying until the wind carried it to her. "Not time yet," her husband said.

Mama opened her eyes.

≈

There was a stillness in the early hours of the morning, mouth dry as chalk and hungry. Mama hadn't felt this kind of hunger in a long time, her thoughts slowly awakening, her arms and legs so stiff it was like swimming through a blanket of seaweed. Her fingers inched away from her body until they traced the deep dip left in the mattress by all the years Nestor had laid next to her. She was relieved to be at home in her own bed, the thought calming her confusion. Mama looked around the quiet room for any signs of Nestor, but even his shadow was gone now. She sighed and tried to push herself up into a sitting position, but her limbs refused to cooperate.

Where had she been all this time? Mama still wasn't sure if she hadn't walked on, to the other valley. She recalled seeing Nestor by the monkey pod tree and walking toward her husband but never reaching him. The rest had been lost in smoke. Mama did feel as if she'd just returned from a long journey, like when she was a child and her parents had taken her to visit her Auntie Kobayashi, her mother's sister, in the village of Honomu, two hours north of Hilo. It was a world away from town back then. In a hired wagon drawn by two horses, she sat on rough burlap bags in the back of the wagon as every hard bump along the dirt road rattled through her body.

Honomu was a small, rural town with wooden walkways, a row of one- and two-story wooden houses, and a general store. Auntie Kobayashi was squat and white-haired; her eyes dark and attentive. She sat on a low chair in the middle of the small, cluttered room that smelled of damp earth and eucalyptus and greeted them. They drank a tepid tea and ate rice crackers. "I see a dark shadow just over your shoulder," Auntie Kobayashi said, looking directly at Mama, her eyes hard and focused. "The spirits are with you, child, you can't outrun them, but they will guide you later, yeah. Always remember that, eh."

"Nestor, you old fool!" she called out louder than expected. Her throat was dry and rusty. "Where are you?"

Mama inhaled. The room was hot and stale, a mix of her own sweat along with the oil and herbs and the coconut lotion that Leia rubbed across her saggy skin. She heard heavy footsteps and then Leia was in the room, the light suddenly too bright and everything too loud as the waking world returned.

"Mama!" her daughter cried out, "You're awake!" Leia rushed to her, touching her cheek before she bent down to scoop her up in her arms. When Leia pulled away she had tears in her eyes, looking relieved.

Mama wasn't sure why Leia was so happy. She hadn't seen her so excited since she was a young girl. *My girl*, she thought, *my talented girl who deserved only the best. Did she ever find it?*

"Where I been?" she asked.

"You've been asleep for almost a week now, yeah."

Her stomach made a growling sound. "Hungry," Mama said.

Leia stepped back and laughed. "Let's get you something to eat and drink, eh. Be right back." She squeezed Mama's hand and stared hard at her as if she were trying to memorize her face before she stood.

My girl, Mama thought again.

Leia then stepped across the room to open the window. "Love you, Mama," she said before she left.

Mama wondered what had gotten into Leia, who looked as if she'd seen a ghost. She shifted toward the sudden breeze, grateful, sniffed the air, something missing. Mama opened her eyes wide and took a deeper breath, but there was no whiff of sulfur that had been in the air day after day. She lifted her head, closed her eyes, and listened, but couldn't hear the snap and crackle she imagined it sounded like; the smooth, slithering heat of the lava flowing down the mountain and swallowing everything in its way had stopped.

"Think I don't know?" Mama said, trying to sit up. "Pele, you a sly one, you finally stopped, eh, showed them fools who's boss, yeah."

Mama smiled then. She lay her head back down on the pillow and waited for Leia to return.

47

THE LIVING

A low hum filled the fish market as Nori watched the crowd from behind the counter. The young, thin geologist had announced that the lava flow had stopped just miles from the watershed. The fissures were no longer spouting hot lava, only the last remnants of steam and smoke. Nori saw him stand straighter as he said, "We're happy to announce that the bombing was a success."

It brought very little response from the locals, who believed it had nothing to do with the bombing, but knew the haoles wanted to make sense of the air show they'd put on. "If the bombs had succeeded, the flow would have stopped a week ago," voices whispered. "No, this was all Pele's doing, yeah." Nori couldn't have agreed more with them. As a little girl, Mama told them all the stories of Pele's power and might. "Pele does as she pleases; her fire is always burning, yeah, moving at her will." She imagined Pele had grown tired of all the noise and nonsense, simply deciding to stop the flow toward Hilo as if she were blowing out a candle. Nori paused to take a breath and steady herself. She was relieved the lava flow was over and they could get on with their lives. She watched the crowd of locals disperse as quickly as they came to spread the good news.

Nori turned, startled when someone touched her arm, only to see Koji standing next to her.

"Saw you standing here staring at nothing," Koji said. "Daydreaming, yeah?"

Nori smiled, clearing her thoughts. "Was just thinking Pele finally had enough of all this foolishness," she said. She looked up at his tired eyes, the glaring raw tracks of his wound above his right eye, and asked, "How are you feeling?"

They never did find time to talk about his accident.

Koji touched his forehead. "Fine, yeah. I had a good doctor."

Nori shook her head and turned serious. "You scared me," she said. "You could have killed yourself up at the lava flow. You're too old for such foolishness."

"Everyone's entitled to be foolish once in a while, eh," he teased.

"Doesn't make it any less foolish," Nori returned. "And selfish, yeah, thinking only about you. What would we have done if you'd gone and killed yourself up there?"

She'd already lost so many; Razor, Mariko, and now Mama, who was one step closer to leaving them. Nori couldn't bear to think of losing Koji, too.

Koji became quiet. "I didn't," he managed to get out.

"Mariko never would have forgiven you," Nori said, her words suddenly caught in her throat. She swallowed, fingering the small scar on the back of her hand. "*I* never would have forgiven you."

What happened next was sudden and completely unexpected: Nori felt a flush of heat, followed by a sudden pressure behind her eyes before her tears came. She turned away, crying, as if she were that child again, only there was no Mama and no Mariko to take away her fear and loneliness. That girl wasn't her anymore, she thought, embarrassed. And still Nori couldn't stop the tears. *It was as if some great welling inside of me erupted like Loa*, she thought. She felt Koji slip her his handkerchief, then wrap his arms around her and hold her tight as she cried and cried.

When he finally did let go, he looked around, cleared his throat, and said, "Folks going to start talking about us, yeah. Don't want Samuel coming after me."

He made her smile. Inhaling, Nori hiccuped and began to laugh, wiping her nose, her eyes, catching her breath.

"Better, yeah?" Koji asked.

Nori nodded, self-conscious. "Don't know what came over me," she said, hiccuping. She felt better letting out the anxiety of the past weeks, the fear she'd been holding in.

"I'll be fine, yeah," he said. "And Mama will wake up," he added.

"You think?" she asked.

Koji smiled. "Like Pele, when she's ready."

Nori didn't question how he would know. She wanted to believe it was true. And then she remembered. "I have news to tell, yeah."

"What's that?"

Nori glanced at the pickle jar filled with nickels. "Never guess who won the pot."

"Who?"

"Samuel," she said.

This time it was Koji who laughed.

≈

Nori left not long after to visit Mama, and for the first time she didn't pause in front of her old childhood house but kept walking. As she approached the Natua house, she heard Leia's voice, happy and animated, coming from the porch. Nori paused before she opened the screen door, assuming they had visitors. She remembered the scared young girl, heart racing, running away from her house, thinking if she just reached Mama everything would be all right. How many times had she flung open the screen door and found Mama stringing leis in the porch, or cooking in the kitchen; rushing into her arms. "Okay, yeah. You'll be okay. Mama's here," she'd tell her. "I'm here."

Nori hesitated now as she rapped lightly before she opened the screen door, something she'd never done before. She saw Leia first; then her eyes fell on Mama, who was awake and sitting up in her wheelchair.

Nori's heart was drumming. "Mama?" she asked, surprised.

"She woke early this morning," Leia said elatedly. "Waiting for Daniel to drop by in a little while."

Nori squatted beside her wheelchair. "Mama," she said, "I'm here."

Mama looked at her, and for just a moment Nori saw the sweet kernel of recognition in her eyes.

GHOST VOICES

MARIKO, 1933

I feel stronger this morning, well enough to ask Koji to take me to Onekahakaha
Beach, where we all met so many years ago. He looks at me as if I'm joking,
but I keep my eyes on his until he knows I'm serious. "Time is short," I say.
The cancer has spread to my bones, yeah, and I've been a prisoner of this bed
so I won't break my brittle limbs. I think back to a time I couldn't stop moving,
and now I'm fragile as a teacup. I slowly push myself up from the bed to show
him just how serious I am. Tomorrow the pain may be back full force, or the
sorrow, or the anger of being cheated out of precious time with the people and
the life I love. There's no time to waste.

"Let's wait for Daniel," he says, hesitating. "He just went to pick up a few
groceries, should be home any time now, yeah."

Daniel is home from Chicago looking thin and tired, ever the serious young
doctor who carries the burden of not being able to save his own mother. "All
the years of medical school," he says, "and there's nothing . . ." His voice caught
as he talked quietly to Koji in the living room last night, or was it the night
before? What they don't realize is that while my body betrays me, my other
senses seem heightened. I can hear their whispers as if they're in the room with
me. "You did save me a long time ago when your father left," I whispered back.
"What would I have done without you?"

"No, we're not waiting!" I say, too sharply. Doesn't he know there's no time to wait? Then I say softly, "Just you and me, yeah."

Koji looks at me for a long moment, then nods. "Stay right here," he says. "Don't move, eh, I'll be right back."

I throw the sheet back and wait.

When Koji returns I'm sitting up. "Anxious, yeah," he teases. He carefully wraps a robe around me before lifting me with ease into his arms as if I were a child, cradling me gently. I lean against him. I've always leaned on him.

Koji carries me outside. It's warm and hazy and I breathe in the daylight as he carefully lifts me into the truck, the front seat a soft nest of pillows and blankets. Sitting up in the truck, I study my house from the outside. It looks as disheveled as I feel, the long grass, the overgrown shrubs, my grandfather's mango tree gloriously full of hard, green mangoes, which delivers another sobering blow: by the time they're ripe I'll be gone.

"The mangoes," I say, and a wave of grief fills me.

"Don't worry," Koji says as he settles into the driver's seat.

I hadn't realized I said the words aloud.

"Onekahakaha Beach, you sure, eh?" he asks.

"Very," I say, glancing at him.

≈

Koji takes the long way, slowly driving down the streets I've known all my life. When we leave the neighborhood and the outskirts of downtown, I roll down the window and close my eyes, letting the warm wind caress my face. How long has it been since I've felt its touch? My mind is racing as Koji drives slowly, carefully over the uneven dirt roads softened by the cocoon of blankets. I know we're nearing the beach even before I open my eyes. There's the sharp salt-fish, seaweed smell of the ocean, the swishing of the palm trees that surround the *beach, and suddenly the past rises before me, and I'm that fourteen-year-old girl standing on the rocks with Nori and Leia.*

"Let's go," Nori says.

We were fishing for bonefish, carrying our bamboo poles and buckets and walking back across the hot sand of the beach.

"Not bad, yeah, we caught two," Leia says.

When I glance across the sand I see the three boys on the beach looking our way, one of them strutting toward us as if he owns the beach.

"Hello, ladies," he says.

We laugh because we aren't ladies, we're still girls.

"My name is Franklin and my friends over there . . ."

I think of that Franklin, so young and handsome, all he did was look my way and I fell under his spell. I think of all the things he could have done if he'd just set his mind to it. Instead, he wasted his talents.

I feel his hand reach out and touch my shoulder, but when I open my eyes it's Koji I see.

"We're here," he says.

"Thank you," I whisper.

"You okay?"

I nod, even though there are increasing flashes of pain.

"Take a breath," he says, knowing.

Koji parks the truck in the shade of the palm trees facing the ocean. He rolls down his window and reaches over me to carefully roll down mine. We sit, comfortable in our silence, letting the wind speak, letting the briny scent of the ocean embrace us. The sun overhead casts an inviting light on the water, and I wonder what it would feel like to just lie back and float out to sea, yeah. I imagine the coolness of the water, the pain and fear gone, the complete calm of drifting off until I simply become part of the ocean. But then Koji reaches over and takes my hand gently in his and draws me back to shore.

"Beautiful, yeah," Koji says, looking at me. "You were always the red lehua blossom to my twisted, gnarled branches."

I squeeze his hand tighter. "Nonsense," I say. "You've never seen just how beautiful you are."

Koji laughs. "I've never been beautiful."

I think of the old Hawaiian legend that Mama had told all of us when we were young, how Pele had been jealous of the young lovers 'Ōhi'a and Lehua, wanting 'Ōhi'a for herself. When he refused Pele, she turned him into an ugly tree. Taking pity on her, the other gods turned Lehua into a beautiful red flower that bloomed on the tree so the lovers could always be together. I can't help but smile to think how our lives have turned around. Koji is now the good and gentle Lehua on my brittle branches. Just the thought brings back the pain that wrings my body dry.

I'm nothing more than pale skin over fragile bones. I rub the callus on Koji's thumb and feel how blessed I am. I gaze out at the ocean and will my thoughts his way. I want you to know that you are the one I loved most. The years with you have brought me such happiness. I won't go far, I promise, yeah. Like this island, I'm already remaking myself. Look and you will feel me everywhere, in the rocks, in the water, in the color of the air.

HILO

JULY 28, 1936

THE MANGO TREE

Even with all the windows of the truck rolled down, the morning air felt hot and sticky, rain likely to come by the afternoon. Koji was already sweating by the time his truck reached Hilo and he turned up the hill toward the green bungalow. He was still getting used to his new life. After leaving the plantation, he'd stayed with Nori and Samuel in town before finding a small house out toward Mountain View. Koji had driven back up to Puli to find Hula, bringing the cat back down in an old wooden crate. He was surrounded by the rain forest, the old lava tube cave that he'd taken Mariko to just a couple of miles away. After spending most of his life surrounded by the hot, flat cane fields, he wanted to be among towering koa and ohi'a trees and the cool, dripping moisture that came after the rains, filled with the scent of damp earth, eucalyptus, and moss. He usually drove into Hilo once or twice a week because he knew that if he didn't, Nori would never let him hear the end of it.

By the time he arrived at the bungalow, Daniel had already filled a couple of baskets with mangoes and was working on a third. He was reminded of the first time he saw Mariko doing the same. Koji watched for a moment from the truck, happy to see Daniel settled in. He had started his own medical practice downtown, but had taken the morning off from seeing patients so they could pick the mangoes together.

"I'd like to carry on the tradition," Daniel had said when he'd asked Koji if he could come over.

Tradition. Mariko would have liked that. She must have told Daniel of their yearly ritual.

"Tradition is good," Koji had said.

≈

"You going to sit there all day, or are you going to get out of the truck and help?" Daniel had stopped working and looked over at Koji, watching from his truck.

Koji shook away his thoughts and smiled. "Looks like you're doing a pretty good job on your own, yeah," he teased back.

Koji got out of his truck and grabbed a basket. The tree was laden with fruit, the warm air ripe with the sweetness of earth and melon and pineapple, the mangoes still firm to the touch. Mariko was right there with them.

"It was a good year," Daniel said, the mangoes falling into the basket one after another with a soft thud.

"Nori will be overjoyed to get a couple of extra baskets this year. She'll be making mango everything for the next few months, yeah," Koji said, and laughed. He leaned the old wood ladder against the tree, climbed up, and quickly began filling a basket. By midday, they'd have all the baskets of mangoes stacked high on the front porch.

"Looks like you've found something you're good at," Daniel said, stopping to watch.

"Your mother trained me well," Koji said.

"She would be happy," Daniel said.

"Very."

Perched on the ladder, Koji looked up toward the now quiet Mauna Loa, which had had the entire community tied in knots for six weeks, only to have the lava simply stop flowing a week after the army bombed the vents, before reaching the river. While the geologists and the army claimed credit, the locals laughed. They knew it was all Pele's doing. She was playing with them, yeah, the locals said. The bombs were no more than a tap on her shoulder.

Koji turned when he heard the front door of the bungalow open. For just a moment he imagined that it was Mariko stepping out to the porch, heart jumping. Instead, it was Maile who walked out, setting down a pitcher of cold green tea. *Still an old fool*, he thought. She smiled and waved to them. In the months since he'd left the plantation, he could feel Mariko's presence, urging him forward. It was time to stay in the present, however much he could. It was Razor who once told him that he needed to live life like the way he cut cane, "move quickly forward and don't look back, yeah."

Koji plucked a mango from the tree. When all the fruit was picked, he'd be sure to cut back the branches, start paying more attention to the yard. Next year the tree would be full of ripe mangoes again, renewing itself for another generation to come. Koji looked around and knew nothing stayed the same, with one exception: he and Daniel would be back here at the green bungalow picking mangoes from the tree next summer and the summers after that.

And for now, it was more than enough.

ACKNOWLEDGMENTS

Heartfelt thanks to Joy Harris, for her unwavering support and dedication; to Tara Parsons, for her insight and advocacy; and to everyone at HarperVia. Thank you always to my *Sistahs*, and to Mary Roach. I'm grateful to Abby Pollak, Blair Moser, Cynthia Dorfman, and Catherine de Cuir, with whom I've shared not only many manuscripts but many Zachary's pizzas over the years. Special thanks to my family and friends, near and far, and especially my brother, Tom.

And to all those who answered my questions, encouraged, and inspired me through the writing of this book, your voices have been invaluable.

Lastly, many thanks to the Hedgebrook Foundation.

Here ends Gail Tsukiyama's
The Color of Air.

The first edition of the book was printed and
bound at LSC Communications
in Harrisonburg, Virginia, April 2020.

A NOTE ON THE TYPE

The text of this novel was set in Sabon. The Sabon® font was designed by Jan Tschichold. Released in 1967, it was inspired by a type cut by Claude Garamond and named after Jakob Sabon, a student of the great French publisher and printer. Sabon is known as a classic font, elegant and highly readable.

HARPERVIA

An imprint dedicated to publishing international voices,
offering readers a chance to encounter other lives and other
points of view via the language of the imagination.